ELI

# CORIN

## AND THE

# COURTIER

Cover by Fiona Jayde

SMOKING
TEACUP
BOOKS

Published by Smoking Teacup Books
Los Angeles, California

ISBN: 9798864824894

# Two Years Ago...

*My dear cousin,*

*I can't tell you how shocked I was to hear what that blasted fiancée of yours had done, and I wish to anything that I could help. Cursed as I am, and with my mother and father breathing fire down my neck as a result, I'm not in a position to come to visit you. Soon I hope to find a home of my own a little farther from their hovering, but at present—well, I really don't think your aunt and uncle would give you any peace, so I wouldn't recommend visiting us.*

*You know she wasn't good enough for you to begin with, don't you? Yes, she's beautiful, and yes, you loved her, but is it really worth running away simply because she—I mean, Belinda didn't <u>really</u> let the fellow have his way with her in full view of the garden party, did she? I simply can't believe it. Not even she would be so brazen. I heard the king was there. I simply can't believe it! You're a wonderful dragon and an honorable knight. It passes understanding that anyone could treat you that way.*

*Anyway, she's not worth it, Cor. No one's going to laugh at you. They'll understand the fault lies with her! And as for that trifling matter of the fellow's scar, what's the bastard going to do, complain to the king? Don't give up everything you've worked and sacrificed for!*

*Much love,*
*Fiora*

# Chapter One

THE SUN HAD FINALLY slipped low enough behind the western peaks that Corin had to either leave off his correspondence until the following day or give in and light a lamp.

He chose to fling his half-completed letter across the desk and slump back in his chair.

No lamps.

Lamps were for people who gave a fuck.

Anyway, his cousin Fiora wouldn't care about receiving a timely letter from him, not when he had nothing whatsoever to say, either about his own situation—dull and lonely, as always—or Fiora's continuing struggles with his curse.

Still. He'd finish the letter eventually, if only to keep Fiora writing to him in return. His little cousin was the only person on earth who could still make Corin smile on occasion, with his melodramatics and his innocence and his vivid, amusing descriptions of the merchant town he'd chosen as his new home after finally escaping the clutches of his overprotective parents.

Even if he'd been as annoying as everyone else Corin knew, he was also the only person who bothered to keep in touch at all. The rest of the family had been distant at best ever since Corin first took up a sword.

A bitterly chilly breeze whispered through the open casement over the desk, rustling the papers and ruffling through Corin's overlong dark hair—which he never bothered to cut these days, letting it go until it hung down into his eyes. Even in a thin linen shirt with the sleeves rolled up, the cold didn't bother him. Dragons ran as hot in their almost-human shapes as in their draconic ones. Corin ran hotter than most.

But oncoming snow scented the air, crisp and damp. Damn it

all, spring had already come and gone again a dozen times, and it couldn't seem to make up its mind. Corin would have to go around the tower and close all the bloody windows again to keep the floors from getting wet, if nothing else, damn it to hell. He'd just opened them a few days before to air the place out.

It felt like an overwhelmingly impossible task.

Maybe he didn't give a fuck if the floors were wet. Did he? He could always shift to his other body and stay scaly and entirely waterproof, as he had for much of the last seven months while winter wailed around him in an endless blizzard. The great hall downstairs held him perfectly well, and he wouldn't need to be in his upstairs bed to be warm. Besides, it wasn't as if anyone would be there to talk to with a human mouth.

Or share the bed.

As if in answer to the thought, the wind picked up a little and shifted slightly, bringing with it a breath of warmth and sweetness, like a rose blooming in the sun that would be shining far down the mountain, across the high valleys, by the coast and in the capital. The scent made Corin long for something…but before he could lose himself in imagination and memory, the breeze also brought him a more prosaic hint of sweaty horse.

His nose wrinkled. What a combination. And if he'd started imagining things, perhaps Fiora was right when he said Corin had been in this remote mountain hideaway for too long, and that only cussedness had kept him here.

As he shook his head, attempting to clear the hallucination, he heard the distant clop of hooves and a jingle of harness.

Well, fuck. Not a hallucination after all. His heart gave a leap and a twist, like a dancer at one of the court balls he hadn't been to in two years or more. Another person. Perhaps someone had come looking for him again, of all the things; he'd thought he'd discouraged any such attempts for good, given that no one had tried in three hundred and seventy-three days.

Not that he'd been counting or anything.

In any case, Corin's sword, let alone the possibility of a blast of fire (not that Corin would use it), tended to discourage even the most determined of guests.

On the other hand, this could be a lost traveler, led to Corin's tower via taking the left-hand branch instead of the right a mile down the mountain.

He jumped up and strode across the messy bedroom, stepping over a pile of clothes and kicking a pair of boots out of the way. The window at the foot of his bed overlooked the steep, winding path that led up to the bridge in front of the tower's main gate. Though Corin doubted a human's eyes could detect him that far up, particularly in the twilight—and while he couldn't be certain the approaching person wasn't some other variety of magical being, he knew for certain no dragon other than himself would arrive somewhere on horseback—he still pressed himself against the wall, peering out from concealment. Why? He didn't quite know. Only it had been so bloody long since he saw anyone face to face, or more precisely, since anyone had seen his human face. He collected supplies at the village at the foot of the mountain in his other body, scooping up the crates he'd preordered in his giant claws and flying back to the tower.

Only once had one of the stupid young men, inflamed with a desire to make a name for himself, leapt out of the shadows and taken a good hard whack at Corin's shoulder with an axe that had clearly spent most of its life chopping firewood.

Corin had blinked at the slight annoyance of the blow, which had glanced off completely, and turned his massive head to stare into the lad's eyes. Another blink, and the fellow had squealed, turned nearly as green as Corin himself, and fled for the safety of his mother, who stood across the village square shouting at him in tones that promised punishment greater than Corin would've troubled to dish out.

Otherwise, the villagers had taken his money and given him food, candles, paper and ink, wine—a great deal of wine—and all the other necessities without any fuss or hassle. It probably helped that they'd figured out exactly who he was. Too many king's knights had come strutting and jangling through the village seeking Sir Corin, the famed dragon knight, for the villagers to have any doubts about his identity. And Sir Corin had a reputation for being gallant and chivalrous almost to the point of idiocy: he wasn't someone who'd lay waste to a helpless village. Not that any modern dragons would. They'd be much more likely to complain about the lack of amenities at the local inn.

So even if the rider coming up the path had taken a wrong turning to reach the tower, he'd know who Corin was. He'd have passed through the village on his way up the mountain, and the locals had nothing bloody else to do but issue dire, completely fabricated warnings about the dragon up the mountain, laughing in their sleeves the whole time.

God. He'd know who Corin was. Or more accurately, who he used to be. And even if he'd never met him previously, if he'd ever spent more than ten minutes in the capital he'd know why Corin had fled to the mountain.

If he'd ever spent more than *fifteen* minutes in the capital, he'd probably seen Belinda naked, too, since she rarely went longer than that without lifting her skirts. And half an hour would've gotten him the tale of Sir Corin's final duel and the way he'd laughed like a madman while he scarred his opponent's face.

Ugh. Perhaps he'd be lucky, and the rider would be some peddler or merchant who'd neither know nor care about court scandal, or would at least be too intimidated to mention it.

When the rider came around the large boulder at a turning in the path fifty yards below the bridge, Corin immediately knew he was not, in fact, lucky—not that that was anything new, of course, damn it to hell. The man seated on a really fine and well-groomed gelding wore a rich woolen tunic and a mail shirt along with equally expensive pants and boots, all topped off with a velvet cloak. The jeweled hilt of the long sword by his side caught the last ray of the setting sun, a ruby gleaming like fire.

A knight or a lord, certainly, which meant someone who'd *know*. Keen as it was, his eyesight couldn't penetrate the shadow of the man's fur-lined hood. That *someone* could be bloody anyone.

*Turn around*, Corin silently begged. *The gate's closed. This tower couldn't possibly be less welcoming. And neither could I. Get lost, you courtly, popinjay prick.*

9

The horse picked his way along the rocky path and then clopped over the bridge, stopping directly in front of the gate and out of Corin's line of sight from the bedroom window. He could still hear, though, and the murmur of the man speaking softly to his horse and the squeak of leather as he dismounted carried clearly.

And then came the sound he'd been dreading: the clang of the large bell attached to the chain dangling beside the gate.

Bother, as Fiora would say.

The bell clanged again, more insistently this time. "Hello there!" called a pleasant tenor voice, as sweet as the scent of roses. Corin froze, his spine fusing into a steel rod, it felt like. He fucking knew that voice. "Hello, up in the tower! Sir Corin, I assure you I come in peace. And I request a night's hospitality, if you please! I've gone too far to retrace my steps tonight before it's dark."

By the end of that, the voice remained pleasant…but strained. Perhaps even a shade desperate?

But Corin didn't give a damn for his troubles, because God. It couldn't be. He wouldn't fucking dare. Hearing his name spoken aloud for the first time in over a year would've been odd enough, but in that familiar voice…

A short silence fell, Corin holding his breath as if his unwanted visitor would be able to hear it and know he stood there listening. He wouldn't, of course. He was as human as could be. Corin eventually had to breathe in, and the rosy sweetness had only grown stronger. How had he never registered that scent as being a part of the man now at his gate? Perhaps because it was such an odd aromatic overtone for a man he'd mainly seen in the palace training yard.

"I know you're there," the voice went on after a few moments. Fuck, he did? How the hell had he— "This isn't the kind of gate you can lock up from the outside! So open up!" A very slight pause. "Please?"

Damn it. Had the fucker no sense of self-preservation at all? Corin had challenged everyone else who'd come knocking, though precisely none of them had taken him up on it. Surely they'd reported their welcome back at court. Not to mention, his last act before leaving the capital hadn't been one to entice people to approach him.

The bell rang again, this time accompanied by a crack of the metal bell hitting the stone of the wall.

Damn it all twice. He'd asked for shelter, which meant Corin couldn't challenge him. And he wasn't fucking taking the hint. Perhaps he could still be shamed or intimidated into slinking away back to the village, and then Corin wouldn't have to let him in.

Of course, Corin would still have to see his face.

Fuck.

With a sigh that rattled his very bones, he turned and stomped away from the window, through the bedroom, and down the stairs, forcing his feet to move.

The lowest two levels of the tower were dug into the mountain bedrock, so Corin stepped off the stairs at the third level, crossed an antechamber, went up and down another little set of stairs, and finally passed through the main hall and down the defensible corridor that led to the gate.

Once there, he paused with his hand on the heavy bar keeping it closed, gathering all his ill-temper and allowing his body to begin its shift to the draconic. His vertical pupils and the faint green tint to his skin always showed the world who and what he was, but if he concentrated, or if he grew too angry to concentrate, a ripple of scales would spread across his face, on his arms and chest; his fingernails would lengthen slightly into gleaming claws. In short, he could make himself even more intimidating than six and a half feet of well-trained knight would be at the best of times.

He had to be able to make him leave. He *had* to, or he couldn't be answerable for his actions. Picking a fight with this particular courtier would be petty and dishonorable and unfair. But he could *answer* a challenge, and he could make himself as unpleasant and unwelcoming as possible.

The bar would've taken the full effort of a normal man to lift. Corin tossed it aside with one hand and pulled on one side of the gate with the other. It creaked open, and Corin stepped forward.

Bright blue eyes gleamed from under the hood of the man who stood expectantly only three feet from the gate. Corin's breath caught, his throat closing up. The most beautiful eyes he'd ever seen, and the last time he'd looked into them they'd been shimmering with tears and malice, they'd been…

And then the man threw back his hood. The last time he'd looked into those eyes, they'd belonged to someone else, and Corin sucked in air, his heart restarting and his lungs unfreezing. This pair of brilliantly blue eyes, fringed with thick gold lashes, ornamented a man's freckled face, bizarrely unsuitable for their plain setting. On Belinda they were perfect. Just like the rest of her, damn her.

The man smiled tentatively, those eyes big and round and hopeful.

His face looked pale and drawn even in the dim light, and painfully young. Up close his fine clothes bore the stains of travel and hung on him too loosely, as if he'd lost weight very recently. Whatever had brought him here, he wasn't on a holiday.

Something Corin feared might be his conscience twisted in his chest.

Fuck.

"Lord Aster," Corin said with heavy resignation. "I guess you may as well come in."

# Chapter Two

ALTHOUGH ASTER HAD HARDLY expected enthusiasm, Corin's greeting achieved some kind of nadir of welcome Aster had never even imagined. If he'd dug a well and buried all the world's excitement in it, and then drowned it for a few years, it might have resembled Corin's downturned mouth and dull dark eyes, and the heavy sigh he let out as he stood aside to allow Aster through the gate.

Corin had always been the most magnificent man Aster had ever seen, with his strong nose and jaw and his (usually) flashing eyes, the faint scales that feathered over his pale bronzy-green skin and gleamed in the sun, his firm mouth and his height and broad shoulders and skill with a sword, and well…Aster would've been there all day if he'd tried to list all the ways Corin outshone other men.

Not to mention, he'd been scrupulously faithful to his own fiancée, unlike the man Aster had been meant to marry…several days ago, now.

And yet Aster's appearance at his gate had managed to make Corin appear older, tired, and *almost* not excruciatingly handsome.

Perhaps making him unhappy was a family trait. No one had ever accused Belinda of having anything in common with her plain, freckled, awkward younger brother. But there had to be a first time for everything.

Or perhaps Aster simply couldn't satisfy anyone, including his own fiancé. He wouldn't be here if he could.

The miserable thought congealed and formed a cold, sad little lump in Aster's gut, joining the much larger cold, sad lump that had been there ever since he fled his home nearly three weeks before. He'd slipped away in the middle of the night without even taking his valet into his confidence, leaving behind a vague note, all his possessions other than what he could carry in his saddlebags, and everyone he'd ever known—except for Corin. He might never see his family again if his father disowned him for running away and snubbing the proud Duke Marellus so thoroughly. He'd never again feel his mother's embrace, or hear her laughter.

Silence had fallen for far too long, leaving an awkward weight to the air. Aster shivered in a breath of the frigid wind that had been at his back the whole way up the mountain and blinked, recalling himself to the present. Everything went a bit blurred for a moment as he did. Fuck, but he'd traveled so far, slept so little, eaten even less. He tightened his hand on the reins he held until the leather bit into his palm, praying that it'd keep him focused and prevent him from passing out where he stood.

"Do I bring my horse inside?" he asked, his words seeming to shatter the quiet and then blow away in fragments on the wind, which whistled over the bridge and through the canyon below in a mournful wail. He didn't see anywhere else to stable a horse, but really? Corin came from a long, noble line of wealthy dragons. His pedigree outclassed Aster's by quite a lot, as a matter of fact, even though he'd given it all up to become a comparatively humble knight in King Theobert's service.

As a not-unimportant side note, Aster had no wish to dine or sleep in the same room as his horse, either, much as he loved the beast. Although he supposed he might be lucky if Corin didn't simply put him wherever he stabled the horse.

"Lead him through and out the other side," Corin said, already leading the way himself into the gloomy bowels of the fort. "There's a lean-to out there you can put him in."

Well, that was a small relief, anyway. Aster followed, Etallon coming along meekly in his wake despite Corin's disturbing draconic presence. For the first time, it occurred to Aster to wonder how Corin managed to be anywhere near a horse, much less ride one, which he'd done constantly while serving the king. Generally speaking and quite understandably, horses—and most other animals—got very, very nervous in the presence of a dragon.

Perhaps the air of competence, strength, and gentlemanly courtesy that humans noticed immediately upon entering his presence translated to something horses could detect with their sensitive ears or noses.

Or, more likely, he'd simply learned how to behave around animals, a skill that many humans also lacked.

Aster might do better as Corin's unwelcome visitor if he could at least pretend to see Corin objectively, rather than through the lens of his own desperately suppressed longings.

Feeling his cheeks flush hot, he ducked his head, hoping Corin wouldn't see his expression in the dimness of the dusty, musty corridor through which they passed. A few steps on, it opened into a hall of sorts, a big rectangular room with high slitted windows, a couple of dark arched doorways in shadowy corners, and a cold, dirty central hearth with a few rough-hewn benches and chairs around it at odd angles.

The fort looked like it'd been abandoned for decades. Not even mice would find any comfort here.

"Good God," he said, startled out of his intention to make himself as unobtrusive as possible. "How bloody long have you lived here, again?"

"You know exactly how long," Corin replied acidly, his already deep voice dipping down to an even lower register that had Aster shivering from the nape of his neck to the backs of his knees. He didn't even favor Aster with a glance, striding without pause toward the other side of the hall, where a large door hung ajar, askew like everything else in this place. "Are you going to ask me *why* I'm here next? Stable your fucking horse and stop talking."

Oh, God. He wished he could sink straight through the floor. So much for Corin's gentlemanly courtesy, but Aster had more than earned some snappishness with his tactless stupidity.

All at once his feet felt like they were cast from lead. His neck could barely hold up his head. It'd simply been a long journey. He needed supper. That had to be it. He couldn't be so weak as to have hot tears prickling at the insides of his eyelids simply because he'd left home possibly forever, and he was alone, and his fiancé utterly despised him, and the one person whose kindness would have made it better…well, seemed to also utterly despise him. Aster had trained as a knight and even fought some duels, not that he'd won many. All right, any. But still. He was better and braver than this. He quickly turned his head and wiped a stray drop clinging to his eyelashes onto the edge of his hood.

"I beg your pardon." He barely managed more than a whisper, hardly audible over the clop of Etallon's hooves. And the hitch in his voice disappeared in the sighing of the wind through all the blasted drafty crevices in this miserable place.

But of course, Corin's hearing was better than a human's.

He spun around so abruptly that Aster stumbled as he came to a sudden halt, Etallon helping not at all by tugging on the reins with a sulky toss of his head. For a moment he overbalanced, one arm flailing and the other caught in the reins—and then in the next moment big hands caught him by the upper arms and tugged him upright again.

Everything seemed to whirl as dizziness assaulted him, and then he blinked at…the surprisingly vulnerable-looking hollow of Corin's muscular throat, his Adam's apple just above it, and the dark stubble all over his chin and jaw.

And then all he could think about was the shocking heat surrounding him. God, Corin's dragon body threw off more warmth than any three humans. After the freezing ride up the mountain, and the lonely weeks of travel before that, sleeping rough so as to avoid being seen and tracked—and not to mention how cold he felt from the inside out—a dragon's banked flame felt like heaven. Corin's touch felt like heaven.

He wanted to sink into it. Sink into Corin. Lean his weary head against that broad chest and go to sleep for a couple of days.

Aster was a *knight*. And a lord, an honorable gentleman, not some lost little boy who needed comforting, least of all from his former almost-brother-in-law. Aster would've given so much to have this for so many years, and now that he did, it was nothing but pity…

Any moment now, he'd force himself to pull away. Aaany moment.

Corin's hands slid down and wrapped themselves above his elbows. They went all the way around, although Aster's biceps were far from dainty.

"What's the matter, Lord Aster?" Corin's voice rumbled out of his chest and seemed to lodge firmly in Aster's, a vibration that had his joints melting and his head drooping forward. For the last two hundred years or more, dragons had essentially been accepted as part of the human nobility, all the ancient feuds and fears resolved. Aster thought of them more as wealthy men and women with the ability to fly and with odd metallic tints to their skin than as monsters, or anything. But the legends of how they could mesmerize humans into obeying their powerful wills didn't seem so far-fetched right now. "You seem…not yourself."

"How would you know? You hardly paid any attention when you were—you hardly know me at the best of times."

Aster winced as the words left his lips. God, he didn't *want* to be rude. Or reveal how deeply it had always hurt that Corin had barely taken the trouble to speak to him even when engaged to Aster's sister. But the energy required for tact and care eluded him in his state of utter exhaustion.

Corin seemed to have heard his misery more than the precise substance of his mumbled words, because he said, "I know I don't. But anyone could tell you're—Lord Aster. There's more to this than travel-weariness. What's brought you to my door like this? What are you running from?"

Corin had run from his fiancée's very public preference for another man. Aster had run from his fiancé's very private preference for another man…only not private enough, because he'd certainly felt free to express it where Aster's valet could hear every word.

A wild burst of laughter bubbled up in his throat and came out something more like a sob.

His head whirled and he had to swallow hard against a wave of nausea as the floor spun out from under him. Oh, for fuck's sake. Looked like he'd be making a closer acquaintance with Corin's chest after all.

At least he'd be warm while he swooned like a fucking idiot.

ASTER'S FULL WEIGHT SLUMPED into Corin's chest all at once,

and only his iron grip on Aster's arms kept the lad from sliding to the floor.

For a shamefully long moment, Corin tilted his head down and breathed deeply, greedily inhaling the scent of another person, the warmth of another life. He'd been so very fucking *alone* for so very long now.

And up close, Aster smelled shockingly delicious for someone who'd been in the saddle for—Corin had to assume a couple of weeks or more, guessing that he'd come from either his family's seat or the capital. Either one would mean a journey of at least that long by land, and Aster didn't smell at all of the sea. He'd been clinging to a futile hope that the scent of summer-warmed roses hadn't been coming from Aster, but had instead been a trick of his imagination or something carried from far beyond the mountains, a waft of a distant southern clime where the flowers bloomed year-round.

Instead it seemed that his senses had chosen to respond to a gangly, overgrown, second-rate courtier with freckles scattered over his cheekbones like spilled paint, and whose only attractive features were shared with the slut who'd broken Corin's heart.

With a jerk, Corin lifted his head and shoved Aster away from him, holding him by his arms and letting him dangle like a rag doll, his feet crumpled on the floor and his head lolling down. A stray lock of silky blond hair, slightly redder than Belinda's but just as soft, brushed Corin's cheek.

Fuck.

His cock had not stiffened slightly. Absolutely fucking not. When Corin fucked men, they were *not* court-bred dilettantes and they were *not* pains in his neck who'd turned up on his doorstep un-invited and they were *not* the brother of the woman who'd allowed herself to be thoroughly rogered in a gazebo during a garden party celebrating the king's fourth nephew's engagement.

Not to mention, they weren't unconscious and entirely at Corin's mercy.

He would never. No matter how much it'd be a sort of revenge, and no matter how often Corin had daydreamed about getting his own back.

His cock…stiffened a little more, fuck, and his hands tightened convulsively around Aster's arms, probably enough to leave rings of bruises by morning.

God. Corin closed his eyes and sucked in a deep breath, trying to calm his pounding heart and all the other parts of him that needed to quiet the hell down. He couldn't stand here all night, and he couldn't drop Aster to the dusty stone floor and leave him there, either.

That left—carrying him somewhere.

Which he couldn't do with the man held out at arm's length like this. Obviously.

Aster's horse snorted and tossed his head, and Corin started and turned, meeting a baleful equine eye. How had he come to focus so completely on Aster that he'd forgotten about a full-sized horse standing there in his hall?

All right. One thing at a time. "Stay there," Corin said to the horse, using an ancient draconic dialect that contained a nearly irresistible command. Well-bred dragons considered it ill form to use it on humans these days, but surely no one could fault him for using it on a horse.

The animal froze as if its hooves had been riveted to the floor.

Which left only one other issue to deal with. Corin mentally braced himself and hoisted Aster's unconscious body up into his arms, one behind his knees and the other around his back. Aster's head rolled against Corin's shoulder, and he let out a soft sigh that tickled his neck.

The scent of roses wafted up, mingled now at such close range with the soft, human warmth of Aster's skin.

"I don't like him," Corin muttered desperately, striding for the stairs. "In fact, I despise him."

Unfortunately, Corin couldn't muster a lot of evidence to support hatred and contempt. Aster hadn't publicly condemned his sister, but then again, who could expect him to? And before that debacle, he'd seemed pleasant enough, if shy, on those few occasions when Corin had spent time with Belinda's family. Aster might be a poor excuse for a knight who'd joined in training at the palace with far more enthusiasm than skill, but he'd been...enthusiastic. Cheerful about his injuries, a good sport when others beat him, gallant on those very rare occasions when his abilities outmatched another man's. Corin hadn't had much to do with him, but he'd noticed. It had been his job to notice everyone and everything in the training yard.

Corin's arms tightened again of their own accord. He took the stairs two at a time, needing to put Aster down before he did something truly stupid, like consider not putting him down at all. Bad enough that the bloody fort boasted only one thing that could be vaguely considered a bed, and even that was rudimentary enough. Half the time, Corin slept as a dragon up on the hill above the tower, or in the hall if he wanted to stay dry.

Well, he could do that again. And Aster could have the bed. Simple.

But when he reached the top and picked his way through the obstacle course of his scattered belongings to get to the bed, he paused.

He could close all the windows, of course, and would...but the top of the tower held the frigid chill of the oncoming storm, and the fireplace was unlikely to be functional, given that it was filled with the caked-on soot and rubbish of decades of disuse and the flue had probably gotten clogged with debris. Sounds coming from it sometimes of an evening suggested it had a family of rodents living in it, too. He suspected chipmunks.

Corin couldn't possibly disturb the little creatures. That wouldn't be fair so close to a snowstorm. No fireplace, then.

Carefully, Corin went to one knee on the edge of the wood frame of the bed. Ropes strung across it held up a mattress stuffed with straw for bulk and pine needles for freshness; not the most luxurious bed, but clean and comfortable enough. Aster had traveled here alone across rough terrain, and he'd certainly slept in much rougher places on the journey. But only one thin blanket lay across the mattress, and Corin knew the tower didn't have another. Even with Aster's cloak wrapped around him too he'd be frozen by morning.

Corin himself, with his dragon metabolism, was the only other possible source of warmth for the bedroom.

He'd been avoiding looking down as he brought Aster upstairs, but as he lowered him to the bed, sliding an arm out from under his knees but still holding him around the shoulders, he couldn't help himself.

No, Aster didn't at all look like someone who'd tempt Corin, not even for a moment, damn it. Those coppery lashes fanned out over his pale cheeks, the spill of freckles beneath, the pink lips parted a little, too dry and still so soft-looking. Plush, even. Far too vulnerable and delicate to be the type of man Corin preferred, someone who could take his full strength without breaking. And far too masculine, with the golden stubble gleaming on his jaw and the muscular weight of him, to be a lady Corin would want to treat with a true knight's gentle chivalry.

Of course, he could always find a middle ground. Half his strength, enough to pound Aster through the mattress, and kisses and caresses to keep him sweet while he took what Corin gave him.

He gritted his teeth together as his cock undeniably went to full mast, pressing painfully against the rough wool of his trousers—he hadn't bothered with anything under them today, as all of his drawers needed mending and he couldn't be fucked about it.

Damn and triple damn. Aster felt glued to his chest, to his arms, because he simply couldn't release him and let him down onto the bed.

What would he look like beneath his fine garments? Smooth and sleekly muscled, perhaps. Strong enough, after all, to withstand the way he'd spread Aster's legs and…

With a burst of willpower born from his total, overwhelming self-disgust, he dropped Aster like his touch was poison, threw the inadequate blanket on top of him as quickly as possible, and fled the bedroom, all but flying down the stairs.

He stopped in the doorway to the hall, leaning his forehead against the wall and closing his eyes. His breath rasped in his ears. One hand twitched toward his cock, still straining, and he clenched it into a fist. Behind his closed eyelids he saw the sprawl of Aster's long limbs in Corin's own bed, and then Belinda's lips and breasts, and then a pair of blue eyes, it didn't matter whose, either of theirs.

Fuck, fuck, something had gone terribly wrong in his brain.

No, *not* fuck. Definitely not fucking anyone, because Aster had to be entirely off-limits.

Even if he hadn't been Belinda's brother. Even if he hadn't been too young, and if at least half of Corin's desire didn't seem to be stemming from some twisted mix of frustrated lust and vengeful fury, and even if he hadn't been *Belinda's brother*, for fuck's sake!

Even without all of that, Aster was helpless for the moment and in Corin's care for as long as the weather lasted—because it would be snowing by morning, he was quite sure, and they'd be cut off from the world except for Corin's ability to change form.

Any human would be helpless in Corin's hands, vulnerable and afraid. Belinda had told him as much, screaming it in his face when she told him how she'd never wanted him, only his lineage and his family's wealth, the envy of her friends for having attracted the attention of a man no one had been able to catch.

Corin swallowed down bile, pushed himself off the wall, and strode into the hall.

Enough. He hadn't even really thought about Belinda in months. He'd been sure his lingering love and bitter hatred had subsided at last. And now Aster's arrival had stirred it all up again, and his brain buzzed like a beehive. He'd been alone too long. Celibate for far too long.

He had to take a breath. Put up Aster's horse, brush and feed the beast, close all the windows. Prepare for the storm.

Prepare to care for his guest, because he had nothing to offer but a hunk of lightly flame-roasted wild boar, which humans couldn't eat, a crust of bread, and possibly an apple or two.

He'd fly down to the village first for supplies and hope the exhausting journey in the freezing gale left him too spent to even think about…anything.

Because when he returned, he'd need to share that narrow bed with Aster if he didn't want him to freeze to death overnight.

# Chapter Three

BEFORE PASSING OUT LIKE an idiot, Aster's last thought had been how incredibly embarrassed he'd be when he came to.

Of course, he hadn't counted on waking up too comfortable and cozy to give a good goddamn about anything at all.

He blinked his heavy eyelids open and curled a little tighter into the perfect warmth that surrounded him up to his chin. In the grim, watery light filtering in through the window near the end of the bed, he could faintly see a plume of his breath steaming in the chill. The frigid air slapped the exposed skin of his face like a duelist's gauntlet, and that pattering sound must be cold rain or snow or some other sky-born misery. Ugh. The weather had clearly taken the turn he'd anticipated as he rode up the mountain.

But it didn't matter. He had a coverlet over him, and a mattress beneath, and he'd melted into goo in between the two. It didn't matter at all that he detested snow and ice, and he missed his home, where it never got cold enough to freeze—and where he might never be welcome again.

A chill went down his spine despite the heat radiating all along his back.

Aster let out a little whimper, and he tucked his chin and tried to tug the blanket all the way over his head without putting a hand out from under.

"Are you all right?"

Aster yelped as his heart flipped sideways and tried to claw its way out of his chest. The galvanic shock that shot all the way down to his toes had him flipping to his back and then sitting bolt upright, the blankets sliding off as he flailed.

"God fucking dammit," he panted, staring wild-eyed at—Corin, who lay at his side in the bed. *Touching* his side, because the bed wasn't really large enough to fit both of them.

Corin. His sister's ex-fiancé. The famed dragon knight. The man he—damn it, Corin. In the bed. With him. Touching him.

He ran through that several more times before his brain really managed to register it. He'd barely ever allowed himself to dream of touching.

They were both fully dressed, albeit disheveled, but the burning heat of Corin's body seared his skin as if he'd been naked. And while his bedmate, oh, fuck, he couldn't use that word or he'd lose his grip on reality, might've appeared to be sprawled at his ease to a casual observer, Aster could feel the tension in him. And see it, too, when he looked into those glittering obsidian eyes. Corin was, in fact, precisely as much at his ease as any lounging large predator would be, particularly when said predator found himself in bed with someone he'd probably like to eviscerate.

"Am I all right?" he gasped, his mind whirling, helplessly trying to land on an acceptable answer. Aster couldn't even really formulate what was wrong, except that he couldn't get a full breath and his skin tingled. "What's—yes, of course, perfectly. Sir Corin, you must know that I frequently—that is—I'm fine!"

God, he must sound like he'd lost his mind. Sharing a bed would be nothing to Corin, who'd spent most of his life in close quarters during training, or on military campaigns. Even if he might've slept with another man for…other reasons…in other circumstances, Aster wouldn't be the one to arouse those particular desires.

Hopefully he wouldn't intuit that Aster had never spent the whole night in bed with a man, and he'd never even come near one who could measure up to Corin.

Corin lifted a hand up and rubbed it over his jaw, a lazy morning motion. Aster could imagine how it would feel if he reached over and did the same, the bristle against his palm. He shivered. The thick dark stubble Aster had noticed yesterday had grown overnight into something more like a scruffy beard.

Not that it made him any less perfect, of course. Aster couldn't have grown a devil-may-care beard like that if he wanted to.

"Good," Corin rumbled, his voice sleep-roughened and

painfully intimate in the small space between them, in the soft silence that underlaid the rush and howl of the storm. "Because the fact that you woke up screaming due to my presence here might've suggested otherwise. And call me Corin, for fuck's sake. Even if I were still Sir Anything, which I'm not, we used to be—"

Corin's jaw snapped shut and his eyes went wide, as if he couldn't believe what he'd almost said aloud.

Related. Brothers. Almost those, anyway. Family, or something like.

The thought of being Corin's brother had always given Aster a lancing pain somewhere below his sternum.

Corin. He'd used the name without the honorific in his mind forever, getting a guilty thrill every time, but it would sound so very different coming out of his mouth.

And feel so very different on his tongue, between his lips.

"Corin," he whispered. And then he snapped out of it, his cheeks going as hot as dragon fire. "I did not scream! For fuck's sake. I didn't—I wasn't—knights don't scream," he finished lamely.

A look of relief flashed across Corin's face, as if he were grateful to Aster for ignoring his slip. "Hah," he scoffed, shoving himself up on his elbows and managing to loom, somehow, despite looking up at Aster from out of a nest of pillows with his hair all mussed and his shirt gaping open. Aster forced his eyes to snap up to Corin's face, his belly clenching. "Look where we are, because knights also supposedly don't—" He stopped himself again, this time so abruptly that Aster heard his teeth click together as he clenched his jaw.

Knights also didn't—and then Aster's fingers clawed into the blanket, going so tight they ached.

Corin had been gentleman enough to cut himself off, but he might as well have said it, because all the humiliation of the previous evening came rushing back at last.

As hot as dragon fire? Aster's face could've been the sun.

"You don't even have to say it, I know what you were thinking." His voice rasped with strain. "Knights don't faint dead away and need to be—" Oh God, oh God, he couldn't say it, he could barely think it. But he *had* to say it, since a gentleman never shied away from the truth, although until this horrifying moment he'd managed to ignore how he must've gotten where he was. "—carried to bed like a swooning maiden! And I may not be very impressive compared to you, Corin, but no one is!"

Oh, fuck, he had to stop his stupid tongue, but now that it'd gotten started it had a mind of its own. He heard more than felt the words continue to tumble out of him, a waterfall of embarrassment. "So that's hardly my fault. And I had a hard journey, very long, and if you'd had to flee your home because your family would've forced you to marry Duke Marellus, who meant to mock and degrade you and make you watch him fuck another man in your marriage bed on the wedding night, then perhaps you wouldn't be quite your usual self either!"

He came to a halt at last, panting, chest heaving, eyes stinging again with frustrated, miserable tears in exactly the way knights' eyes weren't supposed to.

A fraught silence settled over the bedroom. The wind whistled in the chimney mournfully as if in counterpoint.

Corin stared, opened his mouth, closed it again, and then clenched his fists, all the muscles in his arms bulging on either side of his equally massive chest. God damn, how did anyone have muscles like that? It was so bloody unfair. Aster might've been able to swallow his humiliation if Corin had at least possessed a few weaknesses of his own.

And if those hadn't been the arms that had carried him up the stairs.

At last, so quietly that Aster almost couldn't make out the words, he said, "What now? I beg your—*what?*"

God, he'd reduced the mighty dragon knight to monosyllables with his moronic babbling. For a moment Aster was powerfully reminded of his valet's way of leaving him speechless. Pierre couldn't stick to the point if he had it glued to his nose.

A fresh wave of grief would've taken him out at the knees if he'd been standing. Pierre. He'd never again have the opportunity to be furious with the lad for his nonsense—or to apologize for his harsh words in reply to it.

"For one thing, that's not actually at all what I was going to say," Corin continued after another excruciating moment, pinning him with a gaze so dark and deep that Aster's breath caught and held. Were those scales forming around Corin's temples, creeping up his neck from that distractingly exposed triangle of faintly greenish-bronze skin? To Aster's knowledge, that only happened when dragons either meant to change to their other forms or lost control of themselves. And his eyes...Aster could've sworn he saw a faint flicker of orange behind Corin's slitted pupils. He'd never even heard of that.

And yet Corin's tone was so low, so...unnaturally calm, in fact. No one spoke that evenly without trying. Oh, God. Aster was in so much trouble.

"I was going to say that knights—don't house their guests in an unheated room with not enough blankets. Or receive them as rudely as I did, without offering refreshment or any welcome at all. I had no intention of commenting on the way you fainted, in fact." He leaned forward, and then a little more, until Aster could feel the heat of him anew.

Aster's hard swallow clicked loudly enough to make him jump. He practically vibrated with the need to hide, to skitter away and scurry under the bed, to scream and run. Because now Corin knew Aster had come here not by chance, or for some prank, or on Belinda's behalf.

He'd run away from a marriage and defied his parents and Marellus—and by extension, the king, who had to give his seal of approval literally and figuratively to any marriage within the high nobility. He'd made himself one step above an outlaw.

Which meant he could only have one reason for being here.

Aster had meant to reveal the truth later. Much later, or perhaps even not at all. And now, in a fit of stupid, loose-tongued weakness, he'd given himself away.

Corin seemed to grow larger, to fill all Aster's senses, to charge the air the way a thunderstorm would. The storm brewing within the bedroom terrified him far more than the storm raging outside the tower.

"And I'd thought that you'd come here either by chance, or to escape some social faux pas," Corin said as if reading his mind, this time with such a deadly lack of inflection that Aster's spine quivered, and he couldn't do anything but gaze up into Corin's face, eyes wide, frozen. "But unless my ears are broken, I think you've just told me that you're here to escape from—your own intended husband? Duke Marellus. Because he doesn't like you."

Corin's neutral tone gave nothing away. Did he sympathize? Pity him for being so undesirable? Wish him a thousand miles away?

That last one, almost certainly.

Aster could only nod, his neck stiff and the movement jerky. His voice had run away, even if the rest of him hadn't been able to muster the strength.

Corin's lips pressed together tightly, his jaw set.

"Then you're not here for my hospitality, Lord Aster. You're here looking for my protection. Mine. After everything that's—you have the fucking nerve!" Aster cringed back, lungs aching with the effort of holding his breath, as Corin glared at him with a furious flush along his cheekbones and his pupils seeming to glow more brightly.

That clenching in his belly intensified until he thought he might throw up. Or throw himself at Corin's feet and beg. Or—his limbs trembled with urges he couldn't begin to interpret.

At last Corin said, low and rough, "You can stay as long as the bad weather holds. I'm not a monster," and he spat the word as if it tasted foul. Aster flinched. Belinda had called him that. Screamed it, in fact, in front of an audience of dozens, as Corin stood over her bleeding lover with his sword in hand. "I won't throw you out to die of exposure. But that's all. As soon as it's safe, you'll go."

With that, Corin released Aster from his gaze, rolled off the bed, and strode for the door.

Aster all but collapsed, sucking in air and shaking.

Corin turned his head just before he disappeared into the stair-well to add, "And don't think you're going to avoid telling me exactly what happened and how you decided to come here, because that begs for a fucking explanation." Aster winced. "Meet me in the hall, ten minutes. Water in the basin there, garderobe at the foot of the stairs."

He vanished, the sound of his heavy footsteps echoing and then fading away.

Aster dropped his face into his trembling hands.

Well. That could've gone better.

ASTER WOULDN'T BE EXPECTING MUCH, but the meal Corin hastily laid out on a rough board at the end of the hearth still looked unfit for a man accustomed to dining only a few seats down from the king's high table at court. And of course Corin couldn't possibly explain that the effort he'd expended to acquire the dark bread, hard cheese, jar of pickled beets, and wooden bowl of withered end-of-winter apples far outweighed any trouble gone to by anyone who'd hosted Aster in the past. Mentioning his late-night flight down the mountain to the village in white-out conditions, buffeted by high winds, would be fishing for compliments and gratitude.

Or worse, he'd look like he gave a fuck, which of course he didn't. Far from it.

He wished now that he'd simply given Aster the chunk of half-raw pork and told him to fucking eat it or not, depending on whether he preferred parasites or starvation.

How the hell had Aster dared to come looking for his protection from Duke Marellus, from Aster's noble parents, from the no-doubt angry king? The same king who'd been forced to release Corin from his oath of service after pressure from the father of that worthless satin-clad dandy he'd left crying in the dirt with a scar down the side of his pretty-boy face.

Corin *could* protect Aster, of course. Any dragon could, both through sheer unassailable force and through the treaties dragon-kind had made with human monarchs, including King Theobert.

But it made his already awkward position infinitely more so.

And besides, he didn't fucking want to protect Belinda's thrice-damned little brother.

Even if his reason for running away echoed Corin's too closely for comfort. Damn it, Aster was clearly distressed. Distraught, even. And very, very young.

In the abstract, perhaps, he deserved better than Corin's snarling hostility or an interrogation about his reasons for leaving his home. He could forgive himself for that, though.

He wasn't so sure he could forgive himself for what had gone through his mind the night before.

He'd been as tired and chilled as a dragon could get, his fingers aching from the way he'd wrapped his claws around the crate of supplies, and once he'd put his clothes on (at least he'd done that), he'd gone upstairs, drawn as if by a lodestone to the prospect of a bed.

Or perhaps by the prospect of what was *in* his bed, all pale smooth skin and soft pink lips that looked just like—and he suppressed the thought as vigorously as he'd done the night before.

The bed. He'd wanted his own bed, damn it, and to keep Aster from freezing to death. His intentions, at least, had been pure, and he'd stand by that until his dying breath.

The air in the bedroom had been as icy as he'd expected, with frost forming on the windowpanes and the flagstones nearly numbing even his always-warm bare feet. Aster had curled himself into a shivering ball under the blankets, with only the tumble of his red-gold hair peeking out the top like a spill of treasure from a chest.

With no other option, he'd climbed into bed behind Aster and tugged the blanket around both of them, knowing his furnace of a metabolism would throw off enough heat to keep them cozy for what was left of the night.

And it turned out that there was far too much left of the night for Corin's peace of mind. Despite his exhaustion he lay awake for hours, forcing himself to neither toss nor turn so as not to wake Aster. That scent of roses intensified from the heat and proximity. If he moved his head only a little, hair brushed his face, soft and silky. If he'd shifted his own hips only an inch, he'd have been pressing his body against Aster's.

Well, one part of his body, anyway. A part that also refused to settle down and fucking go to sleep.

At last, though, Corin and his most stubborn parts all yielded to weariness, and he slept until Aster stirring around woke him up.

Of course, only Corin knew that he'd spent most of the night rigid and wanting. Aster had woken up shocked to find Corin beside him. How much more shocked would he have been if he knew his host hadn't only lain beside him—he'd thought, in great detail and for two hours or more, about how it would feel to shove him onto his belly, rip his trousers to shreds with razor-sharp claws, and bury himself in that sweet, round peach of an ass? The sweetness might be only Corin's imagination, but he knew how round it was by the way he had to angle his hips to keep from brushing up against it.

Fuck it, it'd definitely be sweet. Soft and hot and slick and open once Corin had finished with it.

God, he had to get himself under control. Even revisiting his scattered thoughts from the night before had him breathing harder, with claws pricking at his fingertips and the faint itch of scales gathering under his human skin.

But how could he stop thinking about it when he didn't only feel guilty for what he wanted, but for *why* he wanted it?

He didn't desire Aster because of himself. It was his resemblance to Belinda, the most beautiful woman Corin had ever met; it was Corin's anger, anger he couldn't take out on her but that still sought an outlet after all this time; and it was sheer deprivation and frustration. He'd stayed away from the village for the last two years, not wanting to take advantage of any of the young folk who would've been only too willing to spread their legs for a famous knight. It'd been longer than that since he'd had anything but his own hand.

In short, Aster himself, as a person, was almost entirely irrelevant.

And that made him feel like the lowest, most despicable bastard to walk the earth. Corin knew how it felt to be wanted for attributes you possessed and not for your own true self. Belinda had treated Corin like a tall, muscular, green and scaled trophy. It still smarted two years later.

Aster would be horrified to find out that the gallant Sir Corin wanted to pin him down and use his body in any case. But if he discovered that Corin only wanted to fuck him out of lingering, festering desire for his sister, and out of boredom…Corin might be angry and hurt, but not wantonly cruel.

The sharp crackle of a damp log catching fire startled him out of his reverie, and he came back to himself to find his fists clenched and his chest heaving as he stared sightlessly down. He blinked the hearth back into focus.

The fire had gotten going well, sending out enough heat that the middle of the hall would be bearable.

Food. He'd put out the food already.

Now to spend a few minutes standing outside in the snow to cool his blood and reduce the chances that he'd have a visible erection when he served it.

But too late. He'd lost the chance to try to school his mind into something a little less brutal and bestial. A soft shuffle of footsteps from above announced that his guest had chosen to accept his not-so-inviting invitation, and a few moments later, just long enough for Corin to belatedly remember something like manners and attempt to straighten the drooping collar of his shirt and rub a hand over the unknightly and unsightly bristle on his jaw, Aster appeared in the doorway.

# Chapter Four

"FORGIVE ME, SIR CORIN," Aster said, his voice nearly as stiff as his shoulders. He'd clearly gone to some effort to make himself presentable, turning his blue tunic inside out to hide the stains of travel, and finger-combing his hair into order with a little water, it looked like. In the firelight, the waves around his face gleamed ruddy gold. "I hope you didn't go to any trouble on my account."

Corin glanced down at the fire, warm enough but hissing and shooting sparks everywhere, at the meager spread that resembled a peasant's daily meal, and at his own shirt, open at the neck and hanging loose and untucked over his trousers. Oh, and with a pink stain where he'd spilled the beet juice. He probably smelled like a pickle.

Fuck his life.

He looked back up to find Aster leaning a hand on the door-jamb as if he couldn't quite maintain that rigid, formal posture without support.

The support of Corin's arms, perhaps, or lying down he wouldn't need it…and no, just no.

A poisonous mixture of pity and guilt and rage and frustration made his voice far raspier and his tone far sharper than he intended as he replied, "I think I told you it's Corin, plain and simple. And no. I didn't."

But he had, of course he had, and although he'd already resolved not to mention it he couldn't help wishing he could flaunt his efforts.

Appearing to be a total thoughtless asshole would have to be his penance for being far, far worse than that.

Aster's face, already too pale except for the black shadows beneath his eyes—fuck, Corin was a monster after all—went a shade whiter, and he bit his lip, brows drawing together in a frown.

"I'm sorry, Corin," he said, so softly that it felt like a punch to the gut. Belinda had been right, and it had nothing to do with his scales or wings or claws or her disfigured lover. "I'm sorry for that and for—for everything. For coming here. I know you never wanted to see any of us again, and I know you didn't want anything to do with the court, and my troubles are bringing that to your doorstep, in a certain sense, anyway. And please call me Aster, too," he added in a rush, his cheeks flushing a pretty rose-pink. Perhaps that would be the color of the roses that had lent him his scent. God, what a nonsensical idea. "I may not be Lord Anything anymore, either, now that I've run away. I'm probably disowned."

His voice trailed off into something barely above a whisper, and he cast his eyes down, blinking as if to prevent tears from falling.

That was more than a punch to the gut. That was a full-force kick from a dragon's hind leg. Someone needed to take care of this lad, badly. And it couldn't be Corin. It couldn't possibly. He could barely take care of himself, and besides, he bloody well didn't want to. He'd already promised once to spend the rest of his life caring for one of that fucking family, and look how that had turned out. Aster might look innocent, but he probably had the same rot at his core as his sister.

And then Aster cleared his throat and lifted his chin. His eyes glistened, bright blue made even brighter, but he held Corin's gaze steadily and even tried to smile, a sad little quirk of the lips. "Again, forgive me. I'm still not myself. Ignore my foolishness."

Those eyes. That voice. That sweet scent. Corin could drown in them.

His heart gave another agonizingly guilty twist. Courage in any form showed a man's character, and despite what so many believed, courage could be far more difficult off the battlefield than on it. Aster might look like Belinda and he might have come here for reasons that made Corin want to throw him out the window.

But he was so young, so alone, and trying so hard to be brave.

"There's nothing to forgive, Aster," Corin said, surprising himself by how close he came to really meaning it. And if his voice dipped a little lower on Aster's name, well. No human would be able to hear that over the aggressive crackle of the fire. "Sit. Eat. Get warm. I've been without company for so long that I've turned into a beast." He tried a smile on for size, hoping it didn't look too feral, and felt a strange lightening in his chest when Aster's lips curled up a little more in response. "But I'm expecting that explanation. You said you might've brought the court to my doorstep, in a sense. That'll be literally true when they come looking for you."

Aster sighed, nodded, and pushed off the doorjamb, coming all the way into the room at last, as if Corin had finally made him feel welcome enough to step over the threshold. "Of course I'll explain," he said. "But I don't think they'll look for me here. This is the last place anyone would look for me."

Corin disagreed completely that no one would look for him here; even if they didn't come this way expecting to find Aster with Corin, they'd ask in the village and end up here by process of elimination.

But arguing about it wouldn't serve any purpose, and he wouldn't get anything sensible out of Aster until he'd eaten and woken up a bit. Corin waved a hand at the food and took a seat on one of the chairs he'd pulled up. That proved to be a sufficient invitation. Aster dropped down onto one of his own, piled half a loaf of bread with cheese and beets, and tore into it like a starving wolf. While hungry himself, Corin ate more slowly, making sure Aster had his fill. After all, he could always change forms and devour the rest of that haunch of pig he had out in the shed.

Besides, the flicker of the firelight on Aster's gleaming hair and on his face, which was slowly regaining color as he ate, proved distracting enough to keep Corin from feeling the force of his hunger. The hall did have open, unglazed windows high up in the walls, but he'd closed the shutters to keep out the snow. Even if they'd been open there wouldn't have been much light on such a stormy day. It left Aster looking like something out of a fairy tale.

He resembled Belinda both more and less than Corin had originally thought. More, in that he'd always thought Aster rather plain and was now forced to revise that opinion, and less in that he'd never spent enough time with him to see his individuality.

The shutters didn't keep out the draft, of course, and every now and then a particularly violent gust rattled them and whistled through their cracks, sweeping down into the room to make the fire dance and flutter the ancient, moth-eaten tapestry on the opposite wall. The small fort had originally been built as a watchtower, and then used as a base for bandits who preyed on small caravans going over the nearby pass. It had eventually fallen into the possession of Corin's great-uncle, who'd used it as a sort of hunting lodge. He'd been the one to put up the ugly hanging of a great gold dragon carrying off a stag.

But he'd grown old enough that he stayed mostly at home, and Corin had appropriated the place, with Great-Uncle Ivar's blessing, as his refuge from the humiliation and violence that had marked the end of his life at court. In fact, Corin's family had rejoiced when he asked permission to come here. They'd made it clear that they hoped he'd finally given up his foolish obsession with human swords and spears and armor and chosen to take a more draconic path in life.

Ironic, given how embarrassed his family had been as he grew and showed far more physically draconic traits than his peers. His cousins, except for Fiora, had whispered and laughed and called him a primitive beast.

Perhaps he'd chosen to live among humans in part to prove he could.

But whatever his reasons, he'd grown to love his life as a knight, and he couldn't choose what he loved, what he hoarded. One couldn't change one's nature, after all, and he'd have thought other dragons would understand if anyone would—but he'd kept his mouth shut. Why argue about it all over again? His family hadn't quite disowned him the first time. Maybe he could keep it that way.

And now Aster had come here to escape a humiliating situation involving a faithless betrothed just as Corin had, with an equally disapproving family lurking in the background.

He set the rind of his piece of cheese down onto the plank he'd used as a makeshift serving platter, no longer hungry after all. Aster had slowed down at last, having polished off most of the bread and cheese and, to Corin's surprise, almost all of the beets. At least now they'd both smell like pickles.

And suddenly his mental perspective shifted, as if he'd taken a huge step off to the side and viewed the two of them sitting by the fire as an outside observer might. Sitting there in his inside-out breadcrumb-strewn tunic with his pink lips dyed even pinker from the beets, Aster had become another refugee from the civilized world— another man, plain and simple, with nowhere else to go.

And they both smelled like pickles.

Corin realized, when Aster looked up sharply with startled eyes, that he'd started to laugh.

"I'm sorry," he said, still grinning. "But it struck me all of a sudden what a pair we are. All covered in crumbs and beet juice and not a clean shirt to be had in the whole ramshackle place."

His merriment faded as Aster didn't laugh with him, simply sitting frozen and staring at him, eyes wider and wider.

"What?" he demanded, self-conscious and fighting the urge to twitch. Did he look even more unkempt than he'd thought? Or maybe he'd completely misjudged Aster's sense of humor. It wouldn't be the first time. Belinda had never even cracked a smile when he tried to joke. Perhaps she and her brother had that in common.

"Oh," Aster said after a long moment. "I hadn't heard you laugh in so long." His natural color had come back with the warmth of the fire and the meal, but now his cheeks flooded with pink, the same color Belinda had…well, honestly, she'd probably used rouge. "Um. I'm sorry, I'm still worn out from the journey."

They'd barely spoken above a dozen words to one another before last night, meeting a few times at the Cezanne family townhouse in the capital and a few more at court or at various parties and balls. There'd always been so many other things to claim Corin's attention. Mostly Belinda, since she'd never appreciated it when his focus wavered. And then once, perhaps, Corin had attempted to correct his form when he'd been sparring with another gentleman at the palace training yard. When had Aster heard him laugh in the first place?

Fuck it. It might put Aster on the spot, but he wanted to know, and so he asked.

Aster's blush went from bright pink to deep scarlet, and Corin watched in fascination as it spread from his cheeks up his temples and to his hairline, like spilled ink. Or beet juice.

"I don't—I mean, that is—you used to laugh when you were training. I was always rather afraid you were laughing at me," he added with disarming honesty. "Although you probably didn't notice me enough for that to be the case. Not that I would've blamed you. You never seemed to laugh when you were with—oh, shit, I mean at court."

Damn it all to hell. No, Belinda hadn't ever made him laugh, either. In hindsight, maybe their lack of anything resembling a shared sense of humor ought to have been a hint.

He wouldn't be touching that with a ten-foot pole. But the rest of what Aster had said, all flustered and obviously ill at ease...

Corin had always been kind if possible but as blunt as necessary during training, because better a discouraged, offended young swordsman safely at home than an overconfident corpse left to rot on a battlefield.

But in the face of Aster's worries about being the butt of the joke—or so insignificant that no one would even trouble to laugh at him—he couldn't bring himself to tell the truth now. "You aren't that bad," he said.

Aster snorted a laugh and his eyes gleamed brilliant blue. Corin found himself smiling helplessly in response. "And you're a terrible liar," he replied. "I'm skilled enough to earn my spurs, and I can defend myself from the average brigand, but I'm never going to be a mighty warrior. Like you."

Corin opened his mouth, fully intending to protest, but Aster held up a hand and actually—shushed him? Yes, that had been a *tchah* kind of sound. Aimed at *him*. Sir Corin, the dragon knight. Unbelievable. He'd never been put so much in his place in his life, at least not by anyone who lived to tell the tale. Or by his Great-Aunt Hilda, who also made that sound, come to think of it.

Although it didn't make him want to put his Great-Aunt Hilda in her place in turn, as it did with Aster.

What that place might be...better not to think about it in detail.

"Don't bother," Aster continued. "I've long since come to terms with it. And trying to reassure me doesn't suit you, Corin. I used to listen as you dressed down those of the squires and bachelors you thought hadn't tried their best. You never gave a word of praise that wasn't earned. Although you did laugh, sometimes."

His wistful tone struck a chord somewhere deep inside where Corin had thought he'd gone numb long ago. The dust and heat, the clang and clash of metal on metal, the shouts and laughter and occasional cry of pain, the shuffle of booted feet. Plunging his overheated head into a trough of water after and shaking the drops out of his hair, sharpening his sword by the fire in the barracks.

And laughing. Because he had, often enough.

The life he'd given up when it turned out to be hollow.

"I was never laughing at you," he managed at last, his throat tight. *You never gave a word of praise that wasn't earned.* That suggested, even to Corin's not-so-sensitive understanding of other people's feelings, a long-held desire to have earned some of those words. He dug deep into his memories, ignoring the sting of loss. "You were always quick on your feet. Not enough power in your stroke, and you simply didn't have the strength to lift your arm fast enough to parry someone who did have enough power, with your sword or with your shield. But you could outmaneuver nearly anyone, given the chance."

Aster's eyes sparkled again. The firelight, or some magic from within? Belinda's eyes had never held that much mischief. He leaned forward, a saucy little smile teasing the corners of his mouth. Teasing Corin, and heat shot straight down between his legs at the sight.

"So what you're saying, Sir Corin, is that I ought to stay the hell out of a fight, but that I'm well-equipped to run away?"

The laugh that startled out of him distracted him somewhat from the very vivid image that'd popped into his mind of putting Aster on his knees and shoving that pretty smile open with his cock.

Fuck, he had to get it together. He'd been fine for nearly two years. *Fine.* And now...

"Ah, no," he stammered, and then added, belatedly attempting to match Aster's light tone, "Don't put words in my mouth, if you please!" *I'd like to put something in your mouth.* Fuck. "You simply don't have the build for combat with a broadsword and shield. You ought to stick to the rapier."

Aster's smile dimmed, and he looked down at his lap, brushing off a few crumbs. Fidgeting, rather than cleaning up. His tunic was probably past help at this point and he had to know it.

"I left my rapier at home, though I do prefer it. I thought a heavier sword would be more practical in case I needed to use it to really defend myself. I suppose I'll have to buy another someday. If I can afford to."

Corin sat back, sucking in a deep breath to try to hide his revulsion. Everything in him protested the idea of Aster *having had to leave his favorite sword behind*. His *sword*. His right hand itched with the desire to wrap around the hilt of his own favorite broadsword, the massive blade that no human man could wield without pulling a muscle at best, and he clenched it into a fist around nothing.

And "if I can afford to." If he could afford it! The spoiled third child of one of the wealthiest nobles in the kingdom, worrying about a future in which he might not be able to buy the necessities of life.

Corin knew, in the background sort of way one knew the sky was blue or that forests had trees, that most people wouldn't consider a rapier a necessity of life. Most people needed every last copper farthing they could scrape together and every working hour of the day to provide themselves with pickled beets and brown bread.

But those were humans, not dragons.

What dragons valued most highly, they needed.

Corin valued swords very highly indeed.

He tried not to acknowledge the nagging thought in the back of his mind that his attachment to well-wrought blades of all kinds wasn't the whole issue, here, and that generally speaking he'd have shrugged at the idea of some pampered courtier losing his fortune. After all, Corin did just fine here in his tumble-down tower with half-raw wild boar and a malfunctioning fireplace full of chipmunks, thank you very fucking much. If he could manage, so could anyone else. And if they couldn't, too damn bad.

But Aster was now Corin's concern.

No, dammit, his *problem*, not his concern, and he needed to keep that in the forefront of his mind.

Either way. If he meant to get Aster back home, into the lap of luxury, and the hell out of Corin's hair as quickly as possible, then he needed information.

"I think it's time you told me precisely what you're running from," he said. "And we'll deal with the question of finding you a rapier next."

# Chapter Five

WHAT WAS IT PIERRE had said when he came running into Aster's bedchamber, breathlessly overwrought and carrying his tale of Marellus's conversation with his lover? *It's so vile, my lord, I can hardly bring myself to repeat it.* Well. Pierre had been forced to say it aloud to the man it concerned, but now Aster would need to say it about himself.

He'd almost rather spend his wedding night the way Marellus had envisioned than tell Corin, of all people, what Marellus had said about him.

But Corin was waiting, and Aster had to look up from the disgusting mess he'd made of his clothing by eating like a wild animal and answer the damn question sooner rather than later.

When he did raise his eyes at last, his throat went dry, any words he'd started to formulate fleeing into the ether. Corin had his own eyes fixed on him, dark and gleaming and entirely intent. Aster had his full attention. And the weight of it left Aster breathless. How often had he half wished for it and half dreaded it? Any word from the king's most illustrious knight, although most often critical, had been prized like gold by the young men at court. Aster hadn't been any different.

In more social settings, Corin's attention had always been riveted to Belinda—and no wonder. Her beauty and her charm snared everyone. Occasionally Corin had spared a word or two of greeting for her plain and dull younger brother before immediately returning to his fiancée.

As he ought to have, of course. The hidden depths of Aster's disappointment didn't make that feeling more rational, only more painful.

And now he'd had more of Corin's words than he knew what

to do with and couldn't find any of his own. Corin had laughed. He hated to ruin what felt like a moment of genuine rapport with a serious discussion.

But he had to. Corin's brows had started to draw together into an impatient frown.

"Do you know Lord Dericort?" he asked finally. "Marellus's...closest friend." To the rest of the world, anyway.

Corin's frown deepened. "I've come across him once or twice." His tone didn't suggest he'd enjoyed those meetings much, which encouraged Aster a bit.

"My valet overheard them when they arrived at Cezanne." Corin nodded. Aster drew a deep breath. He could tell this, he could. "Dericort complained about Marellus marrying me, he said that I, I was too plain for anyone to get it up when we—and that Marellus would need to put a bag over my head." His voice broke, and he stared down at his fists where they sat clenched on his knees. He couldn't possibly look at Corin's face, and most likely see nothing but agreement there. "Marellus said no, because that'd block my view of the two of them taking their pleasure. That he wouldn't betray Dericort with me. And kissed him."

Corin didn't speak. The fire crackled, the shutters banged.

At last Aster dared to look up. Oh, God. Corin's expression showed exactly as much disgust as Aster had feared. He'd never recover from the humiliation of this, not in a thousand years.

"You said your valet saw this conversation? Heard them? Where? How trustworthy is this servant of yours?"

Aster blinked at him. That was not at all what he'd expected Corin to say—not that he'd been able to imagine anything at all without his brain shutting down.

"Pierre's very loyal to me, and he's not excitable at all," Aster said. The opposite, in fact. Pierre tended to the placid, cultivating his slight rotundity with a great deal of quiet, contemplative snacking. "He wouldn't lie to me. He—didn't want to tell me. But he felt like he had to."

"All right," Corin said slowly. "Fine. Let's assume for the moment he was telling the truth. What the fuck are you doing here? Lord

Cezanne could've dealt with Dericort. Gotten him out of the way somehow, exiled or out of favor with the king. I know Marellus, he's not sentimental, to say the least. He wouldn't choose his lover over whatever reasons he had for marrying you in the first place."

Aster swallowed hard, his throat painfully tight. "I didn't tell my parents, but—"

"The fuck do you mean you didn't tell them!" Corin's voice snapped like a whip, recalling all the times he'd told off some unlucky squire for showing up to training hung over, or failing to check the straps on his armor properly. Aster fought the urge to shrink back in his seat as Corin leaned forward, eyes blazing. "Your betrothed doesn't want you and has a lover. It's an arranged fucking marriage, Aster! What did you expect? True love?"

The nasty twist of sarcasm Corin put on those words burrowed into Aster's chest like a blade. He *did* want to be loved. Didn't everyone? Did he really deserve Corin's contempt for thinking he ought to be treated with respect, at least? But of course…*whatever reasons he had for marrying you in the first place.* Corin couldn't think of any, clearly. Perhaps he agreed with Marellus and Dericort after all.

"And so you ran away," Corin went on implacably, "with nothing but your horse and your sword. Did you at least leave a fucking note, or are they dragging lakes and arresting anyone who's ever looked at you sideways?"

Oh, God. Corin made Aster's flight sound like such a childish overreaction. So unnecessary, so irresponsible and thoughtless.

"Of course I left a—a note," he stammered. "On my dressing table. Telling them that I'd had to leave for personal reas—"

"You had to leave for personal reasons?" Corin hadn't raised his voice much, but—oh, fucking hell, that puff of smoke had come from his *mouth*, not from the fire in the hearth. And limned as he was in flickering orange he looked more draconic than he ever had, the faintly metallic green undertone of his skin brought out in the light. "Personal reasons. You had to leave. You didn't bloody well have to leave, Aster. You had to back out of the marriage if you couldn't stand to live with a man who loved someone else. You had to refuse to go through with it and tell your parents why. Instead you didn't even try to deal with the situation before you simply fled. What the fuck were you thinking?"

The power of Corin's anger seemed to fill the room, a heavy pressure—that same sensation of walking into a thunderstorm that he'd had earlier in the bedroom. And it had the same effect, of making his mind shut down completely.

He wanted to accuse Corin of being horrifically unfair. Hypocritical, even. He'd run from Belinda's betrayal just as Aster had run from Marellus's.

Except that Marellus hadn't done anything publicly. And Corin and Belinda's engagement had been, supposedly—*true love*. Not a political match made to ally his family with one of the most powerful of the king's favorites and at the same time end the simmering feud that'd existed between their houses for the last eighty years or so. He'd been assured by his father that it would be wonderful, and by his mother that he'd find contentment in marriage eventually just as she had. Since Aster had never managed to find more than mediocre pleasure with another person, giving Marellus a lackluster rogering couldn't be much worse. And as he'd never expected to be happy the way married people outside of the nobility were supposed to be, he'd thought that he might as well marry someone who'd make everyone else happy.

And he'd hoped that if he kept gritting his teeth and repeating it, he'd believe it eventually.

But he also knew no one should have to live that way, no matter what interests were at stake for the Cezanne family.

And Corin ought to understand that. He, of all people, ought to understand, and it was so terribly unfair that he didn't. Perhaps the crux of the matter was that Corin didn't believe someone like Aster, who didn't have beauty or charm or anything special about him, deserved anything better.

"Well?" Corin prompted impatiently. "Nothing to say?"

He had so much to say. How he'd gone downstairs to greet Marellus and his entourage after hearing what Pierre had told him, because he didn't know what else to do. How Lord Dericort had lounged at Marellus's side like a poisonous snake, all graceful long lines and glittering dark eyes fixed on Aster with obvious hatred and scorn. How Marellus had laughed at Dericort's sly asides, leaning in to allow the man to whisper in his ear, and hadn't favored Aster with so much as a smile. Marellus had been coldly, scrupulously polite—but barely.

And Aster's parents had seemed perfectly happy with the meeting and with their guests' behavior. They loved him dearly, though they showed it oddly sometimes. But they didn't love each other and saw no reason why aristocratic spouses ought to do so. By giving him to Marellus they believed they were assuring him of wealth, a high place in society, the favor of the king. Everything they valued. As long as Marellus's manners remained correct in public, they'd never believe Aster could be as unhappy as he claimed.

Surely Corin would understand why he'd had to go, why he couldn't have confided in his family, if he explained all of that.

Instead, all he managed was, "I don't—I don't—it wasn't only what he said, it was how he said it! He has nothing but contempt for me, Corin. I know it."

Corin's eyes closed for a moment and he blew out a long, deep breath. Two small tendrils of smoke escaped from his nostrils. His lips moved slightly.

Counting to ten. He'd reduced the mighty Sir Corin to counting to ten like a schoolmaster trying to keep his patience with an unruly student. Of course, your average schoolmaster wouldn't breathe fire when his patience ran out.

When Corin opened his eyes again, he said, very slowly and evenly, "You didn't hear him say it, Aster. Your valet did. Or did I misunderstand you?"

Oh, for fuck's sake. Aster's head felt light and floaty, dismay and frustration swimming in circles in his skull and putting him all off-balance. "Yes, it was my valet, but—"

"Your valet heard him. And then told you how he'd sounded. And from the hearsay of some eavesdropping servant, you constructed the need to run away from a betrothal that I'm guessing had been carefully negotiated by all parties and approved by the king? A betrothal you'd agreed to?"

Aster's face went so hot it hurt, cheeks prickling and eyes burning. He clenched his hands on his thighs to try to quell the shaking in his limbs, but his fists trembled too.

All of that was true on the face of it, and yet…it ignored everything that really mattered. The way he'd felt when he'd returned to his own chambers and had a few minutes to think and to face the reality of what the marriage would mean. The shuddering horror that had come over him as he'd imagined his wedding night in visceral detail.

He had to think carefully and explain himself in a way that Corin wouldn't disregard. Because he wasn't an idiot, and he knew Pierre, and his own observations had only confirmed Pierre's story.

Instead, all that came out—and in a sulky tone to boot—was, "I didn't negotiate anything. They decided it all without me." Corin stared at him silently, jaw set and one eyebrow raised, saying more without words than he could have with a whole tirade. Fucking hell. "It's not because I didn't have a say that I had to leave," he went on, knowing he was only making it worse, but starting to trip over his words as they tumbled out of him. "It was—you weren't there. You didn't see them. Marellus hates me. It would've been a living hell. Corin, please. You have to believe me!"

After a beat, Corin's face softened, and he said, "I believe you." But he didn't sound sincere, and Aster could practically feel his heart cracking in half. He'd lost his family with his little stunt, and none of his friends who wanted to keep their social standing would take him in. In other words, all of them. Corin was all he had.

Hell. Corin really was all he had.

And the man barely knew him despite how closely they'd almost been related, despised his whole family as far as Aster knew, and couldn't even convincingly pretend that he thought Aster hadn't played the fool.

Far worse, Corin's doubt only fed his own. He'd wondered if he'd made a terrible mistake over and over again on the cold, hungry, homesick journey here.

This might all have been for nothing. He couldn't believe that, he couldn't. But…

Aster stared into the fire until his eyes hurt. At least then he could pretend it was from strain and not the stinging of unshed tears.

"But it doesn't actually matter at all if I think the marriage was a bad idea or if you were right to want to get out of it," Corin went on when the silence had stretched almost to the breaking point, making Aster jump. He looked back up and immediately wished he hadn't. Corin's frown hadn't lessened at all. He still loomed in front of the flickering flames like a ferocious storybook dragon, the kind who used to eat annoying knights who turned up at the door uninvited. "It only matters that you gave your word."

"But I—"

"Your *word*, Aster. As a knight and a gentleman. Too many other people were involved. Your family. His. The king. If you weren't going to marry him, no matter why, it was your responsibility to honorably end the betrothal. And that's all there is to it."

Aster raised one shaking hand and rubbed at his temples, trying to soothe the headache that had started pounding into life.

Corin's voice rang in his ears. *Your word, Aster. That's all there is to it.*

Of course that would be Corin's perspective, and he'd never been a yielding, flexible type of person; when he had a moral stance, he stuck to it as stubbornly as any mule. He'd expect everyone else to follow the same code, because it was the *right* code. Aster couldn't even argue the point in the abstract.

Still. He had to make Corin understand that right or wrong, the die had been cast.

"I agreed to the betrothal, yes," he muttered. "But I can't go back. Even if I wanted to. Marellus would never marry me now. Not after I've humiliated him like this. And my parents won't forgive me either, so it's not like I could just go back to the way things were."

Corin's eyes flashed with a sudden fire. "Is it a family trait to publicly humiliate anyone you're engaged to?"

Oh, God. His limbs went cold as a horrible jolt of hurt and shame shot through all of them. "But I—he—I'm—sorry," Aster stammered. "But *he* humiliated *me*, he—he would've made me watch!" he ended in a wail. "Watch him with someone else!"

Corin's jaw dropped, his face going pale. "Fuck," he said, sounding choked. "Fuck. Forget I—fuck." And he slumped back into his chair, resting an elbow on the armrest and dropping his head into his hand, rubbing his bristly chin and his temples.

Aster sucked in a deep, gasping breath, feeling like he'd been released from an enchantment without the weight of Corin's gaze on him.

But that relief only lasted a few seconds. "You're right that the fault here isn't all yours. But you have to go back," Corin said heavily. "And you will. Not tonight, obviously. And not while the storm lasts. You can wait out the weather here. But that's all."

That cold lump in his belly that'd melted away a little bit in the warmth of the fire and the meal formed again with a vengeance. Aster nearly doubled over from the pain of it, regretting every bite of his food. He tasted beets, and not in a good way.

"Please, you have to—"

"No," Corin said with absolute finality, and he stood up, brushing the crumbs from his knees with a brusque gesture that felt like a dismissal of Aster himself. "I'm sorry." And he did sound sorry, which made it even worse. Corin would never pity someone he saw as an equal. "You can't run away from this, and I won't be involved in it. I need to go and see to your horse. No, stay here where it's warm," he said as Aster made to stand up. "The cold doesn't affect me."

Before Aster could muster another word, Corin turned and strode off across the hall to the door at the back. When he opened it, a gust of frigid wind roared into the hall; he slammed it shut, leaving Aster alone.

More alone, in fact, than he'd ever thought it possible to be.

He stared at the remains of breakfast, wishing it'd been a little later in the day and that Corin had brought out wine to accompany it.

If he had any, of course. This miserable place might not even be supplied with any. Though surely there had to be at least a jug of ale about.

Aster had never been able to hold his liquor. He didn't get

violent or belligerent, more's the pity. That at least would've been understandable for a knight and a lord. No, he became maudlin, sentimental, and foolish, and the likelihood that he'd have drunkenly slurred his admiration for Corin's physical, mental, and moral attributes—at great length—before weeping over his ill fortune was unfortunately extremely high. That, or begin begging Corin to let him stay.

He felt close enough to sobbing on the floor even stone-cold sober.

But now he desperately longed to numb his brain.

Brandy. Aster could destroy a bottle of brandy if opportunity allowed. He might be sick, but at least he'd stop hearing Corin's voice saying *You can't run away from this, and I won't be involved in it* or *Is it a family trait to publicly humiliate anyone you're engaged to?* over and over again.

Aster had always known he had very little in common with Belinda. And the first time someone ever suggested they might be similar, it wasn't for shared beauty or charm or wit, it was for this. Of course. And it didn't matter that Corin had realized he'd been unfair. He'd still thought it and said it in the first place.

The minutes stretched. The fire crackled and spat, and Aster added another couple of small logs from the pile on the floor. The hissing and popping became unbearable, and Aster moved his chair back to avoid getting little holes in all his clothes from the flying sparks.

Corin still didn't return.

The wind howled around the tower, banging the shutters wildly. The tapestry on the opposite wall flapped and sent up a massive, choking cloud of dust. Aster eyed it suspiciously. Was that supposed to be a golden dragon? Probably, by the wings, but it looked more like a lumpy sort of scaled flying cow.

Ugh. What a horrific thought.

And with that, Aster had exhausted all of the hall's available options for avoiding his situation, Corin's opinion thereof, and anything else he desperately didn't want to think about.

He looked around the room, but no. The fire, the tapestry, the shutters, the door. There really wasn't anything else to absorb so much as a moment's attention.

And Corin *still* hadn't returned. If he'd been human, Aster would've gone looking for him long before now, concerned that he might've gotten lost in the blizzard, or injured himself, or fallen victim to frostbite. And if their conversation had been any less fraught, guilt and affection would've had him out there too to pet and reassure Etallon.

But a dragon wouldn't be subject to any of those dangers. Not in his own courtyard, anyway. And if Corin wanted to be anywhere near Aster, he'd have come back. His protracted absence sent a very clear message of *Leave me the fuck alone.*

Well, message received. And it hurt, no matter how much Aster himself didn't want to continue the discussion. It could only end with him begging or shouting and Corin calling him a great deal of things that would be both insulting and mostly true, like *coward* and *idiot* and *liar* and *just like your faithless bitch of a sister except that she's gorgeous and you're not.*

Screw it. He simply couldn't sit there any longer—he'd go mad. So he stood, stretched, moved the board that'd held their breakfast to a bench further from the flames so it couldn't kindle, and set off to see what else the tower held, if anything.

People generally kept their wine downstairs.

Perhaps he'd explore the cellar first.

# Chapter Six

CORIN TOOK HIS SWEET time caring for Aster's horse, telling himself that the beast deserved a little petting and soothing after being installed in a strange shed during a snowstorm. The horse might be warm and fed—Corin had also carried back a bale of hay from the village the night before—but he hadn't exactly been able to provide the kind of equine luxury the animal would be used to. It was common decency to spend more time grooming him.

And if the horse's snorting and eye-rolling suggested he knew damn well Corin was using him as an excuse to hide from his master, he chose to ignore it.

Maybe the horse didn't know anything at all and Corin's guilty conscience was really the one rolling its eyes and snorting.

Fuck.

He rearranged the horse's blanket yet again to make sure it covered his withers. Even though it was late morning and both the warmest and brightest part of the day, the light filtering into the shed made it look like evening, and the air hadn't gotten above freezing. The snow showed some signs of slowing, though. Corin might be able to get Aster on his way back to his family sooner than he'd thought.

Aster. Corin knew he was in the right. He *knew* it. If a man gave his word, he had to retract it directly if he changed his mind and stay to face the music. He couldn't simply run away.

*But you ran away.* For the tenth or perhaps thousandth time, Corin told his conscience to go fuck itself. His situation had been entirely different. No one would've expected Aster to go through with the marriage if Marellus had been seen fucking someone else in public. If that didn't constitute a tacit breaking off of an engagement, Corin didn't know what did. Corin had been running from the humiliation of his engagement being broken that way. Not from the task of breaking it off in the first place.

But he had to take Aster's age and experience, or lack thereof, into account. Like most dragons, Corin looked younger than he really was to a human eye—although dragons weren't considered fully mature until their mid-thirties, which made up the difference a bit. His relatives still saw him as a callow youth even though he'd utterly failed to celebrate his thirty-seventh birthday a few months back.

Still. Fifteen of those years had been spent in King Theobert's service, and those years hadn't all been peaceful; no one could call Corin inexperienced or naïve. Corin didn't know Aster's exact age, but Belinda was twelve years his junior and Aster even younger than that. Twenty-three at the most.

For fuck's sake. Marellus was an asshole, and everyone knew it. Aster's valet had probably exaggerated what he'd heard to its greatest possible extent; gossips always relished the drama of it all. And no one with an adult's common sense would expect a wealthy nobleman entering into a convenient marriage, like Marellus, to have any sentimentality about his husband-to-be.

But that didn't mean Corin couldn't sympathize with Aster's very real misery and disappointment and shame, his fear of a future that offered nothing but unhappiness. And it also didn't mean Corin had any excuse for the way he'd snarled at him, the way he'd taken out his own lingering anger on an innocent object. The look on his face when Corin had told him he'd need to leave...those eyes. Aster's huge, pleading blue eyes would haunt Corin's fucking dreams, damn it all. And not only because of their resemblance to his sister's. On their own account.

But Aster couldn't be Corin's problem. He had to go home and sort it out himself one way or the other.

Aster's horse had started giving him sidelong glances that suggested imminent kicking if Corin didn't clear the fuck out and leave him alone to munch his hay in peace, and the smell of horse had gotten a bit thick anyway.

He shoved the door of the shed open and stepped out into the whirling snow, wedging the door shut again behind him. For a moment he simply stood there with his overheated face tipped up to the stormy sky, breathing deeply to let the invisibly tiny flakes of snow slide down into his lungs and extinguish some of his overproduction of draconic flame. He'd gotten agitated enough to start breathing smoke at Aster, an unforgiveable faux pas. If his family could only see him now: half-dressed and grubby and unshaven, unable to control his flames or his scales, not only still cowering in the mountains to escape his own shame but harboring a human fugitive.

Enough stalling. No trace of Corin's bootprints showed between the door to the tower and the shed, which meant he'd been bothering Aster's horse far longer than warranted. Like it or not, Aster would be his guest for another couple of days until the weather cleared. Sleeping in his bed. Looking at him with those eyes.

Fucking hell.

Stomping back to the door didn't feel quite as satisfying with every step cushioned by inches of snow, but he gave it his best shot all the same. And he wrenched the door open with enough force that he heard an ominous crack from the hinges.

God, he really needed to control his own strength, not that he cared if he ripped this fucking place to shreds with his bare hands.

Aster would care, though. He might be frightened at worst and disappointed in Corin's behavior at best. And that was enough to make him shut the door more gently behind him.

But Aster wasn't there. Where the hell could he have gotten to? And why? He could've gone to the garderobe, of course—but the garderobe was empty. Corin ran up the stairs and checked each floor. Nothing.

Now driven by something Corin would've denied with his dying breath could be incipient panic, he ran back down the stairs, taking them three at a time, heart pounding. He'd been dismissive, angry, even cruel to the lad. What if he'd pushed him over the edge?

Possibly literally. The bridge in front of the gate went over a deep canyon, too steep and jagged to climb down even in the best of weather. A fall, or a jump, from that bridge…and if a man felt he had no options, nowhere to go, no future…

Corin nearly ran into the gate face-first in his haste and got halfway through lifting the bar when he realized.

The gate would be open if Aster had gone through it.

God, he was an idiot.

He leaned his forehead against the rough wood, his own harsh breaths echoing in his ears.

The soft scrape of a footstep behind him had him spinning around, sure he'd turned a dark bronze from the blood he could feel flooding his face. Fuck, how incredibly embarrassing to be caught like that. Aster smiled at him sunnily from the doorway to the hall.

"What?" Corin snapped, relief making him irrationally angry. If Aster had simply stayed where he'd been bloody well supposed to—something that didn't seem to be his strong suit—no one would've had to go temporarily insane with worry and guilt. "Where the hell were you?"

Aster's smile widened, ratcheting Corin's blood pressure up another painful notch and making his temples throb.

No one should be that pretty when you were furious with them, it simply wasn't fair. Maybe not everyone liked freckles and a wide mouth and broad shoulders above a slender body. In fact, Corin would've sworn up and down that he wouldn't, that he strongly preferred small features and luscious curves.

But Aster's eyes would've been enough to draw anyone's attention. Bright and long-lashed and the color of the sky when Corin had flown so high the clouds were little puffs below him. Sometimes he'd do tricks, flipping and rolling, tumbling down and then soaring again. When he went to his back and stared straight up, he gave himself vertigo sometimes, feeling as if he might sink upward into infinity.

That was the color of Aster's eyes.

No, not everyone would appreciate Aster's unassuming beauty. Marellus had overlooked it completely. But apparently Corin bloody well liked it, damn it all to hell.

And then the smell hit him. Brandy, and lots of it.

Brandy. *Corin's* brandy, that he'd had stashed behind the wine where only someone very determined to get drunk would find it, and where he'd hoped he'd forget about it so as not to get very drunk himself.

ELIOT GRAYSON

"Hello," Aster—purred. There really couldn't be another word for that low, smooth tone. "What's got your knickers in a twist?" And then he slumped against the doorjamb and dissolved into helpless-looking giggles, absurdly lovely eyes even brighter and pink mouth hanging open in a way that should've been unattractive and really, really wasn't.

As Corin stood staring, more nonplussed than he could ever remember being in his life, the giggles started to morph into long, sobbing hitches in Aster's breath.

No. No, he could in fact become more nonplussed. Appalled, even.

His mind moved slowly, as if stuck in some kind of nightmarish goo.

Aster had started to cry.

When people cried, someone had to take care of them—that was simply decent.

(And while Corin didn't disdain men who cried, as so many did—one of the most ferociously hardbitten men-at-arms he'd ever served with wept into his gin and sang about a shepherdess's lover who'd been lost at sea after every battle—he also ran like hell to make them someone else's problem.)

There was no one else around whose problem Aster could be.

*Fuck.*

"It's not so bad," Corin ventured, brow prickling where sweat would've been if he'd been human. "You don't need to—I mean—it'll be all right."

"No," Aster gasped, slumping lower, hands on his knees now. "No, it fucking won't!" He burst out laughing again, shoulders shaking, sliding down the wall—oh, God, no, not again—Corin dashed forward just in time to catch Aster as he nearly collapsed to the floor.

And for the second time in less than a full day he had a double armful of unwanted guest, all firm in the right places and yielding everywhere.

Only this time Aster was conscious, which he showed instantly by bringing his arms up and looping them around Corin's neck, pressing their bodies together tightly in the process. One of his hands

56

slipped under the collar of Corin's shirt, fingertips tracing his skin with delicacy despite their swordsman's calluses.

The resulting shiver went all the way from the crown of Corin's head to the backs of his knees. Touching Aster had been one thing.

Being touched, it seemed, was quite another.

Aster clung to him, wriggling closer, rubbing his body against Corin's in a way that had to be entirely innocent and yet only succeeded in making his skin prickle everywhere and his cock start to stiffen with every glancing bit of contact. And then, with a long, contented-sounding sigh that ended in one last hiccupping sob, Aster went limp, apparently counting on Corin to take his full weight.

He did, having to fumble one arm down and wrap his hand...under Aster's ass. One of the cheeks fit perfectly in his hand, his fingers dipping toward the crease.

That hand went so rigid he was probably leaving bruises.

*Bruises.* On Aster's ass, in the shape of Corin's fingers...

Aster had to be able to feel his erection against his stomach by now, since Corin didn't think it would be possible to get any harder. He stood frozen, bathed in the rosy sweetness of Aster's body mixed intoxicatingly with brandy fumes, trying desperately not to push his fingers deeper between those round cheeks. Silky waves of hair tickled his jaw.

"I think I want to lie down," Aster murmured into his neck. "You carried me up those stairs last night, didn't you? You can do it again."

He certainly could, if Corin didn't wring his neck first.

"You can make it on your own."

Aster giggled again, rubbing his nose against Corin's neck. It tickled, like a spider on his skin...ugh, all right, that made his erection go down a tiny bit. One firm thigh pressed between Corin's legs, nudging up against his cock.

Corin bit back a groan, his arms tightening against his will. So much for that.

"I really can't." And now Aster had started purring again, damn him, sounding like sex on legs. "I need you to carry me. You have such strong arms. Always watched you when you were training."

All right, that was it. Every man had his limit, and Corin had officially reached his. He bent down and hoisted Aster behind his knees, regretfully sliding his hand off his ass in the process, and swung him up into his arms.

His strong arms that Aster had always admired while Corin wielded a sword, apparently.

Aster laughed, whooped, and tightened his grip around Corin's neck, tipping his head back on his shoulder and grinning up at him dizzily.

"How the fuck did you get so drunk so quickly?" Corin demanded, striding for the stairs. Fuck. This. He had to get Aster into bed and out of touching range in the next thirty seconds or he'd cross the line of gentlemanly restraint and then some.

The question had been mostly hypothetical, but Aster laughed and said, "I drank half the bottle like you'd drink a glass of water."

"Half the bottle." He could only take the stairs two at a time while going up and burdened with the weight of a full-grown man, but he'd be there in a second. Hopefully before Aster threw up on him or he took him right there on the stairs. "You're joking." God, he hoped he was joking.

"No, I'm serious," Aster said, turning his face into Corin's shoulder. "Mmm. You're really warm. I left the rest for you, it's downstairs."

"I don't—I don't need any brandy." He desperately needed all the brandy. "You're going to bed, and I'll—I'll go drink that brandy," he finished lamely. Because he certainly would.

He jumped up the last few stairs, crossed the landing, and shouldered the bedroom door open. Thank God. A couple of steps across the room and he could dump Aster down on the bed and beat a hasty retreat. Get downstairs again. Drown himself in liquor. Go for a drunken flight around the mountain in the storm, that'd be fun, he hadn't done anything that irresponsible in years.

There. The bed. He dropped one knee, leaning down and laying Aster out more gently than he'd planned to. He couldn't really help it; Aster tipped his head back against Corin's arm and blinked up at him with wide, shimmering eyes, now the color of the clear sea around the southern islands where Corin had spent a few years in his early youth. He'd swum in that sea. Now he feared he might drown in its likeness. The arm behind Aster's knees came away easily enough, but the arm under his shoulders lingered. He couldn't help that either. Aster's arms stayed around his neck, one hand playing up into the hair at Corin's nape.

He couldn't break Aster's gaze, his breath coming quicker, and Aster's heart hammering against him where their chests were almost pressed together.

He had to go. Now, he had to go, because warm, brandy-sweetened breath wafted against his mouth and he could read his welcome in the flush on Aster's cheeks and down into the hollow of his throat. If he kissed that soft pink mouth, Aster would open and allow him in, probably moan, go pliant, spread his legs. Corin could plunder him until he'd discovered every sweet secret he possessed.

And for all the good judgment Aster had at his disposal at the moment, Corin might as well go downstairs and fuck that half-empty bottle of brandy.

"Let me go," he said, voice hoarse. "You need a nap."

Aster smiled, intimate in the scant inches between their faces. A lover would see him like that every day. Or a husband would. And Aster had the next best thing to a husband, to whom he'd given his word. Even if he'd been sober it would've been wrong.

The thought should've given Corin strength to resist. Instead, it made his chest hurt.

"Only if you lie down next to me. You're so warm," Aster said again, snuggling up against him. "Or you could lie down on top of me like a blanket."

"I'm too heavy to be a comfortable blanket," he gasped, hoping that logic would suffice for a drunken man. "Now let me go, if you please."

Corin squeezed his eyes shut for a moment, praying for strength and that when he opened them, he'd be a thousand miles away with his cock in a nice soothing snowbank. Or that Aster would let him go.

When he opened them, Aster had tilted his head at an

impossibly coquettish angle and bitten his rosy lower lip, and he'd wrapped his arms more firmly around Corin's back. For an instant he resembled Belinda so strongly that Corin's vision went sideways, a jolt to his nervous system.

"I'd like you on top of me, even if you're heavy," Aster said. "I think you should stay. You can do anything you want to me."

And that was when something in him simply snapped.

# Chapter Seven

WHEN ASTER GOT VERY drunk, he could hear the words coming out of his own mouth. Sometimes he could predict them. But he could never, ever keep them in.

Even when they really ought to be swallowed down, stomped on, and then lit on fire. Even when he knew he'd regret them terribly in a few hours.

But Corin had his arms around him, and he'd carried him up the stairs, and this time Aster had been awake to enjoy it, and it'd been as lovely as he'd thought it would. Those arms didn't shake at all holding him up, and then Corin had actually run up the stairs without breathing hard. Well, he had been breathing hard. But maybe that was because of the terrifyingly large cock Aster had felt pressing first into his belly, when they were standing, and then into his hip.

Could Corin have...a tree branch in his trousers, or something? Or a broom handle? Except that was too thick to be a broom handle. How the hell had Belinda coped with it? She certainly had more experience than Aster did by a factor of a hundred at least, and that probably accounted for it.

But it didn't matter, because he doubted Corin wanted to use it on him or with him. An erection was a normal reaction to having someone squirming around against you. At least for most men, probably. And besides, you didn't need to like someone very much to get off with them, and when you did it usually wasn't that fabulous anyway.

*That* didn't matter either, because he had his arms around Corin's neck and he was bending over him, his eyes fixed on Aster's face and his lips right there, and he'd watched and admired the mighty Sir Corin for so long. And now he was right here. Touching him, all big and warm and safe, a haven from the snow outside and all the people who held him in contempt. Everyone, basically.

Except that Corin didn't want to be his safe haven. He wanted him to go home and get married to someone who hated him so he could watch his husband fuck someone else, who also hated him.

Case in point, Corin said, "Let me go. You need a nap."

Aster smiled up at him helplessly, because Corin's voice sent little shivers down his spine. It always had, even when Corin had belonged to Belinda and Aster had been forced to strain his ears to catch a few words here and there, since they were pitched low for his sister's ears only. He'd always felt like such a creepy voyeur.

Now no one was here but the two of them, and Belinda, more fool her, had thrown Corin away.

And a nap sounded like a wonderful idea, come to think of it. "Only if you lie down next to me. You're so warm." He wiggled a little, enjoying the solidity of Corin's body above him. The liquor had made him so fluffy and floaty. It felt good to be kept stationary. "Or you could lie down on top of me like a blanket."

Corin's eyes went wide, deep and dark enough that he could've drowned in them. Dragons in their human forms often had hair and skin to match their scales, or at least in a similar shade, toning together. Corin's greenish-bronze tinted skin and jet-black hair and eyes were striking even for a dragon, and the vertical slits of his pupils held Aster fascinated, like a snake's prey.

"I'm too heavy to be a comfortable blanket," Corin said nonsensically. He'd be a perfect blanket. "Now let me go, if you please."

Corin's eyes shut, giving Aster a moment to really stare at him. Of course Aster wouldn't let him go, and he shifted his arms, getting a better grip—not that Corin couldn't get away if he wanted to, of course.

But…fuck. Maybe he *didn't* want to. Could he really…desire Aster? It seemed so unlikely, a man like that who could have anyone. A man who'd already had the only beautiful Cezanne. Aster couldn't hold a candle to her.

On the other hand, it'd been more than two years since Corin had fled the capital in the wake of the scandal. If he'd been here by himself that whole time, maybe even a plain, cut-rate, taller and less soft version of the woman he'd desired so passionately would start to look good. Aster hadn't even known Corin took his pleasure with men. But perhaps that was just another way in which two years of exile had made him more flexible in his tastes.

He tipped his head, considering, chewing on his lip, trying to get a better view of Corin's flushed face. An aroused flush? Or anger? Both? Aster had never been particularly adept in the art of flirtation.

But if he wanted him, then maybe he'd let Aster stay. For a while, anyway.

And Aster could finally find out how it felt to really, truly have all of Sir Corin's formidable attention on him and him alone. To be, even if only for an hour, the most important person in the world to him.

That might require him to flirt, though. He had to say something clever, something witty and seductive and charming.

Corin's eyes opened. God, he was so handsome.

Clever. Charming. But instead, with a vague sense of horror, he felt the words, "I'd like you on top of me, even if you're heavy," tumble out of his mouth. Followed by, "I think you should stay. You can do anything you want to me."

Corin stared down at him, that dark, bronzy flush spreading over his entire face.

And then, between one breath and the next, he went from complete stillness to moving so quickly Aster's head spun. He wrenched himself out of Aster's grasp and ripped his arm out from under his shoulders, dropping him to the bed. Corin seized his wrists and shoved them down onto the mattress above his head, pinning them there with his huge, callused hands, and then leaning down and looming over him as only a dragon could.

Oh.

Oh, God.

That was...his pulse raced against Corin's palms, the thin skin of his wrists feeling like no barrier at all, as if he and Corin had become one at those two points of contact. Corin had twisted further onto the bed to pin him. Aster lay splayed beneath him, helpless.

He'd never lain with anyone who handled him like this. He'd

never even known he was allowed to want it. He only knew that the pit of his stomach had clenched tight, the way it often had when he'd been near Corin in the past, and that his cock had gotten hard somehow without his even noticing, and that his nipples ached where they rubbed against the fabric of his shirt.

"Well?" Aster whispered, not sure whether or not he truly wanted the answer to his next question. "What *are* you going to do to me?"

Corin's eyes seemed to glow afresh with the light of the flames banked down inside him, wild and hot, the slit pupils flickering orange. Aster knew he wasn't imagining it now.

"I'm not going to do anything to you," he growled, in a low, feral tone no human throat could've produced. It didn't make the words sound very convincing. Aster felt his voice the way Corin had to feel his heartbeat, as a part of him, something that thrummed through his body and his blood. "Nothing at all. Because you're drunk. Because you're Beli—*fuck*." He squeezed Aster's wrists hard, hard enough that it hurt. In that moment, Corin's thoughts weren't for him. That hurt a thousand times more. "Because I'm a fucking gentleman, and a knight, and you're my guest. Do you fucking understand me?"

He understood. He really, truly did, and the disappointment might kill him, but he'd tell Corin that it was all right, and to please never mention this again or Aster might spontaneously combust from the force of his own humiliation.

Instead he said, "You could fuck me. You should probably fuck me, isn't that what you want? I've been fucked before, but it wasn't particularly—"

"No!" Corin said harshly, and hung his head down between those massive shoulders, his back heaving like a bellows.

Aster blinked up at him, mouth still open, words dying in his throat.

When Corin looked up again Aster's remaining breath caught.

He'd never seen Corin like this. His features had sharpened, somehow, maybe an effect of the scales now visibly creeping up his neck and wreathing his face, his ears—shrinking, maybe? Dragons didn't have ears like humans, Aster knew.

"Fuck you?" Corin snarled, and his teeth had changed too, sharpening and lengthening into something more like fangs. Aster should've been terrified, probably. Had Belinda ever seen Corin like this? If she had, then Aster wasn't surprised she'd called him a monster. He'd have appeared like one to her, for certain. Aster's heart pounded, his cock trying to bore a hole through his trousers. "I'd fucking destroy you, Aster. You don't want me to fuck you, because I wouldn't stop. I'd fuck you unconscious. And I still wouldn't stop. You'd wake to find me still inside you, wrapped around you, my hand around your throat, and you wouldn't even be able to scream."

Corin leaned down, and on his breath Aster caught a hint of flame, of smoke, something rich and drugging like incense. He tipped his head back instinctively, showing his throat. For Corin's hand to fit around, or for his mouth, his teeth. Dragons really could mesmerize their prey. Maybe he'd write a memoir so scandalous it'd make everyone forget the garden party and the duel...if he survived.

But he still wasn't afraid, because this was Corin, the most gallant and honorable knight living.

Aster heard himself saying as much, slowly, as if he really had been drugged. But his heart raced faster and faster, pulsing in his cock, in his bollocks, behind them. The two times he'd been fucked before he hadn't seen what the fuss was about.

Now he thought he could feel every atom of the skin of his hole individually, tight and hot and eager.

"You really believe that about me?" Corin asked, some of the wildness fading out of his eyes. "That I'm too gallant to hurt you. Too honorable to take advantage of you?"

"Of course you are. There's no one in the world I trust more than you. Because you're trustworthy. Why else would I come here, of all the places in the world?"

"Oh," Corin said, a soft, almost hurt sound. As if Aster struck him rather than complimented him. Of course, he hadn't really meant to admit that, had he? That he'd sought Corin out because if he wouldn't protect Aster, no one would. Because Aster had no one. Even though he knew Corin hated Belinda, and their family by extension, when he'd been fleeing his home in a panic only one man had come to mind.

Because he'd intended to try to take advantage of Corin, in short.

Oh, God. He was the worst person in the world.

His eyes prickled with tears again. Oh, for fuck's sake, he'd ruin everything…

"Don't, don't cry, fuck," Corin said, sounding desperate—and not in the hopelessly aroused kind of way. "Look at me."

No human could've resisted that command. Aster stopped, gasped, and met Corin's gaze, pinned as thoroughly by that as by the hands still wrapped around his wrists.

"I'm not going to take advantage of you. I'm not going to do any of those things. Do you believe me?"

"Yes. Because you don't really want to any more than Marellus does." Aside from everything else that might make Corin not want him, no one—sane, anyway—wanted to fuck someone who couldn't stop laughing and crying by turns. Even Aster knew that much about human, or human-adjacent, sexuality.

Corin laughed, a low bitten-off rumble. "Oh, yes I do," he said. "Fuck Marellus. Fucking moron. You're right that I wouldn't really hurt you, though. I'd take my time. I don't know how long it'd take me to get inside you, to make it fit. But I'd take all the time I needed."

"Uh," Aster said, no real words forming in his mind, which had gone blank except for a vivid image of Corin kneeling between his legs and slowly, ever so slowly, forcing his unnaturally large cock into Aster's body. All his blood had rushed away from his brain and into his own cock, apparently. It throbbed and stirred, begging for a touch. For the first time since Corin had pinned him down, he squirmed and struggled, trying to get his arms free.

Corin's fingers flexed around his wrists, casually, as if Aster's strongest efforts were barely noticeable. Aster squeezed his eyes shut. He wouldn't. He *wouldn't*, fully dressed and with Corin not even kissing him or anything at all…

"You'd probably tell me you couldn't take it," Corin went on, and he'd bent down to murmur right into Aster's ear, and Aster started to pant, little whining moans coming out with every breath. "But you'd be lying. I'd ignore you, even when you begged me not to break you in two. Or perhaps you'd beg me to do it after all."

Aster's whole body trembled, his spine arching and his bollocks drawing up painfully tight.

Apparently he would.

"Oh," he moaned. "Oh, please. Corin!"

Release hit in a wave of relief and humiliation, followed by pleasure so intense and pure it washed the rest of it away.

"Fuck," Corin breathed. "Are you...? Fucking hell, you are."

Aster managed to crack his eyes open. Everything had gone all blurry. That was fine. Tremors raced through every limb. He shifted his legs and the slight movement of fabric against his oversensitive cock set him off again into a new spasm that left him squirming and whimpering.

When he blinked the world back into focus he found Corin leaning down, mouth open, eyes wide. Awestruck, perhaps? Not disgusted, anyway, or contemptuous, as Aster had mostly expected.

He'd just spent in his trousers, writhing on the bed like a slut with his hands pinned down, from no more stimulation than Corin telling him how he'd use him like a whore.

And instead of mortified, he felt...powerful. Beautiful, for the first time in his life. A thrill tingled through every part of him, light and buzzing.

An illusion, of course. It'd wear off as soon as Corin got over whatever sexual desperation had brought them here in the first place.

But for now...

"You should finish too," Aster managed. "I can—"

"No," Corin said with absolute finality. And also regret, Aster was glad to hear. "No."

And then Aster had perhaps the cleverest idea that'd ever graced his brain, and he grinned up at Corin smugly.

"All right, I won't. But you can. Bring yourself off? I promise not to touch if you don't want me to."

He wanted to, badly, to run his hands all over Corin's body and feel his heat and the patterns of his scales beneath his skin. Not to mention some of his other parts. But the liquor and the orgasm had left him so limp he didn't know if he'd be able to lift his hands even when Corin released them. That was a promise he could actually keep.

Aster could see the exact moment that Corin gave in, his shoulders slumping in resignation but his eyes kindling with fresh heat and desire. Slowly, he released Aster's wrists, leaving them tingling. Aster wanted those big hands back on his skin. But of course Corin would need them in a moment for his own skin—and that thought had his cock stirring again, impossibly, even in the damp confines of his clothing.

Even more slowly, Corin shifted his weight, rising so that he stood upright with one knee still propped on the bed. The bulge in the front of his trousers was nothing short of astounding at this distance and angle. The fabric strained, absurdly tented. Aster watched avidly, heart pounding in suspense, as Corin popped the first button.

The thick, shiny head of his cock pushed out through the top. Thicker than any human prick Aster had thought existed, in fact. It had flushed a deeper green than any other part of Corin's body he'd seen thus far. And it had...those were two ridges, each curved, the edges bronzy-purple... Aster moaned helplessly, his belly clenching into a painful knot, and Corin said, "Fuck this," and tore the trousers open, the other three buttons popping and flying, landing who the fuck cared where.

Corin had a hand wrapped around his shaft instantly.

Aster's hand went up too without his conscious volition. He stopped just in time, fingers outstretched and almost brushing Corin's cockhead. His hand tingled, as if even that proximity was too much for his nervous system. Both men froze.

"I'm sorry," Aster said. "I really won't so much as lay a finger on you." *Please let me.* "But take your hand away for a second? I want to see you."

Corin hesitated, and Aster watched in fascination as even more color flooded into his cheeks.

He couldn't quite meet Aster's eyes, either.

Oh, for crying out loud. Aster was about to hyperventilate

himself into unconsciousness over Corin's massive, gorgeous, oh-God-double-ridged cock, and Corin was, what? Self-conscious? Sympathy twinged through him. Aster knew damn well how embarrassing it could be to disrobe. What if you didn't measure up? Not that Corin needed to worry about that, but most worry wasn't rational by its very nature.

"You obviously don't have anything to be ashamed of," Aster said helpfully. Corin's gaze snapped right back to his face, now sharp and focused. And clenching his fist around his own cock like that might actually hurt him. Oh God, had Corin taken that for sarcasm? He had to correct himself! "Uh, other men, they don't have much to brag about. I mean, the ones I've seen. I've never had anything nearly that big, in me, or, or, in my mouth, or even to touch, and it's certainly larger than Lord Fan—oh fuck, I'm sorry! Please don't—please finish what you started?"

Corin's brows furrowed alarmingly and his jaw went tight.

Shit, no, what the hell had he been thinking? Lord Fanfelle, Belinda's lover...whose (only moderately sized) cock Aster had seen at the garden party at the same time half of the court had, when he pulled it out of Belinda, right before he'd closed his eyes in horror and prayed not to have nightmares.

And then Corin's lips started to twitch. A low rumble started in his chest. Had he decided he'd had enough and it'd be easier to simply light Aster on fire? Aster dug his fingertips into the mattress and braced himself as best he could.

"You're unbelievable," Corin said, and that was when Aster realized he'd started to laugh. "Bringing up—right now?" His smile widened into a grin, showing all those sharp teeth.

Even though the air in the room was cold enough to show his breath and raise goosebumps on his skin, a flush of heat nearly as powerful as Corin's flames spread through his cheeks and lips, his chest and belly, all the way down to his toes.

Nothing, nothing in this world could compare to Corin's smile. Had all those young squires and knights felt like this when they won his approval? How had none of them ever torn their own clothes off and gone to their knees on the spot? If Aster had ever been on the receiving end of that smile in the training yard…

"I'm sorry," he said belatedly, realizing that Corin had been waiting for an answer. "I choked instead of finishing his name?"

Another low laugh rolled out of Corin. "Fair enough." The grin turned wicked, his eyes gleaming. Aster's cock had started getting hard again—despite the brandy. He'd never had a refractory period this brief, even sober and even as a green youth.

Corin moved his hand at last, a leisurely stroke down that showed off a couple of inches of his shaft along with his cockhead. With his other hand, he pushed the trousers down a little.

Fuck, now Aster could see almost to the base.

But not quite.

Despite the impressive number of ruddy green inches revealed, Corin had still more, and how thick would that be all the way down, God, it had to be as big around as Aster's forearm, and then there would be his heavy balls, and his muscular thighs, and curly hair that would match the jet-black of the hair on his head and his chest, and…oh, God, that gasping, high-pitched sound had come from *him*.

"That's the sound you'd make when I opened you up," Corin growled. "Isn't it? Fucking say it."

Eyes fixed helplessly on that massive cock, big enough that even Corin's huge hand barely kept it in check, what could he do but choke out, "Yes, it is, please!"

Corin ran his hand all the way up again, and now Aster could see the lower part of his shaft. Darker green there, and some-how…more textured than a human's? Were there scales? Maybe. That didn't look like the skin of Aster's cock.

His fingertips itched with the urge to trace those double ridges and to see if that skin felt rough or smooth or hard or soft, to taste…which he couldn't do with his hand, could he? The slap of skin on skin and the scent of sex filled the room, making Aster's head spin. He didn't want to beg Corin to let him lick his cock, did he? That wasn't in his nature. That neediness, that desperation. His previous lovers had complained about his lack of enthusiasm.

God, but he couldn't touch Corin. He'd promised. But his hands were free. He could touch anything else he wanted.

One hand flew to his own cock, palming and gripping through his damp trousers, too eager to try to open them. Aster arched up, moaning, eyes slipping shut at the relief of it despite how much he didn't want to miss a second of this. Of Corin kneeling over him, tall and broad enough to blot out the light from the windows, gazing down at him avidly as if he didn't need to see, or think about, anything but Aster to get himself off.

Frantically groping his own cock and balls, squeezing, wishing he could get his hand down to push lower between his legs, he was so close—and then Corin groaned, yanked the loose folds of his shirt over the head of his cock, and bent in half, shoulders shaking.

God fucking damn it, he'd covered up right when he—oh, God, he'd come, Aster had been the one to make Sir Corin of Saumur, famed dragon knight and victor of a hundred battles, spend every drop of his sweet, salty—Aster cried out as a second climax knocked him nearly unconscious.

The fabric under his hand wasn't just damp now, but soaked. And Aster might never be able to breathe again, all the wind knocked out of him, lungs laboring. His heart raced like he'd run up the whole mountain.

He needed to open his eyes. Say something.

And please, please God let it be charming and witty and debonair this time.

Aster opened his mouth, and all that came out was something like "Uhhh."

Well. So much for that. He didn't have the strength left to try again. And the eye-opening thing really had to be abandoned, unfortunately. He'd have loved to know what a post-coital Corin looked like, but it simply wasn't in the cards. He seemed to be sinking down into the bed, deeper, farther, spinning…

Snow tapped gently against the windows; the force of the storm must have been abating, because it'd been banging and howling earlier. Both of their breaths sounded very loud in the relative silence, a raspy melody and harmony, gradually slowing. The bed dipped as Corin took his knee off, and Aster managed an incoherent murmur of protest.

Somehow Corin must've understood what he meant by the whiny tone alone, because he laughed softly and said, "Nap, Aster. No argument. I won't go far."

*I want you to go so not-far that you're wrapped around me with your cock up my ass and your hand around my throat, like you promised.*

Probably luckily, that came out as a little moaning mumble. Reality had started fading away, though the spinning sensation had only increased. Fucking brandy.

"Sleep," Corin said, and Aster did.

# Chapter Eight

TUGGING A BLANKET OVER Aster and leaving him there alone, all sprawled out and sticky and flushed and sweet, had to have been one of the noblest sacrifices Corin had ever made.

Not that he'd made all that many, truth be told. He much preferred winning to martyrdom.

Still. He lingered for a moment, finding a clean pair of trousers that also had all the necessary buttons, listening to Aster's soft breathing and shamelessly savoring the intertwined scents of roses and sex. He knew damn well Aster's murmurings had been pleas for him to stay. The tone, for one, but also simple inference.

Or perhaps it'd been his own desires projected onto Aster.

With one last look from the doorway, he forced himself down the stairs, taking them several at a time.

Bloody hell. He regretted what they'd done. Not quite done. Whatever. Of course he did, because Aster had been too drunk to really know what he wanted.

Worse than that, Corin couldn't be sure how much of his desire had crawled, dark and twisted, from the ugly part of his nature that wanted to punish his former fiancée and fuck her into submission in equal measure. He wouldn't touch her even if he could, no matter how often he'd fantasized about her coming back to him on her knees.

But he could have Aster. If Corin seduced and debauched her younger brother, how she'd feel if she knew...the sick thrill of the thought left him dizzied and nauseated and hating himself.

And yet his blood sang through his veins and his nerves fizzed, and that had nothing to do with his rage or his desire for revenge.

Shimmering blue eyes, wide and fringed with red-blond lashes even longer than Belinda's. Long, slender limbs, an ass that fit perfectly in his hands and in which his cock wouldn't fit at all without significant and extended effort. That wide pink mouth, gasping out Aster's orgasms.

Two of them. Fuck. He'd made the lad come twice and hadn't even touched him. Corin's hands twitched and he had to force his feet forward rather than giving in to the sudden urge to run back up the stairs.

Belinda had never allowed him to make love to her—in retrospect, probably to ensure he'd marry her, though she'd claimed to be afraid of what he might do to her. That had kept him humble, gentle, obedient. He hated himself even more for that.

But he could take and ruin her brother. Wreck his pretty body, make him scream, show him how draconic and how monstrous he could truly be. Show him the differences between a human's body and that of a dragon claiming what he wanted.

Fuck, he'd never have held it against her if she'd simply broken it off, even though it would've broken his heart. She didn't owe him her body or her touch or her love, only her honesty.

Aster had been honest. Too honest. Naked, even, in his wide-eyed and low-voiced commentary on Corin's strength and prowess. And he hadn't seemed afraid at all.

Corin had paid little enough attention to Aster before he arrived yesterday. Apparently Aster had been watching *him* much more closely.

He strode into the hall and stopped, assessing the situation. The fire had burned down to embers. As promised, the half-empty bottle of brandy had been left on Aster's chair. Slightly brighter daylight than before seeped through the cracks in the shutters. He'd only taken a moment to look out the upstairs windows, but the snow had appeared to be slowing down.

All at once claustrophobia had him breathless and too hot inside his skin. He had to get out. Dragons had adapted to human life in many ways since the father of their shapeshifting kind had first taken another form some two thousand years ago, but the confinement of a human dwelling still chafed at times.

And became unbearable at others.

The fire didn't need attention and no one would come to the tower in this weather. Corin could leave without the slightest risk to Aster, or that stupid, disapproving horse of his, or even the chipmunks in the chimney. For a couple of hours, he could shrug off his responsibilities to any of them, for fuck's sake.

He stripped as he all but ran for the door to the back courtyard, his shirt flying to one side, his trousers to the other, his boots tossed somewhere into the dimness of the hall with a double thud. Out, out, he needed to get out, and his first breath of frigid, snow-dusted air felt like fucking heaven. He sucked it in, letting his own fire ramp up to melt the ice, plumes of smoke and steam rushing out of his mouth and somersaulting up toward the sky.

Scales bled over his skin. He slammed the door shut behind him and took three long steps into the center of the courtyard, spreading his arms as his bones lengthened and took on mass, as his face transformed, as his own natural armor wrapped around him from head to toe.

Corin threw his head back and roared out a gout of flames that sizzled and spat as the snow fell into them, that lit every corner of the courtyard. His claws dug all the way through the snow, and he curled them, scritching against the stone beneath.

With a massive shrug that rippled all the way down his spine and into his long spiked tail, Corin unfurled his wings. They filled the courtyard.

What felt like limitless physical and magical power thrummed through his muscles and veins. He crouched, allowing the potential energy to build to a crescendo, and then launched himself into the air, soaring over the edge of the chasm behind the tower, buffeted above and below and sideways by the icy winds, his body more than equal to the challenge.

Up, up, wings flapping and tail extended, the sharpness of ozone in his snout and nothing but the roar of the gale to be heard, until dark clouds wrapped around him, crackling with lightning—and at last he popped free, blinking into the sudden onslaught of brilliant sunlight. Below him the clouds lay dark and heavy, gilded at the edges like the pages of an expensive book. Above, the sky vanished into an infinite dome of nothingness.

Corin wheeled in lazy circles between the storm and the void. He owned the expanse of it all; nothing else would venture so high or so far. His mind expanded with it.

And for a little while, he could be at peace.

THE SNOW HAD STOPPED AT last when Aster opened his eyes to a frigid and empty room. Even the wind seemed to have run out of willpower; he'd never heard such silence in his life, ringing in his ears and pressing him down into the bed.

Of course, that could've been his incipient hangover. Six of one, half a dozen of the other, perhaps. He pushed himself up onto his elbows, groggy and dizzy and blinking and frowsy-feeling. No amount of sputtering dislodged the tendril of hair stuck to his lip. For fuck's sake. He gave up and looked around him now that his eyes had started to clear a bit. The light hadn't changed. That didn't mean much; it couldn't have been past noon when he…

When he…

"Oh, fuck," he groaned, and he fell back onto the bed and shoved his hands over his eyes.

Well, not fuck. Even though he'd begged for it.

Hands covering his eyes weren't enough. Aster rolled onto his belly and screamed into the pillow.

No, that didn't help much either, especially since it twisted his still-damp drawers and trousers around his hips and tugged on everything in a particularly uncomfortable way. His erection pulled to the side, straining up toward his hip and pinned by his thigh.

Another erection, even though he'd come his brains out twice however many hours or minutes before. He'd been hard more since he got to this miserable place than he had in the last six months.

There had to be something in the air or the water, because not only had he been hard more than he ever had, he—shy, plain, dull, not-at-all-charming Aster—had mustered the courage or the recklessness to get drunk and beg the mighty and renowned Sir Corin, his former almost brother-in-law, to fuck him up the ass.

Corin had brought himself off while watching Aster spend in

his trousers.

Those double ridges. Corin's huge hand looking entirely in proportion to its surroundings for once when wrapped around that intimidatingly thick shaft.

Hangover or no, Aster's hips had started to move without any conscious intent on his part. Even smothering himself in the pillow as much as possible, he couldn't shut out the rustling of the sheets and the straw in the mattress as he rutted into—Corin's bed, which smelled like him, faintly smoky and spicy and masculine beneath the fresh scent of pine.

Aster barely managed to get a hand shoved down into the front of his trousers, awkwardly trapped by his chest, before he soaked the fabric all over again.

He spent all over his hand and *also* soaked his trousers all over again, subsiding limply into the bed with a moan, head spinning. Opening his eyes gave him the edge of the linen pillowcase and a bit of stone wall, also spinning.

But as his heart rate slowed, so did the movement of the bed and the wall and the pillow, and his stomach settled with them. Fine. He'd come a third time without Corin's touch—or even much of his own. He could accept that without having to crawl into a hole and hide from everyone in the world forever.

Although to be fair, living in this tower might not be much of a step up from that.

Deep breath in. Corin's scent blended with the faintly bitter aroma of his own come, a heady mixture that had his eyes trying to flutter shut.

God.

He shoved himself up, determined to stay that way this time, and rolled out of bed before he could change his mind.

Time to get it together. Who knew where Corin had gone, but Aster might not have long to get clean, organized, and…not quite as pathetic? His hungover brain struggled to come up with anything less nebulous than that, but he knew what he meant. Basically, the next time he saw Corin he needed to smile, say something suave, and not come in his pants.

There. He had a plan. Now to implement it.

Of course, that turned out to be easier said than done. A first trip all the way down the stairs to use the garderobe and fetch his saddlebags, which he'd seen near the back door of the hall, turned into several minutes of puzzlement over a whole set of Corin's clothing which appeared to have been scattered around the hall by a high wind. And once he'd hauled his bags all the way back up again, he found that the water pitcher and basin on Corin's dressing table were both empty.

He made it all the way down again before remembering he'd forgotten to bring the pitcher. And he had no idea where to find a water bucket downstairs.

God, his head hurt, and now so did his thigh muscles.

Back up. Get the pitcher. Still cold, still with throbbing temples and an unsettled stomach. And at last, he shoved open the back door, freezing air smacking him in the face. The wind had died down completely. Everything lay still and blanketed in snow.

At last his head started to clear. He tipped it back and sucked in deep, cleansing breaths, washing away the fog of brandy and sex and confusion and embarrassment.

Aster squinted and shaded his eyes with a hand, peering at…the great trampled area in the center of the courtyard, looking as if an army had marched through it. But wait, no. No army could've left that massive claw-tipped track in the snow.

Well. That explained the discarded clothes. Corin had stripped and transformed while Aster lay drunkenly sleeping it off. He gazed up at the sky again, staring until his eyes burned and he could see nothing but unfathomable pale gray, not so much as a speck that could've been Corin, wheeling above in his dragon's body. Sometimes the vastness of the heavens could make a man feel tiny and insignificant—but never more so than at that moment, when he knew Corin had the freedom to glide through it all, master of the air.

Aster shivered and turned his attention down again. Corin could soar above him, above the clouds, even, but Aster was stuck down here plodding through the churned-up snow to the pump across the courtyard. And perhaps that was as it should be.

But he'd never felt so small and cold and lonely all the same.

Finally cleaned up a bit, and with the fire stirred for later, he went back out again to spend a few minutes petting and soothing Etallon in the little shed Corin had set up for him. Corin had fed and brushed him, too, while Aster lay snoring, yet another source of shame.

Etallon's whickers and nuzzlings comforted him more than he'd have been willing to admit, though; the ten minutes he spent with his arm around the horse's neck left him almost calm.

Several cups of water and an apple—shared with Etallon, of course—left him feeling almost human.

He could do this. When Corin returned, Aster would be cool as a cucumber, unmoved, wearing trousers and drawers that didn't have any come in them and a sophisticated, sardonic smile.

To that end, he went back down to the cellar and retrieved a bottle of what looked like a lightish wine, something restorative. He carefully arranged a chair by the fire, poured himself a cup of it, and sipped.

Yes. Mmm. All right, all the cells in Aster's body sat up and took notice as that hit them. Corin might have fled the court and chosen to live in a dirty, drafty hole in the mountainside, but he'd clearly not lowered his standards in *every* way. The pale wine had the faintest hint of a far-off summer orchard, soft and fruity. Perfection.

The sudden banging of the shutters in a gust of wind startled him into nearly dropping his cup, and he sat up, alert, heart pounding. A heavy thump echoed from the courtyard.

Corin. The urge to run to the door and catch a glimpse of him in his dragon form nearly overwhelmed him.

He resisted, distracting himself by refilling his cup with a shaking hand and settling back in his chair, assuming a carefully casual pose. While he hadn't precisely packed a full wardrobe when he fled home, he had managed to dig out a relatively pristine pair of pale gray trousers and a light blue tunic that brought out his eyes. Dark colors would've been more practical for a journey, something he'd only considered once he'd spent a couple of days riding and then sleeping on the ground and marinating in dirt, but now he was glad he'd brought

ELIOT GRAYSON

these foolish garments. He might even look more or less handsome in them. For him. Anyway, they were doing their best.

Several tense and silent moments passed. Surely Corin had shifted back to human by now, especially because there would've been more noise if he hadn't: of heavy clawed feet, of flapping wings.

And then the door slammed open.

Aster had noticed the clothing on the floor. He'd even figured out its cause.

Somehow, though, that hadn't prepared him for the idea that Corin, when he came home, would do so entirely nude, hard muscles gleaming with melted snow and with shimmering malachite scales still rippling and melting into his skin.

Aster's jaw fell open and his hand went lax. His cup of wine tipped, and the contents sloshed directly between his legs to soak him from navel to thigh.

# Chapter Nine

IT TOOK EVEN CORIN'S dragon eyes a moment to adjust to the change in lighting as he strode into the hall, kicking the door shut behind him. Once he came through the cloud layer, the glare of gray all around and above him and an endless expanse of reflective white below had forced him to use his inner eyelids the rest of the way down. But the glow of the fire...

The fire.

Aster had risen, then, because Corin had left it as coals. And the hall reeked of wine, which...

He stopped, blinked, and brought the scene before him into focus at last: Aster sat by the newly blazing hearth, an open bottle at his elbow and a cup in his hand. He was gaping at Corin as if he'd seen a ghost, and a wet stain was spreading across his groin.

The tilted cup with a last drop falling from the rim clearly showed the source of the wetness.

But the combination of that and Aster's surprised, horrified face finally pushed Corin over the edge.

He felt it first as a juddering in his stomach and then as a hitch in his breath. And then he bent over, braced himself on his knees, and howled with laughter. Corin's belly and chest heaved, his shoulders shook, and puffs of smoke laced with an edge of flame huffed out of his mouth as he wheezed.

"It's not—it's wine!" Aster's mournful wail set him off again, helplessly. "You startled me!"

With one last paroxysm, Corin managed to straighten up and rub his eyes. "Sorry. But you..." And he gestured at Aster's indignant face and soaking-wet pants, barely managing to restrain himself from another cackle.

A long flight tended to leave him loose, relaxed, less human than usual—for good or ill. His senses were heightened and his interest in human proprieties lowered. Somewhere in the back of his mind he knew he ought to say more than that, to try to put Aster at his ease. They'd come damn close to fucking. That would've been awkward enough. Aster's total lack of any kind of poise or dignity pushed the awkwardness into the realm of absurdity.

Aster's elder brother, the heir to the title, had already distinguished himself as a diplomat, probably because he had all the straightforward honesty of an oiled weasel. And Belinda…well, she might be a bitch, but she ruled any ballroom she deigned to enter and any conversation she chose to dominate. Her clothes were always perfect unless she'd rucked up her skirts to get fucked by someone she wasn't engaged to.

Whether running away from home or spilling wine on himself or doing anything else foolish, Aster didn't lie as far as Corin could tell. And he certainly lacked his brother's and sister's elegance. But he had something a lot more important than that.

"How did you turn out so unlike either of your siblings?" Corin asked.

Aster's eyes went even wider. "Oh," he gasped. The corners of his pretty, mobile mouth turned down. Fuck. Corin hadn't meant it badly. How could he take that as anything but a compliment? "I suppose—everyone wonders that. I once overheard my aunt say that the third time's apparently the lack of charm. Maybe there's no better explanation than that."

What the…? Corin's temples throbbed trying to process that. He'd met Aster's aunt once or twice, and he didn't think she had much room to talk, personally. The woman was a shrew. A beautiful shrew, but apparently that ran in the family…except for Aster.

Who couldn't seem to meet Corin's eyes, his gaze directed down in shame, possibly?

Or no. No, perhaps partly shame, but mostly…

Fuck, mostly at Corin's cock.

Which started to thicken under the attention.

Corin's breath was coming a bit faster, tension seeping back into him. He'd spent the whole flight, a long one, hoping Aster would be in his right mind when he returned—and hoping the same for himself. He'd desperately wanted to rid himself of the desire to pin Aster face-down and fuck him unconscious. Aster had clearly sobered up. And Corin had thought he'd succeeded in the other part of his plan, too.

One minute was enough to undo it all, apparently. Especially since Aster being sober meant that one of Corin's greatest sources of reluctance had been removed.

The firelight flickered over Aster's wide-eyed face and heaving chest, on the white-knuckled grip he had on the arm of his chair and on the cup—a bit belated, that. Aster might have been offended by Corin's tactless question, or upset by having to give an answer to it, but it certainly hadn't affected his physical desires. The fire cast enough of a glow to highlight the growing bulge underneath the damp fabric in Aster's lap.

He could've been on a stage set by a particularly clever director, the only thing really visible. The only thing Corin could see, anyway, and that probably would've been true even if he'd been in the midst of a sunlit crowd.

Corin flexed his fingers and toes, fighting back the claws that tried to sneak out. A faint, ice-cold breeze through the broken shutters and under the door whispered over his exposed skin. It did nothing to take the edge off of the heat building within him; it only emphasized his nakedness and the fact that he had no barrier at all between him and what he wanted.

What he definitely, desperately wanted, the longing smacking him out of nowhere with renewed force and leaving him grinding his teeth and clenching his fists with the effort of not simply *taking it*. He could hear Aster breathing, little needy pants. He could smell his arousal mixed with the spilled wine, sweet and salty and intoxicating.

One leg moved without his volition, and then the other. A third step, and then a fourth. Every nerve ending prickled. Each speck of grit in the stone floor pressed palpably into the soles of his feet. His erection hadn't reached its peak, but it stuck out in front of him like a dowsing rod searching for Aster's body. The fire crackled. With a soft little gasp, Aster shifted in his chair, and the cup fell from his hand and clattered to the floor, rolling away into the shadows.

Corin didn't stop until Aster's breath brushed his abdomen. Corin looked down and went lightheaded for a moment, almost swaying on his feet. Those softly parted lips were only a couple of inches from his cockhead.

God damn it, he'd had no intention of doing anything like this. He'd meant to apologize for the way he'd behaved and then keep his fucking distance.

And now he watched his left hand rise, watched it cup the side of Aster's face, fingers sliding into the silk of his hair. He heard Aster's tiny, bitten-off moan, saw his tongue dart out to wet those plush lips.

Pressed his thumb against the corner of Aster's mouth as his hips moved forward, a small motion that set his cock bobbing, the sensitive double ridges gleaming in the firelight.

Monstrously large and inhuman.

What would Aster think of the way he looked now that he had the most intimate of front-row seats?

"Uh," Aster said, and he lifted his hands in a quick, jerky movement, laying them flat on Corin's thighs, the cool touch sending a shockwave up and down his body and centering in his balls. All the blood still remaining in his brain went rushing to his cock, which stood up practically straight now, straining toward Aster's face. "Oh, oh God."

Aster sounded wrecked already.

Corin was such an asshole. So much older, so much more experienced, in control in every possible way.

Except that when those long fingers dug in, Corin felt his control fading away like mist on the mountain. They weren't claws, but they were similar enough to set off Corin's draconic instincts, the part of him that knew mating ought to be a fight. His own fingers curled. He swallowed hard, forcing his own very real claws to stay in through sheer force of will. He wouldn't hurt Aster. A fight, yes, but only on terms Aster could meet.

Aster tilted his head slightly, constrained by Corin's grip on him, gazing up with eyes turned to pools of black by his dilated pupils, only a shimmering ring of blue remaining visible around them. His tongue slipped out between his lips again.

Only this time he turned his head—into Corin's grip, fuck, *toward* him, not trying to escape his touch at all—and that tongue slid over the pad of Corin's thumb. A shudder rippled up his arm and all the way down his spine. Soft and wet, delicate and sweet, too perfect for him to bear. Far more perfect than he deserved. The tip of Aster's tongue caught on the callus left by years of gripping the strap of his shield.

It'd catch that way on each of the ridges of his cock. Tease between them.

If his hand tightened any more he'd leave bruises at best. He had to—he couldn't—his claws tried to come out again—

Instead, he pushed his thumb deeper, angling up to press into Aster's soft palate and force his jaw open.

Aster moaned, low and long, his fingers pressing into Corin's thighs almost painfully. Aster couldn't really hurt him. Corin wished he'd try.

"You like having your mouth open for me?" Corin liked it. He liked it very fucking much. The world had started to retreat, going distant and hazy, a dull setting for the jewel that was Aster, all golden and creamy pink and bright. "I'll fill it for you if you do what you're told."

"Yeth," Aster slurred around Corin's thumb, his lips caressing Corin's skin as he did—and that was more than enough. He wrapped his other hand around the back of Aster's head and pulled him in, bending his knees slightly to lower his cockhead to the level of Aster's open mouth.

He'd stop if Aster pulled away, if he flinched...not that he could, because Corin's grip would've been unbreakable for a much stronger human.

Fuck it. He hadn't said anything when he had the chance, and Corin could feel the heat of Aster's mouth luring him irresistibly. It'd been years since he'd had this. And he doubted he'd ever had anything he wanted as much as this to begin with. He shoved his cock in next to his thumb, stretching Aster's lips to their limit and resting it on his tongue.

Aster let out an odd little gurgling moan. Corin tugged on his hair and angled his head back. Aster's eyes glistened, all sheened with moisture.

Corin's cock gave an almost painful throb.

And he froze, unable to move a muscle, cold horror turning him to stone.

That shouldn't arouse him. Even if the victim of his monstrous lust hadn't been Belinda's little brother, it shouldn't tighten the pit of his stomach and send a thrill of triumph through him to see someone so much at his mercy.

Aster wiggled his tongue, sliding it back and forth over that unbearably sensitive spot on the underside of Corin's glans.

He shivered and pushed a little deeper, drawing out a soft whimper that rose up headier than the scent of wine.

Oh, God, there was only so much a dragon could take before he didn't fucking care about doing the right thing anymore. He'd spent a decade and a half filling the mold of the perfect honorable knight, the perfect gentleman—and then the perfect betrothed, gallant and thoughtful and gentle. And those he'd believed loved him for himself had never seen him as anything but a dangerous beast.

Perhaps they were right.

But fuck it. Fuck the way he kept making an effort to be something that no one appreciated anyway—if they'd even been here to see it.

"That's right," Corin growled. "Use your tongue. Lick every inch of me, Aster."

Aster's soft tongue started moving faster, desperately trying to comply even though Corin's cock weighed it down almost too much to let him do what he was told. Fuck, fuck, the tip of it between the ridges felt almost too fucking good, too much, he'd finish like a teenager if Aster kept it up, making those little *uh uh uh* sounds in the back of his throat, his body moving subtly as his hips shifted around in his chair.

"Don't even think about it," Corin said as Aster's hands started to lift away from his thighs. Not only did he want those hands on him, but he'd be damned if he'd let Aster start focusing on getting himself off instead of giving Corin every ounce of his attention. Fuck it twice. He'd decided to be selfish, he might as well go all the way. "If you're bored I'll give you something to do."

Aster's hands pressed back against Corin's skin like they'd been glued there, and Aster moaned something slurred that sounded almost like, "Maybe you should."

Corin stopped, stared, and tilted Aster's head up another notch, caught somewhere between disbelief and admiration and irritation. The motion rubbed his cock against the inside of Aster's mouth and nearly made Corin moan too. He forced himself to sound calm and in control as he said, "The fuck did you just say to me?"

Aster raised his eyebrows, fluttered his eyelashes, eyes glinting: firelight or mischief, who could say?

All right then.

Corin adjusted his grip so that he had both thumbs prying open the corners of Aster's mouth, dug his fingers into his skull, and thrust.

Incredible heat and softness, the constriction of Aster's throat…Corin's vision blurred and his head dropped down, every other muscle going rigid. Only a few inches of his shaft fit in Aster's mouth. He wanted to bury himself, impale Aster's throat on his length.

A soft choking sound brought him back to reality, and he pulled out enough for Aster to breathe. But only enough, keeping Aster's head immobile and dragging the head of his cock back and forth over his tongue.

The legs of the chair made a horrible screeching noise as they dragged a few inches along the rough flagstones; Aster had moved again, his hands still obediently in place but his body shoving the chair. He gazed up, eyes unbelievably wide, and Corin couldn't look away.

Anything more than the plain facts were beyond Corin at that moment, caught and held as he was, desperately close to spending as he was, with his bollocks drawn up tight and his cock pulsing.

"I'm going to come in your slutty mouth, Aster," he said, and

Aster let out a groan that rose to a high-pitched wail. His eyes rolled back in his head as his hands convulsed against Corin's legs.

Fuck, fuck, and Corin knew that if he could look away from Aster's ecstatic face he'd see more wetness spreading on the front of his trousers, and the heat of that perfect mouth still surrounded him, and when he thrust one more time Aster tightened his throat and sucked and let out a final strangled moan—

He kept his word, almost toppling forward as he came hard and long, pumping Aster's mouth and throat full. His vision whited out, his blood rushing like a river in his ears. It went on and on, over-whelming, a humming through every nerve.

At last the final shock hit, a full-body shudder, leaving him wrung-out and tingling from head to toe. He couldn't feel anything at first but the heat around his softening cock. Then awareness came back to his lungs, laboring away, to his feet grounded on the gritty floor, to…his hands still buried in Aster's hair, his thumbs caught in the corners of Aster's lips.

Fuck.

Slowly, so slowly, he slid his thumbs out, withdrawing his cock-head at the same time. Aster's eyes had fluttered shut, lashes spread out and gleaming against his flushed skin. His mouth looked like someone had—well, like someone had used and abused it beyond what it ought to have had to take.

Not someone. Him. He'd done that, left those rosy lips swollen and shiny with saliva and—fuck. A trace of his come sheened the center of Aster's lower lip where Corin's cock had passed over it as he pulled out.

The urge to lean down and suck that lip into his mouth, abuse it a little more, taste himself in Aster's mouth, hit like a fucking tidal wave, nearly knocking him off his feet.

And then Aster's tongue flickered out and swiped it off his lip.

Everything went hazy again.

Corin let go of Aster's head, seized him under the arms, and hauled him up against his chest.

And then he did what he'd been wanting to do for—no, he wouldn't think about when he'd first suppressed this desire, because it was probably years ago, and that way lay madness. He took Aster's mouth with his, tongue diving in to chase the taste of his own come and Aster's summer-rose sweetness.

# Chapter Ten

THE WORLD SHUDDERED AROUND him as the hands on his face went away all at once, and he wanted to cry out but couldn't, and he was hauled up and pressed to Corin's unyieldingly hard and muscular chest. He'd have new bruises simply from Corin's body.

He opened his eyes a slit just in time to see Corin's dark eyes flashing with something that took Aster's breath away—and then Corin's mouth covered his, and the world went spinning off in all directions, disintegrating into fragments.

Fucking his mouth was one thing.

Kissing him was something else. Something Aster would've thought Corin would reserve for someone beautiful.

Oh, God, Corin had spent in his mouth, his slutty mouth, and now his tongue tangled with his, opened him up the way he had with his cock, only more passionate and more intimate. Aster sank into it. Corin's big hands still held him in place with a grip like a vise. If he'd wanted to he could've crushed Aster's skull in those hands. He could've choked Aster with that massive cock, forced it into his throat and fucked it.

Instead, he'd chosen to spend in him, hot and metallic with a flavor like smoldering sugar, and then kiss the traces of it out of Aster's mouth.

Aster couldn't bring himself to care if he kissed him or choked him or fucked him. No matter which one Corin chose, Aster would be able to imagine he wasn't just a convenient placeholder for something better.

When Corin pulled back enough to suck his sore and swollen lower lip, a shock of pain shot down through him, melting every joint and bone along the way and lodging right between his legs.

If he hadn't been inescapably crushed against Corin's chest he'd have slid to the floor. But he didn't need to hold himself up, and so he wriggled closer to that wall of heat, rutting his half-hard cock against a very hard thigh.

Oh, he'd never been kissed like this, never had his lips bitten and his tongue sucked, his mouth so thoroughly explored.

And then Corin wrenched his mouth away.

Aster blinked up at him, shocked by the sudden chill of the air on his lips.

Their eyes met, Corin's black slits of pupil on black: not remotely human, and too mesmerizing to escape.

Reality seeped back in, though, starting to reform around him in bits and pieces. His hands had landed on Corin's chest. A faint tracery of scales and a dusting of hair roughened the skin under his palms. A chilly draft rattled the shutters gently and brushed over his burning cheeks. And Corin's arms around him felt like the most solid thing in the world.

Corin's cock nudging into his stomach wasn't far behind in terms of solidity, now that he noticed.

"Why did you stop?" The words came out before he could think them through. God, he sounded pathetic. But he didn't understand. That kiss hadn't been lukewarm at all; Aster still couldn't get a full breath. And if Corin wanted him again, why hadn't he kept going?

"It's not—fuck," Corin said roughly, a frown furrowing his brow.

"Exactly," Aster said. "It isn't. If you stop, it definitely isn't."

Oh, God. That hadn't been smooth, or sultry, or seductive, or anything resembling sophisticated. If he needed an applicable word that started with S, he'd be going with shameless, actually. And possibly stupid.

Could he still be drunk after all? He'd only managed half a cup of that wine before he spilled it all over himself.

Corin's frown deepened. "I thought you'd sobered up." His accusing tone rankled, but—how the fuck…?

"Are you reading my mind? Tell me the truth. Do dragons read minds?"

Corin glowered at him. "No, of course we don't, that's—are

you drunk or aren't you?"

"You didn't take advantage of me, if that's what you're asking." Aster's cheeks burned. He managed to choke out, "I wanted every bit of that. And I'm completely rational."

Corin simply stared down at him without answering, something measuring in his eyes. Aster wanted to close his own, or hide, or squirm…actually, he could squirm, and he did, getting a little more friction on his cock, even though it wasn't the most comfortable with the wet fabric in the way. Holding Corin's gaze while he rode his thigh had him panting for air in seconds, heart pounding, everything between his legs aching.

Those iron arms tightened around him until he could practically hear his ribs creaking with the strain.

But he didn't look away, didn't stop, couldn't stop, rubbing himself up and down and straining to spread his legs further in the constriction of his pants, his bollocks catching a little painfully and only making it better, and then he found that if he tilted his hips he could almost get the pressure of Corin's leg on his hole.

Almost.

God, he was like a cat in heat.

It made it all the more humiliating that Corin hadn't moved. His expression hadn't changed.

But his cock pressed into Aster's belly now, fully hard again, and he hadn't loosened his grip.

"I really did sleep it off," Aster whispered. Although it seemed like the horse had really left the barn on that one even if he'd been twice as drunk as before. "Why did you stop?"

For a long moment Aster thought he wouldn't get an answer.

And then Corin said abruptly, "It'd be wrong, and we both know it. I stopped because we need to stop. I lost control. It won't happen again."

Except that he was still holding Aster so tightly it felt like he'd never let him go, and they were both fully erect.

"If I'm not drunk, then there's nothing wrong—"

"You're her brother," Corin gritted out, his teeth clenched. "I'm not—this isn't honest."

"Not honest," Aster repeated, not understanding. And then it hit him like a slap to the face. "You mean you want her." He tried to pull himself out of Corin's arms, shoving against his chest. Corin didn't seem to notice. "I'm some kind of substitute—"

Corin flinched. "You aren't!"

"Of course I am, that's the only thing you could mean, and not that I blame you, but—"

The arms around him gave at last, but only so Corin could grasp him by the shoulders and shake him until his teeth rattled. The whole world went topsy-turvy, and he flailed uselessly.

The shaking stopped. Aster blinked. Corin leaned down until their faces were scant inches apart. "I don't want her," Corin said very slowly. "Not after—you think I could still want her?" Yes, in fact. Aster knew very little about the workings of the human heart—or a dragon's heart. But he did know love wasn't rational at all, and it didn't simply vanish because the object didn't deserve it. "You're not anything like her. I don't see her when I look at—if anything, I'd want to hurt her," he said in a rush. "It's not something I'm proud of. I can't, Aster, you deserve better than that."

Hurt her? Corin fucking Aster wouldn't accomplish that, even if she somehow found out. Or did he want to hurt Aster himself, making him a substitute after all, only for a different reason?

Aster swallowed hard, pushing the pain down along with the words that wanted to spill out. He couldn't allow himself to care why Corin wanted him. Not if he wanted it to continue. Which meant he needed to convince Corin that he was allowed to take what he wanted, no matter why he wanted it.

"Fine, then this has nothing to do with her," he said. A lie, but if they both pretended to believe it... "Which means you don't need to stop because of her, either. We knew each other outside of me being her brother and you being her betrothed, didn't we? Training. As knights. And now we're—" Damn it, damn it, he couldn't say *lovers*. He knew instinctively that Corin would shy away from that word as if it had fleas. "—not only connected through Belinda," he finished.

Aster peered hopefully up into Corin's face. He nodded slightly, but his expression didn't change.

Fuck, not quite enough.

"We had a connection totally apart from almost being related. By marriage! Not really related!"

Oh, for God's sake, why couldn't he keep a rein on his tongue? But Corin's face softened, one corner of his mouth quirking up. "Not related at all," he said softly, his tone making Aster shiver pleasantly. "And that's probably a good thing, considering."

The heat of Aster's flush spread all the way down from his hairline to his throat, his stomach sinking with it.

"There's really nothing stopping us from—"

"No," Corin said, with absolute firmness.

His stomach fell all the way to the floor. Aster's mouth opened and closed again. "No?"

"No. There isn't. We are both men of the sword, to some extent, anyway. We have that in common." Well. At least he knew Corin really was being honest. Ouch. "And I've always liked you, as far as I knew you."

"You have?" Maybe it made him pathetic to a degree that even Marellus would pity, but *I've always liked you, as far as I knew you* would be something Aster would listen to over and over again in the privacy of his own mind, possibly for the rest of his life. He cleared his throat. "Right. So…you might as well. I mean, if you wanted to?"

He stuttered to a stop, now that it had come to it unable to look Corin in the eye and say *If you really liked me, you'd bend me over and fuck me raw.* Perhaps he ought to have stayed drunk after all.

And as if reading his mind *yet again*, Corin said, "You begged me for it when you were drunk earlier. I guess you really are sobered up if you've gone shy on me. But I'm not doing anything at all until you tell me what you want." Corin's voice went low and husky as he added, "In detail."

"You what?" Aster gaped up at him, and Corin's infuriating little smile broadened into a wicked grin.

Fucking smug asshole.

Except that Aster had never been so hard in his life, or so incredibly frustrated. He squirmed, pressing his legs together to try to soothe the ache, since the bastard still had him held out at arm's length.

"Tell me what you want me to do to you now that you're completely in your right mind, Aster." Corin's hands tightened on Aster's shoulders, and he drew him a few inches closer—but not close enough, damn him.

"Why?" Aster demanded. "What—I don't want to!"

Corin shrugged, the motion shaking Aster too. "Why? Because I want to be sure it wasn't the brandy talking. And because I want to hear you. Do it or don't, but I can always get myself off without any help." Strongly implying, of course, that he didn't give a damn whether Aster wanted to or not.

Aster had been trying with all his might to keep his gaze up, knowing he'd lose the power of rational thought if he looked down. But now, screw it. He sent a pointed glance down at Corin's...oh, God, his massively erect cock. Intimidatingly thick at the base above his heavy bollocks, the huge cockhead with its two pronounced ridges, all of it a deeply rosy, almost iridescent green, glimmering in the shifting firelight.

Even thinking about doing what Corin wanted gave him a giddy sense of swooping through the air, the same way he'd felt when he'd dared Corin to give him something to do with his mouth.

He smiled up at him, batted his eyelashes, tipped his head the way he'd seen the coquettes do at balls back home. It probably looked absolutely absurd, but if he tried to do this with a straight face he'd spontaneously combust with embarrassment.

"You mean you'd be just as happy bringing yourself off as you would spend—spending in my—" Oh God, this wasn't working. But he took a deep breath and... "—my very tight ass?"

That sound Corin made, God, like he wanted to eat something, and he yanked Aster close at last, wrapping an arm around him so he was bent backward with his head tipped at a painful angle.

"More," Corin said, eyes flashing.

Aster's chest rose and fell too quickly with his shallow breaths, and he swallowed down a weird little bubble of panic.

Corin bent his head, down, down, tilting Aster even further

back until he went dizzy, he'd fall—and pressed his face to Aster's throat, open-mouthed, searing hot.

"More," he growled, voice gone so low it didn't sound human any more.

"Oh, oh, I don't—" A nip to his Adam's apple had him flailing and crying out. "More, all right, I—my tight ass. Oh, God, Corin, please, you'll get it, get it wet first?" Corin growled again and bit down, and everything went a little reddish and cloudy as Aster's eyes rolled back in his head, and he was really falling—no, not falling. Being lowered. To the floor, Corin's arms around him and his heavy body pressing him down, a massive weight between his legs.

He wanted to keep giving Corin what he wanted, terrified that if he stopped, so would the hands sliding over his chest and the mouth on his throat, biting and sucking and tormenting him with teeth that felt sharper than a human's. But his mind only gave him a series of fractured images: his clothes torn, Corin kneeling over him, searing pressure inside him, a dragon's heavy heat on him and cold floor beneath him and being pinned between.

He couldn't organize it into words, and all that came out was, "Please do what you said you'd do. Earlier, what you said. Please."

Corin lifted his head from his throat, hands resting on Aster's hips. When they flexed, he could swear he felt the slight prick of claws. And his eyes…those red flickers behind his pupils weren't Aster's imagination.

"What I said I'd do," Corin repeated. "The part where I open you up slowly while you beg? Or the part where I hold you down?"

"Yes," Aster said.

The grin that won him had a feral edge to it that promised more than he'd bargained for. But then Corin—knelt up and moved off of him, leaving him bereft and cold and—

"I'll give you one out of two. You're going to ride me," Corin said before he could muster a protest. "Strip for me. I'm going to watch."

And then he lay down on his back, careless of the rough flagstones, cock standing up straight like a knight's lance, and crooked a beckoning finger.

# Chapter Eleven

"ARE YOU—YOU CAN'T be serious," Aster stammered, startled out of his fugue of obedience by Corin's incredible nerve. Did he really think Aster would simply, what, strip for him like a paid whore and then—impale himself on *that*? There were limits!

The thought of letting Corin use him left him breathless with desire. But using himself for Corin's pleasure, climbing on and riding him?

That also left him breathless with desire, damn it all, but he hated himself for it.

Not bothering to answer, Corin slid a hand behind his head, displaying an upper arm as thick as Aster's thigh to mouthwatering advantage. His eyes flickered, perhaps a reflection from the fire in the hearth…and perhaps not. He lifted the other hand, lazily stroking his cock from tip to root, lingering to play with his bollocks.

Aster's hands were moving too without any conscious input, undoing his trouser buttons, with his breath coming faster, his cock painfully stiff, a strange piercing ache behind his bollocks and between the cheeks of his ass. He'd removed his boots when he came inside, and his trousers and socks peeled down easily, leaving him only in his drawers from the waist down. Corin's eyes were truly alight now, red slits in black. Aster slid his hands under the hem of his shirt, and he hesitated.

*Strip for me. I'm going to watch.*

Distantly, he knew no one spoke to Lord Cezanne's son that way, even a disregarded and mostly useless younger son. He oughtn't to allow it.

But no one from court could see them now. Only Corin could see him. And it wouldn't be enjoyable for him to watch someone simply pull a shirt off willy-nilly, would it? So he toyed with the hem, lifting it with one hand, sliding the other hand teasingly over his own stomach.

Corin's low growl vibrated the air.

Aster tipped his head back and pushed the shirt up to the middle of his chest, sliding the other hand up. The chilly air brushed over his nipples. Had they always been this sensitive? Or were they responding to Corin's attention? Because he wasn't looking at Aster's face anymore, eyes fixed avidly on his chest.

"Pinch them, Aster." His deep voice wrapped around Aster like smoke. "One and then the other."

He winced. His flat, muscular chest had small nipples—not a lot of flesh to pinch. Of course he didn't strictly *need* to obey, but...

He pulled the shirt up even more until the fabric bunched around his neck. The other thumb and forefinger went unerringly to his right nipple and pinched it, gently at first, circling around, squeezing. Little sparks of sensation radiated out and shot down, seeming to pool between his legs, increasing that bizarre tightening and stabbing feeling with every touch.

The tender skin grew oversensitized almost to the point of pain, pebbled and sore, as he kept pinching and pinching, but Corin hadn't told him to stop, and somehow it felt even better this way—knowing this wasn't for him. Those soft gasps he let out every time he dug his finger and thumb in couldn't be pleasure, could they?

"Stop," Corin said. "Enough."

Aster started, his eyes fluttering open. He hadn't even realized he'd closed them.

"Oh," he said, fingers stilling. His nipple throbbed. Corin had propped himself up on his elbow, the other hand throttling his cock like he needed to keep it in check by main force. The tip of it glistened with fluid.

"Come here and straddle me," Corin said, his voice less smooth than before, bordering on desperate.

But that didn't change the irresistible strength of his command.

Aster shuffled the couple of feet to where Corin lay, and then hesitated despite how much he longed to obey that voice. Three lovers. Three. That comprised the sum total of his experience. Two had fucked him, once each, with neither time memorable except for moderate discomfort.

He hadn't really enjoyed anything he'd done, in fact, and it'd been far from creative or acrobatic.

Where did he put his hands? Or his legs, for that matter? He'd do it wrong, and Corin wouldn't want him after all...

He let out a startled yelp as Corin muttered something under his breath and sat up, lunging forward to seize him under the arms and lift him bodily into place. He landed in a shaky sprawl, legs splayed to either side of Corin's hips, his bollocks nestled against Corin's. It felt shockingly intimate, that masculine softness.

In one swift motion, Corin released him and seized his shirt, ripping it off of him as easily as Aster would tear a piece of paper and flinging it away in ragged threads. He lay back down again before Aster could do more than gasp in shock. His body felt so big between Aster's thighs. And when he looked down, there was that cock, even longer from this angle.

He bit his lip, gaze flicking back up to Corin's face...which softened, oddly, the flames behind those dragon eyes going orangey-yellow instead of crimson. "You've never done this before, have you."

It wasn't a question. It didn't need to be. Aster bit harder, the sting of it something to focus on, and shook his head.

"Mmm," Corin said, a low rumble that he could feel in his bones. The flames in his eyes flared blood-red. "I'll do the work for now, then. And you can take over in a while. Lean down. Brace your hands on either side of my head. And stay there."

Feeling more ungainly and awkward than ever before in his life, Aster slowly leaned down, setting his hands gingerly on the floor, wincing at the chill and the gritty dirt. Ugh. Corin had that all over his back and legs, too.

"Oh," he said, as it hit him.

"What?" Corin nuzzled into his chest as it came into range, breath nearly searing.

He tipped his chin down. Corin's hair brushed his face, and he dared to lean a little further. The scent of him was more soothing than temple smoke and as intoxicating as wine, like incense and heat and a trace of the icy storm Corin had flown through in his other body. Tenderness welled up in him, as heartwrenchingly unwanted by its object as it was impossible to smother.

"You're putting me on top so that I don't get hurt on the flag-stones." His back would be black and blue immediately and the skin stripped off agonizingly within a few minutes if Corin fucked him like that. "You won't be?"

Corin froze. "No," he said after a moment. "Dragons were birthed from stone, did you know? Thousands of years ago. And I'm more of a dragon than most." He shifted, lips brushing Aster's right nipple, the one he'd pinched into a throbbing bud. Aster held his breath, squeezing his eyes shut and trying not to whimper. "Much more," Corin whispered. "A throwback of sorts. You'll see."

And then his hot mouth closed over Aster's nipple, a hint of teeth, and the sounds trapped in Aster's throat poured out, little cries and pants as Corin sucked hard, flicked with his tongue, sucked again, made Aster writhe and buck and moan.

As he rocked his hips, his cock met Corin's, kissing and retreating. Even though he'd spent enough to last longer, if this kept up it wouldn't be very long at all.

"I thought you were going to fuck me?" he gasped. Corin's mouth left his nipple with an audible pop as he lowered himself down to his back again. God, he didn't want to look—but he glanced down, unable to help himself. His nipple stuck out obscenely, red and swollen. "What did you—oh, God!"

The air went out of him in a rush as Corin seized him around the waist and yanked him down, chest to chest. He couldn't help squirming and struggling as Corin's other hand slid between his cheeks, a finger pressing into him.

Corin pinned him more firmly. "That's better," he said. "Now you can get held down after all, just the way you wanted."

It felt so undignified to be positioned so strangely, sweaty and clumsy and embarrassed—and yet he tingled with the need for more of anything Corin wanted to give him, to take from him, to do to him.

Corin stroked his finger in a circle around Aster's rim, prodding a little into the ring of muscle, making Aster clench. Everything had narrowed down to that. The pressure of the powerful arms around him, the texture of Corin's chest hair under his cheek, the way his arms were bent oddly over Corin's shoulders—it was all window dressing to that thick finger touching him, almost penetrating him but not quite. His other lovers had simply put it in.

"What are you doing?" he panted.

"Seeing how tight you are," Corin replied, and moved his hand, taking a firm grip on Aster's ass and shifting him up his body. It rubbed their cocks together again, Aster's bollocks catching between them. Corin's cockhead lodged between his ass cheeks and pressed firmly against his hole, so much thicker than the finger that had been there a moment ago.

Too dry, it'd hurt, and it didn't even feel like it'd fit without tearing him open, but he'd take it if Corin made him. He didn't know what he was begging for as he said, "Corin, please—"

"Not yet, I won't hurt you." Corin's voice dropped into that low, commanding register again. "Look at me." Aster lifted his head, helpless to resist. Besides, why would anyone not want to look at Corin, with his dragon's eyes and his firm human lips, his perfection? Their eyes met and held. "See how it feels," Corin said softly. "Rub yourself on me. Get yourself wet."

It wouldn't get him wet, he wasn't a woman, for fuck's sake.

But his hips started to move, little circles, up and down, massaging his hole with Corin's cockhead.

And he *was* getting wet. He stopped dead.

"Is that you or me? Corin?" His voice rose an octave, shaky and weak. His body didn't do that, it couldn't—

Corin's low laugh and shake of the head were enough for him to let out a breath. "Me," he said. "I told you, I'm more of a dragon than most. Keep going. It feels fucking incredible, Aster. You feel fucking incredible."

Well, then. He moved again, tilting his ass up, spreading his thighs. Making more room for that thick cockhead that didn't feel like it could ever penetrate him, letting the double ridges tease the sensitive skin of his bollocks and the inner curves of his cheeks. Keeping his eyes locked with Corin's made everything more intense. As if the world contained only the two of them and their rough, uneven breaths.

"I told you I'd take all the time in the world to open you up," Corin said. He pushed up, his stomach muscles contracting under Aster's, his cock nudging Aster's inner curves open a little and making him gasp. God, he was strong, to half-sit like this with his arms around Aster's body. Aster had never really wanted someone stronger than he was, someone who could physically master him so easily.

Then again, he'd never been able to look away whenever Corin was in view.

Maybe he should've realized sooner what he really wanted.

Corin curled his body again, and this time, Aster's body yielded. The head of his cock sank into him to the first ridge, a monstrous stretch and burn. Aster's eyes went wide and his mouth dropped open as he froze, transfixed by the shock and pain. How had he thought he could do this—and then it popped out again with an obscenely wet squelching sound, another burst of pain and surprise, and Aster couldn't do anything but collapse and rest his sweaty forehead on Corin's collarbones, panting for breath, shaking.

"Oh, God," he choked. "Oh, fucking God. How did that fit?"

"Magic," Corin said, sounding nearly as wrecked as he did. "Or just your body wanting me. Sit up and take it, Aster. Now."

He'd wanted it, he had—but now that it came down to it, fear froze his mind and slithered down his spine, tingling in his hands and feet. Shame followed. He'd put on such a show of confidence, and now he'd be disappointing Corin as well as himself.

"I don't think I can," he said, the words scraping his dry throat raw.

Corin's hands wrapped around his hips. "You can." And gently but irresistibly, he angled Aster's lower body to aim Corin's cock right at his hole. "Sit up."

He might not have been able to obey on his own, but Corin took him by the shoulders and levered him up until he had to scrabble to get his knees under him before gravity impaled him on Corin's cock.

All the way, anyway, because an inch or two had surely gone in. It felt like balancing on a fencepost. So stretched and full, his thighs aching from the angle he'd had to spread them.

Corin's eyes were fixed intently on his face. He gazed down into them, saw the flames dance there, caught the glint of a sharp fang behind Corin's curled lip.

And his fear bled away. Corin had him. He was the strongest being Aster had ever met, the most honorable, the most trustworthy. With him in charge, Aster could do anything.

It wasn't necessarily comfortable, though. His hair hung around his face in a wavy mess, stuck to his temples, hanging into his eyes. He wanted to push it out of the way, but if he did that he'd lose what little leverage he had from bracing himself on Corin's chest. His legs shook. One knee slipped a little to the side, and Aster cried out as he lost his balance and another inch, maybe, shoved inside his body.

"Corin." His voice didn't even sound like his own, too thin and high. "Do you really think I can take it? Take you?"

The toothy, feral grin Corin flashed at him raised the hair on the back of his neck. His cock gave an eager jerk, and God, there was something wrong with him if a predator showing his fangs made him harder.

"I promised you I'd make you, didn't I?"

Aster could only nod.

"I keep my promises," Corin growled, and his hands grew heavier on Aster's shoulders, inexorably forcing him to slide down. And down, inch by inch, thicker and deeper until Aster couldn't feel anything else but the cock filling him completely. He caught at Corin's forearms and clung to him. "Almost there," Corin said, tone so oddly soft and kind for someone who was ruining him forever. "A couple more inches."

A couple more…he tucked his chin and stared down, past his own straining cock—he couldn't even feel it through the waves of sensation below, but apparently the little bastard enjoyed this—and his bollocks, to…he saw the base of Corin's cock between his thighs, massively thick and with a faint green shimmer of scales, and everything went all swimmy.

Oh, God. He really could do this, take Corin all the way, satisfy and please him…

With a breathy little moan, he closed his eyes, relaxed his legs, and gave in.

His ass pressed down against Corin's body as the thickest part of his girth filled Aster up. Corin's big hands slid down again, pausing to tweak Aster's swollen nipples and make him jump and whimper, and then settling on his hips again and giving him a squeeze.

"There you are," Corin said. "Hot and wet and perfect inside. You fit me like a sheath for a sword, Aster."

If any other man had said that to him he'd have protested. He wielded his own sword, didn't he? Literally and figuratively. He'd often been the one to do the fucking.

Not that he'd done it particularly well, he didn't think.

Apparently, he was doing *this* well. All he had to do to be…perfect…was to be Corin's sheath. Allow Corin to do as he pleased. God, he was *pleasing* him, although he almost didn't have room for the fluttery pleasure of having done so around the massive cock embedded in his guts.

But he didn't know what came next. He felt restless, strange, as if he wanted to move. But moving seemed impossible.

Experimentally, he shifted forward and back, rocking on Corin's cock. Forward felt odd, but when he rocked back, shoving Corin's shaft against the front of his body—painful, incredible pressure built and twisted in him, everything clenched below the waist, and he curled over himself in a rictus.

That sound was him, that whining moan. God. And that was Corin growling, hands sliding up to wrap around his waist, thrusting up while Aster rocked.

Corin's cock pounded so deeply into him it felt like it nudged his ribs, he couldn't catch a breath, every motion hit him so perfectly and drew his bollocks up painfully tight. He could barely see, everything a blur, and the cock in him blazed like dragonfire sparked from granite, impossibly hot and hard, pounding him into nothingness…

And then Corin lifted him like he weighed nothing at all, holding him up so that only half his cock was left inside, letting him hover. Aster's eyes focused at last as he came to stillness. He breathed in, deep and shaky, and tightened his death grip on Corin's arms. They weren't even trembling from the strain.

Well. Corin's weren't.

"Corin?" He squirmed a little, testing how it'd feel. It felt like he was stirring his insides with an enormous dragon cock, what a surprise. "What are you doing?"

Corin smiled, teeth flashing, and slammed Aster back down again, thrusting up at the same time. The girth of the base wrenched him wide, stuffing him, putting almost unbearable pressure on that spot behind his cock. And again, up, hovering, while Aster writhed and squirmed, and then down, and then again, and again.

Using him like a wet, living sheath.

The pressure exploded at last and the world turned inside out. He came and came, painting Corin's chest, letting out a wail that ended in a sob, wetness streaking his cheeks. Corin's growl of triumph echoed through the hall.

When Aster collapsed down, limp and wrung-out and with his mind drifting sideways through a fog, trembling with aftershocks, Corin wrapped him in his arms and pinned him down to his chest, a hand buried in his hair and cradling his skull. Corin's chest rose and fell hard and fast, his still-hard cock shifting inside Aster with his breaths.

Aster closed his eyes and allowed himself to melt into Corin's hold. No purpose. Nothing he needed to accomplish. Cocooned in warmth, gently rocked by the force of the massive cock filling him up. His whole body had turned into trembling, pleasure-wracked jelly.

"I'm almost there, Aster," Corin gasped, hips flexing and pushing his cock even deeper. "I told you I'm—more of a dragon than most."

More of a dragon than most? He was almost…where? What—

And then Aster felt it. The base of Corin's cock had—had expanded somehow, growing even more, stretching Aster's rim to the utmost limit of what he could take.

He tried to push up, but he'd been pinned. "Corin, please, what's happen—"

"Fuck, just a second—" Corin shoved him down, and no, that hurt, it hurt so fucking much that his vision whited out, but then the base of Corin's cock somehow popped inside. All that thickness was pushing on the same spot that'd made him come so hard he nearly passed out. Inescapable, no matter how he wriggled, no matter how he writhed and moaned and scrabbled at Corin's sides with his fingers, the pressure building again—

With a low, bitten-off groan, Corin thrust hard and then stilled.

Almost stilled.

His cock moved, pulsing inside him, his come almost searing Aster with its inhuman heat.

Aster convulsed, cried out, and came again, except that he'd been milked dry. His cock twitched, still soft, his bollocks feeling like they'd twisted into a knot.

Corin went still, gasping for breath, his arms so tight around Aster they could've been carved out of that stone he claimed his kind had come from. He thrust again, rubbing his huge thickness against Aster's inner walls again.

It was too much, and Aster let go, everything going red and gray and then black.

# Chapter Twelve

MAYBE IT MADE CORIN A ridiculous cliché of a man, but for several long, overwhelming, luxurious minutes he couldn't focus on anything but the sensation of tight, wet warmth around his knot, the pressure and the slickness and the smoothness of the lovely body surrounding him.

Fuck, *fuck* but that felt good. He hadn't knotted in years, not since the last time he'd fucked another dragon. At least his kind knew such a thing was possible, even if they didn't all form knots themselves—it was a bit of a genetic abnormality, something that had been bred out over millennia of occasional matings with humans. When you did have a knot, good manners and common sense suggested keeping it under control most of the time when you were lying with a human.

It felt a lot less good—downright disturbing, in fact—to acknowledge that it hadn't been a choice this time so much as a necessity. He hadn't tried to suppress it. He hadn't even planned to try. He'd gone into this with the full intention of splitting Aster open on his knot, because anything else would have been unthinkable.

Long ago, when all dragon cocks had knots, dragons only knotted their mates.

At that, his eyes were wide open, staring up at the shadowy ceiling. His knot hadn't gone down at all and wouldn't for at least a quarter of an hour. It still throbbed, and he felt as if every muscle, bone, and joint in his body had been melted.

But he wasn't adrift in a haze of pleasure anymore.

And his knot wasn't just in a wonderfully tight hole, it was in Aster. Belinda's brother, someone he would never mate and who shouldn't have tempted him into knotting in the first place.

Not to mention, a real person with his own thoughts and

feelings—which Corin had totally disregarded in favor of satisfying his own basest urges.

He lifted his head a fraction and peered down at the man sprawled across his chest. Aster's golden hair glinted redder than usual in the dim light of the dying fire in the hearth, and it had tumbled into a glorious mess, completely obscuring his face. Beyond that, the long, smooth curve of Aster's back, with Corin's arms around it, softened into the much more pronounced and delicious curve of his peachy ass.

Corin shivered. God. If he wasn't already buried to the hilt inside that ass he'd want to fuck it. His cock gave a hopeful little twitch.

Damn it, he was a dragon, not an animal. He had to get it together.

Aster's warm weight felt delicious too, not nearly enough to impede his breathing or inconvenience him, but a substantial, satisfying armful.

A very quiet and still armful.

"Aster?" Corin gave him a gentle shake, careful not to jostle him too much with Corin's knot inside him. Aster's head rocked limply from side to side. No answer. "Aster?" he asked a little more loudly. Nothing.

All right. He could hear Aster's breathing, deep and even, could feel his heart beating against his own chest. He hadn't killed him.

Had Aster fainted?

From the overwhelming sensation of Corin's knot?

Fuck, fuck, no, he would not feel a deep, satisfied sense of possessive triumph that he'd managed to fuck and knot Aster unconscious. That would be *wrong*. His hips lifted slightly, pushing his knot a tiny bit deeper. Aster let out a soft whimper.

It was by far the most painfully arousing thing that had ever happened to Corin in a life, the past two lonely years excepted, spent with few inhibitions and plenty of very attractive partners. He wouldn't do it again. That would be more than wrong.

His hips moved again, his knot rubbing against Aster's insides.

This time, Aster made a sort of *mmm* sound and snuggled into Corin's chest, the fingers of one hand trailing gently along his ribs. A tendril of his silky hair drifted across Corin's neck, almost ticklish.

Corin thumped his head down onto the flagstones hard enough that he saw stars.

No, he couldn't do this. He had to think about Aster's comfort. Care for him. Aster had wanted Corin to fuck him, but he hadn't expected a knot and he hadn't signed up to be fucked twice on a cold stone floor, his hole stretched so wide and open and pink—

All right, no.

Yes, all right. He could acknowledge the part of him that wanted to rut into this pretty boy until he owned him, but that part had to shut the fuck up for all the reasons he'd already enumerated.

The other part of him, the decent part, knew that Aster needed a soft, warm bed, and when he woke a bath and clean clothes and the attentions of a gentleman, not a beast.

With infinite care, as if he could make up for what he'd done, he made sure he had Aster cradled against his chest and sat up, bending his knees and planting his feet flat on the floor. Rising took careful balance, but he made it upright with only a small jostle, one arm wrapped under Aster's ass and the other around his shoulders to keep him from falling backward. Once he got going it was easier, across the hall and up the stairs, much more slowly than usual since every time he lifted one knee his knot pushed to the other side.

It was awkward as hell, in fact. But he made it to the top and through the bedroom door without anyone falling down or over. Luckily Aster had left the blankets thrown back with a nobleman's disregard for anything servants would usually do, and Corin was able to lower him down directly into the bed.

Which revealed the weak point in his excellent plan.

Now Aster was in a comfortable bed instead of on a floor, yes. His head lolled on the pillow, his arms had flopped down by his sides, and his legs sprawled out to either side of Corin's thighs. He could be completely at his ease.

But Corin was stuck on top of him, with his knot still stretching Aster open and the rest of his cock buried deep.

Corin gazed down at Aster's slack face, his flushed cheeks and parted lips, the crescents of his eyelids and the fanned-out lashes. So young, and in sleep, so incredibly sweet. Too young and sweet to be subjected to the darker, more draconic side of Corin's lust.

And yet here they were, with Aster unconscious on Corin's knot.

He rocked forward an inch. In the silence of the bedroom, it made a slick, wet sound. Corin's come. That was Corin's come, filling Aster's body and kept inside by his knot.

Another adjustment of his hips made another squelch. Aster stirred, moaned, tensed around Corin's knot, squeezing it like a vise and making Corin tremble.

He shouldn't. He couldn't.

And yet he was, moving faster and deeper now, shifting his hips in little circles, propped on his arms to keep his weight off of Aster's smaller body, gazing down at his lovely face.

When had he finally understood how lovely Aster truly was? Maybe all along, only he'd been distracted by flashier beauty. Aster had been like one of his wild namesakes growing in the shade of a peony, neglected by those who didn't have the discrimination and taste to recognize its perfection. But the peony, to overextend a metaphor, had proven to be a cheating bitch. No beauty made up for that. Aster…God, look at him. And feel him. And…Corin leaned down and pressed his face into the curve of Aster's throat.

No clue what actual asters smelled like, or if they even had a scent. But this Aster smelled like roses and sex, like sweat and salt and his come and Corin's, like *his*.

He nipped gently at the corded muscle in the side of Aster's neck. Aster sighed, squirmed, subsided again. Corin thrust one more time, just once.

Fuck, he had to stop.

Or he could stuff his knot even deeper, fuck Aster with it harder and harder until he woke fully erect and moaning helplessly, startled and disoriented and about to spend all over them both. Aster's cries of shock and desire would taste so delicious when Corin licked them out of his sweet mouth.

Corin froze, even his hips stilled at last, chest heaving with his rasping breaths.

He could abandon every principle he'd ever held dear and use and abuse Aster for his own pleasure, excusing it on the basis that he'd give Aster pleasure too—whether he liked it or not.

No. Because he might have given up on being the perfect knight, given up on sublimating his own needs into those of the people who depended on him but never appreciated his dependability. But that didn't mean he lacked standards and morals of his own.

All right. He couldn't pound Aster to bits before he woke. But he couldn't pull out, either, not without inflicting physical damage worse than his transgressions.

And nothing prevented him from enjoying his current situation within some reasonable boundaries, after all.

Corin lowered himself to one elbow, holding up enough of his weight while still pressing his body down onto Aster's, savoring every inch of his soft human skin. His own wasn't rough, precisely. But it did have the faintest texture of his scales permanently embedded. Aster felt like silk.

The other hand, he slid under Aster's back and down, down, until his palm smoothed around the curve of Aster's equally silken ass. A gloriously soft handful that he could squeeze and knead, pushing it in and pulling it away from the other cheek, the motion massaging his knot at the same time and making him lightheaded. He settled down on the pillow beside Aster and nuzzled his soft hair.

It wouldn't hurt to slide a finger between Aster's cheeks and feel where they were joined, would it? God, he felt good, inside and out. Even with Corin's knot stuffing him full and keeping him from leaking too much, he was slick around his rim, the skin taut and stretched to its limit.

Corin shuddered and thrust once, just fucking once, eyes closed and face pressed to Aster's hair, savoring having him wrapped up and enclosed and filled and possessed.

Aster made a little sound—and Corin felt his body come back to awareness, that slight increase in tension that meant consciousness. Corin froze, eyes popping open, breathing as lightly as possible.

"Corin? Are you—oh," he said, sleepy and confused on the first word and much sharper at the end. "You're still inside me."

"Yes." His voice sounded bizarrely rough, not like his own at all. Corin cleared his throat, belatedly remembering he had his face right next to Aster's ear. He pulled back an inch. "My knot hasn't gone down yet."

"Your knot. Your—I think I fainted. I had no idea that was possible. Corin?" His lost, plaintive tone felt like a kick to the chest.

Aster shifted his weight, and Corin went rigid with the effort of not thrusting into him again. Gentle hands settled on Corin's sides. Not soft—a swordsman's hands; even if Aster hadn't gained much skill, he'd put in the time training. But his touch seemed tentative, as if it wouldn't be welcome. Careful, even though he was the one who'd been plowed open in a way no human would expect or probably even want.

And that was unacceptable—heartbreaking even. More than Corin could bear.

He vibrated with the need to do something, to fuck Aster into next week or to say the right words, to soothe the anxiety and fear he knew underlay Aster's pitiful uncertainty and doubt that Corin wanted his touch.

Words—the right ones, at least—had never been his strong suit. And fucking Aster again might send the wrong message. An honest message. But wrong.

Corin pushed himself up so that he could look down into Aster's face. Blue eyes all clouded with worry and confusion met his, irresistible in their appeal.

He had only one answer to that, to any of it. Before Aster could say anything else that'd make him feel like a fucking monster, he bent down and pressed his mouth to Aster's softly parted lips.

This kiss couldn't have been more different from before. He'd claimed Aster's mouth earlier, forced him open. This time he teased him, coaxed him, nibbled so softly at Aster's swollen lower lip that he opened easily, with a sigh that sent a shiver down Corin's spine. The hands on his sides grew bolder, fingers digging in, one sweeping up to cradle the nape of Corin's neck.

And then he lifted his hips, moaning into Corin's mouth, spreading his thighs wider to let Corin push that tiny bit deeper.

Fucking him while he lay there insensible would've been a wicked pleasure all its own, but this—this was infinitely better, thrusting down into such incredible tight softness and feeling Aster arch under him, bodies straining together. Aster's cock had even gotten half hard again and pressed against Corin's stomach in a way that suggested he didn't hate having a knot buried in his ass after all.

He sank deeper and deeper into Aster's body: with his cock, with the kiss he couldn't seem to keep sweet and gentle anymore, with his body half-crushing Aster into the bed, with the hand he still had clutching Aster's ass in an increasingly possessive grasp.

Corin's knot made any really vigorous movement impossible, but he drove his knot and his cock a little further in with every shift of his hips, forced Aster's legs a little wider.

Pleasure built and built until he couldn't tell how much was his and how much was Aster's, an almost intolerable tension building in his knot and his balls, every muscle taut. His fingers hurt and even his shoulder blades itched, claws and wings ready to force themselves out, his skin too tight and too hard and crawling with the need to transform. Heat flared in his belly and rose up into his chest.

Fuck, he was going to—going to—

Corin's knot swelled impossibly larger and he came again, filling Aster to the brim in pulse after pulse, his spine arching as he threw his head back and roared a gout of flame to the rafters. Under him, Aster cried out and pulled him down, arms tight and legs wrapped around his hips.

For a long moment, Corin couldn't do anything but let his head hang down, eyes closed, the world tilting and whirling around him. At last he was able to look up and make sure the ceiling hadn't lit on fire—good, his flames hadn't quite reached that far—and then collapse down, forehead on the pillow beside Aster's head.

God damn, he was done. If it hadn't been for all of Aster's long limbs around him he might have floated away, or rolled off the bed and fallen to the floor. He couldn't quite seem to get his bearings, with up and down not having resolved yet into distinct directions.

Aster squeezed him harder, inside and out, and Corin shuddered, nuzzling into the side of Aster's head and pressing a kiss to his hair. That was possibly the very best thing he'd ever felt.

Fuck it, Aster seemed to need all the praise he could get.

"That," he said hoarsely, throat raw and singed, "was possibly the very best thing I've ever felt."

And then he closed his eyes and let himself rest.

# Chapter Thirteen

IF SOMEONE HAD ASKED Aster how he'd feel toward a dragon who'd fucked him unconscious, knotted him—and the hell was that, anyway, he felt like he'd gone into some kind of fantasy world—and then woken him by fucking him again only to *breathe fire* when he spent...well, "protective" wouldn't have been on the list, let alone at the top.

Stunned. And intimidated. Both of those would have been on the list for good reason.

But with Corin enclosed in all of his limbs, collapsed on top of him and breathing deeply in his ear, he felt such a swell of tenderness and care that he could hardly contain it.

Not that he had much more room available to contain anything, to be honest. Before Corin had lain down on top of him and blocked his view, he'd tucked his chin and peered down at his lower body, shuddering with something between desperate desire and horror at the sight of Corin's massive shaft stuck between his legs. And when Corin had come inside him the second time, Aster's belly had visibly rounded. The pressure of it had finally stopped making him want to come again. Instead, it had him trying to squirm to relieve it, although he knew he couldn't. Not with Corin's dragon cock still buried in him.

God. So much come would rush out when Corin...uncorked him. It'd be so disgusting. Maybe Corin would laugh at him.

Aster bit his lip to keep from groaning.

But there was nothing he could do about it. And surely, surely if he was sweet enough, accommodating enough, Corin would be kind in return. That honeyed kiss when Aster woke had been the most loving of his life.

Despite the fact that love had nothing whatsoever to do with it.

He tightened his arms, stroking along Corin's spine, hooking his ankles around Corin's thighs to relieve the ache in his own, which had been exercised more in the last couple of hours than they had in three weeks of riding a horse. Corin's skin had the slightest texture all over. Not rough, exactly, but Aster could infer the shapes of scales beneath his fingertips. He hadn't had to infer anything when Corin had let off his spout of fire; his skin had rippled with metallic green scales, his face transforming for a moment as he threw his head back and shook the walls with the force of his roar.

Aster had a dragon in his arms. A fire-breathing, armor-scaled dragon with a double-ridged and knotted cock.

Aster had a double-ridged and knotted cock in *him*.

He turned his head and brushed a kiss against Corin's shoulder, the skin so much hotter than his lips. Of course, all of Corin felt that way. The sun had started to go down at last, the day's gray light fading out of the bedroom windows, and any warmth in the air had faded with it, leaving the tower bitterly cold. Aster's breath steamed when he let it out.

But he couldn't have been cozier underneath his enormous dragon blanket.

*That was possibly the very best thing I've ever felt.*

Well. Aster squeezed him even tighter, wishing he could kiss him all over. Same for him, only without the *possibly* qualifier. He'd never felt like this, so replete and satisfied that he couldn't stop smiling and longed to stay precisely where he was, swollen belly and all, forever.

Mmm. God, he couldn't. But he could spread his legs later and ask Corin very, very nicely to swell him up again, fill him until he couldn't breathe.

At that moment, the pressure inside him eased slightly for the first time since Corin had gotten his cock all the way in. The knot shrank; not much, but a little. Enough that…oh, God. Wetness seeped out all around, hot and slick, on his thighs and in the crease of his ass and on the underside of his bollocks. Fuck, Corin's bed would get all wet. Of course, if Aster's wetness disgusted him that'd be a bit unreasonable—but most of the time men *were* pretty unreasonable when they were inconvenienced, if they'd already gotten off and weren't hypnotized by lust anymore.

Had Corin gone to sleep? He wasn't snoring. Maybe he simply didn't snore at all. That seemed unlikely for someone who could blow fire out of his mouth, but what did Aster know? Could he slide out from underneath as soon as Corin's knot went down enough, and perhaps…tighten himself up to hold it all in until he could get out of bed? Oh, God, that would be so much worse, somehow, and he had no idea what to do, and instead of perfectly relaxed and happy now he teetered on the brink of panic, heart pounding…

He nearly jumped out of his skin when Corin lifted his head and blinked down at him, pupils narrowing to slits as they adjusted to the light. God, that wasn't fair at all. Most people's rumpled post-coital hair didn't look as if it'd been styled by a court valet. Aster's certainly didn't.

"My knot's going down," Corin said casually, as if it weren't a disaster in progress. "What's wrong? Your heart started pounding like you'd been running up a hill."

Aster swallowed hard enough that he heard it click.

Damn it. How the hell did he answer that? "Your—knot—*is* going down," he managed to repeat, although his voice wavered on "knot," a word he still couldn't quite believe he was using in this context. "And I, I," fuck, fuck, "think I'm leaking," he finished in a whisper, staring at a point past Corin's shoulder. A tomato probably would've been jealous of the color of his face.

Corin hummed thoughtfully and gave Aster's ass a gentle squeeze—oh God, he still had a hand down there—wiggling his fingers into the slick crease. "You are, actually."

"Get off of me," he gasped, flustered and irritated, starting to try to extricate himself, letting go of Corin's back and planting his feet on the bed to get a little leverage. "Pull out. I don't care if it's not, if it's not ready and you hurt me, I don't care—"

"Aster, stop. Aster, for fuck's—look at me!"

"Damn you," Aster snarled, but he turned his head and looked. Because Corin had used that voice of his, the one that he couldn't seem to resist, the one that had to be a part of his draconic magic.

117

Corin had slid his hand out from under Aster's ass, at least, and propped himself up on both arms, looming over him and staring down with eyes that flickered anew with a vermilion glow.

This time, Aster couldn't even pretend it was a reflection from the fire. They'd left that downstairs.

Corin pinned him with his fiery gaze. "I came in you twice," he said, cheeks flushing dusky-brick-green despite his matter-of-fact tone. That made Aster feel even worse. If it embarrassed *Corin* to talk about it... "So if you—"

"Don't," Aster snapped. "You're disgusted by the mess, fine, but you don't need to—"

"God damn it, it makes me want to fuck you and fill you up all over again, Aster!"

Aster stammered to a stop. It did? "It does?"

"Yes, of course it fucking does," Corin said, sounding far less embarrassed and far more harassed. "That's my come, Aster," and his voice dropped down to a rasp that had Aster shuddering and melting all at once. "You're full of my come. Dripping with it. I want to wait until my knot slips out and then fuck it right back into you."

"Oh," he choked. All other words in his vocabulary had deserted him. "Oh."

Corin leaned down until their faces nearly touched. "Yes, oh. Tell me not to touch you again if you want," he said, and now he sounded a little less certain. "I know you didn't expect—I told you I'm more dragon than most. I'm sorry. But don't think I'm not dragon enough to enjoy every bit of what I've done to you, too."

"Then you're not going to be angry when I, fuck." He licked his dry lips and wished he could tear his gaze away. "When I get the bed all wet and sticky?"

Corin's eyes darkened, and then he leaned down even further, nudging Aster's chin up with his nose and pressing his lips to the curve of his throat, caressing, gentle. One soft kiss, and then another a little lower down, and then up again, nuzzling under his ear. His breath heated Aster's skin and paradoxically left a trail of goose-bumps in its wake.

"You can get the bed wet and sticky," he murmured between

kisses. "You can get me sticky. And if you get yourself sticky, I'll lick it off."

Lick it...

"Fucking God," Aster choked. "Lick my—"

"With great pleasure," Corin purred into his ear. "Very great pleasure." His tongue flicked out and curled around Aster's earlobe, and fuck, but it felt so much longer than a human tongue when he extended it like that. It could go...and if he thought about it, he'd combust. "But right now, I think maybe you've had enough. And I'm going to leave you alone for a few minutes and fill a bath for you by the fire." Another kiss. "Don't worry about anything."

Aster opened his mouth to protest that he absolutely had *not* had enough, and that he could take as much as Corin could give him, thank you very much.

And then he snapped it shut again. What did he have to prove? If he'd been in bed with another human man, maybe he'd have tried to compete with his prowess.

But he wasn't. The man currently kissing the side of his neck, rocking his hips, gently starting to disengage from his body as more and more of his come trickled out of Aster's incredibly well-used ass, was a dragon. Magical. Far stronger than any human, and presumably with more staying power too. Since Aster couldn't possibly compete, why should he try?

Because he had, in fact, had enough for the moment. And he wanted nothing so much as for Corin to put him in a hot bath and pour him a glass of that lovely wine he hopefully hadn't spilled all of.

Wait a moment. A *hot* bath.

Damn it.

"Maybe wait a while on the bath," he said with great regret. "Mmm. That spot is—I'm a little ticklish. Corin—" He broke down laughing as Corin licked under his chin. "Stop! Thank you. I don't think I have the fortitude for a bath as cold as the water that comes out of the well. It'll have to sit by the fire for a while. And even then."

Corin lifted his head and grinned down at him, eyes bright, and Aster's heart did a helpless double-flip.

"I have a metal tub for a reason. I'm going to fill it with snow, takes less time that way. And yes, I will put it by the fire. But it'll be steaming hot in a couple of minutes of me breathing on it." And then he—winked. With both of his eyelids, the human outer and the draconic inner.

Nothing in Aster's past had prepared him for being fucked up the ass with a dragon's knotted cock.

But even that paled in comparison to being winked at mischievously by Sir Corin, dragon knight, disheveled and flushed and unshaven, offering to personally fill and then heat Aster's bath with his flames—after fucking him up the ass with his magnificent knotted cock.

Something squeezed oddly in his chest and stomach, a sensation of twisting and floating and sinking all at once.

If he put a name to it, even inside his own head, he'd be so very, deeply fucked in an entirely different and much less enjoyable way. And if he'd had a chance in hell of believing that strange feeling had been born of the extreme circumstances of his flight from home, it wouldn't have been so bad. But he'd known Corin for years and years, first as King Theobert's most illustrious knight and then as his prospective brother-in-law. And he felt no different now than he had then.

A tremor went through him. No, he couldn't think any more about what that meant.

He smiled up at Corin, praying that none of what he felt would show on his face. Corin would be horrified.

"Thank you," he said, with an effort to sound just the same as he had a moment ago. "Can you also put what's left of that bottle of wine into a bowl of snow? While you're bringing snow inside anyway?"

Corin rolled his eyes, but his grin didn't fade. "Your wish is my command, my lord." He swooped down to press a swift kiss to Aster's lips, and then rose up, shuffling back on the bed as he carefully withdrew from Aster's body.

Ugh, *ugh*, but after a moment the slick, heavy slide out of him ended, Corin tactfully saying nothing about the sound it made, and then he'd tossed the covers over Aster and turned his back, rummaging for clothing, it looked like.

He waited, perfectly still and heart hammering away, until Corin had tugged on a pair of trousers and loped out of the room and down the stairs, shirtless and whistling.

He continued to wait until the surprisingly off-key whistling had faded—and at least now he knew of one thing the mighty Sir Corin did shockingly badly, which shouldn't have been so painfully endearing—and he'd heard the distant creak and thump of the courtyard door.

Then, and only then, he put his hands over his eyes, rolled onto his side, and groaned into the pillow.

The worst part was, he didn't think his feelings for Corin had changed much, if at all, from what they had already been when he ran away from home. Or from what they'd been when he used to end up even more black and blue after a day of training than his skill level would've gotten him, since he kept looking for Corin instead of keeping his eyes on his opponent. Or even from what they'd been when Corin used to squire Belinda to balls and parties in the capital. Aster had followed them about, standing on the edges of the groups in which they laughed and conversed, hoping for a moment of Corin's notice and pretending to be simply accompanying his sister—who probably hadn't even known he was there.

Now he knew how it felt to have more than a moment of Corin's notice. He'd had all of him.

All of him except for the only thing he really wanted, of course.

He wouldn't put a name to it. Corin had fucked him, and he wanted to do it again. Aster could be happy with that for as long as it lasted.

And if he waited a few extra minutes to go downstairs until he was sure his eyes were dry and he could keep his voice from cracking, no one would ever know.

# Chapter Fourteen

WATCHING ASTER TAKE A bath by his own fireside gave Corin a set of disturbing sensations that he couldn't attribute to simple lust.

Yes, those pale shoulders with their curves and shadows of muscle made him want to lick them. And yes, the way Aster tipped his head back against the side of the tub, showing off the long line of his throat and then below that his nipples, still peaked and pink, made him want to...well, lick all of him.

Corin had never claimed to be a complicated or a subtle man.

But Aster's little sighs as he settled into the water, the way his hand hung over the side, his faint smile as he tipped his head back...every sign of comfort and satisfaction, of ease and contentment, soothed something in Corin's soul he hadn't even known he possessed. Corin had made Aster happy, and that made Corin happy, and that was...fuck.

He'd have sworn up and down that he didn't give a good goddamn if any Cezanne ever felt happy again.

And yet.

When he helped Aster out of the bath and into what passed for a towel in his mountain hideaway, and God, but he'd never even thought about the quality of his towels before, he had to viciously stuff down the urge to toss him over his shoulder and start all over again with making him filthy.

Not that Aster needed help getting out of the bath. But he'd blushed and smiled when Corin took his hand, and that was reason enough.

Now Corin had him all tucked in upstairs between the clean sheets that he'd put on the bed while Aster dried off by the fire, and he'd resisted a sleepy plea to join him and instead come back down to polish off what Aster had left of the wine.

If he got in that bed he'd also get in Aster. And judging by the way he'd winced when he bent over to adjust a pillow, that really needed to wait a day or two.

But all of that was simple. Easy to deal with.

The way he rather wanted to climb into bed behind Aster and hold him and keep him warm and safe all night, now that he'd fed him supper and chilled his wine and heated his bath and made his bed, was a lot less simple.

Fuck it. He'd spent two years brooding, and he refused to spend another night on such a useless occupation, especially when his blood fizzed hot in his veins and his limbs practically vibrated with energy. Corin hadn't felt like this, like *himself*, in years.

Even with the day's activities, the evening was still youngish. Down in the village the inn's taproom would still be open for hours yet. Not that Corin needed to have another drink necessarily, but he did need to restock more supplies, and since he hadn't sent word down to the village in advance, he'd have to do something he'd only done two or three times before: appear in person wearing human skin and clothing instead of scales.

How annoying, but no time like the present.

It took all of a minute to strip and bundle his clothes, tip the bottle over his open mouth and get the last few drops, and bank the fire. And then he only had to step outside and allow the transformation to flow through him, reshaping everything so swiftly he almost couldn't track the individual changes.

Corin shook out his wings, lit up the night with a burst of flame simply because he could, and launched himself up toward a twinkling star peeking through the ragged clouds.

Even though he'd spent hours in the air that morning, he still indulged himself by circling north and then spiraling in toward the village rather than taking the direct route. Beneath him the earth gleamed with the scattered diamonds and rubies of snow catching the last of the sunset and the first of the pale moonlight. Tiny dots of flickering yellow and orange showed him where the village clustered along the bank of the river running down from the mountains, and only his dragon eyes allowed him to pick out the more regular shape of his fortress from the tumbled edges of the natural rocks around it.

At last he swooped down, wings spread to allow the updrafts to buffet him as they chose, and landed with a muffled thump on the far side of a grove of oaks at the edge of the village. The trees hid him well enough as he shifted and dressed, the work of a few moments. Since the inn's patrons tended to the informal, Corin didn't even bother tucking in his shirt or lacing it at the neck, striding through the snow toward the village square with his trousers bunched at the tops of his boots and not a care in the world.

He passed only one person on the way, a man standing in the doorway of a house across from the inn and taking the air. The fellow started, stared, and said, "Sir Corin! Is that you? You should probably—"

"Evening!" Corin called back over his shoulder, speeding up a bit so as to avoid whatever dull nonsense the man wanted to say to him.

The inn yard was deserted, and he pushed the door open and stamped his way into the taproom unimpeded, thank God. He'd speak to the innkeeper, who doubled as the manager of what passed for a general store here, lurk out of sight while they put his order together as quickly as money could induce them to, and then be on his way.

In the taproom, two fireplaces blazed away, thick tallow candles sat on the tables, and the bar boasted a large oil lamp. It took even Corin's dragon eyes a moment to adjust.

When they did, he found himself the target of a whole room full of other sets of eyes: the barman in the act of pulling a pint, several tables of village yokels, the innkeeper standing by the best table in the room that sat right in front of the larger fireplace...

And the two haughty gentlemen, both decked out in velvet, silk, and furs, who lounged at their ease on either side of that table with a tall bottle and a deck of cards between them.

The older of the two, the one with the absurdly brushy mustache and arched eyebrows that suggested perpetual surprise, lifted the quizzing glass hanging around his neck and peered at him through it. Corin had hated the pompous and self-important Sir Gustave Perron at court, and he found that somehow, after two years of not having to see his fucking face, he hated him even more.

The younger one Corin couldn't put a name to, though his face looked familiar. But anyone with a ruffed lace collar that high—while traveling through the back ass-end of nowhere, no less—had to be an insufferable prick. His curled lip and up-tilted chin as he stared at Corin didn't help the impression.

*You should probably...* Fucking double fuck. Tuck in his shirt, wear a coat, turn around and leave as quickly as possible—or maybe apologize to the fellow across the street as soon as he had the opportunity.

"Sir Corin!" Sir Gustave blinked and cleared his throat. "In the flesh, I do declare."

"*This* is what the legendary Sir Corin is reduced to?" the other put in, his drawling tone a perfect match for his appearance. "My word."

"Shut it," Sir Gustave hissed in an undertone as he went as pale as the snow outside and shoved to his feet in a flustered rustle.

Corin smiled sourly. Sir Gustave might be an ass, overly conscious of his position as one of King Theobert's household gentlemen, but stupid he was not. The younger idiot had already given Corin enough reason to take him outside and beat him to a pulp, if he even chose to let him live.

"Sir Corin, what a pleasure to see you," Sir Gustave went on much more loudly, as if declaiming to a crowded throne room. Men like that needed an audience, and it didn't matter who they were, apparently. "We are here on King Theobert's business, long may he reign. We bear a royal proclamation intended for your eyes!"

Here he paused, emphasizing the drama of his announcement, Corin supposed. What a windbag. And fucking bloody hell. There went Corin's last gasp of hope that these court popinjays would be here for reasons entirely unrelated and irrelevant to him.

"Bully for you," Corin growled. "I suppose there's no way to prevent you from telling me what's in it. Because if it's anything to do with summoning me back to court, I won't go."

As Sir Gustave almost certainly knew perfectly well, he had every right to refuse such a summons, too. He'd always served at his own pleasure rather than the king's. He'd taken an oath, yes, but out of a desire to be honorable rather than out of necessity, and he'd been released from it officially when he left court. Dragons owed no fealty to human monarchs, only the courtesy of not eating anyone under their protection. And even that could be negotiable.

Hmm. Corin eyed Sir Gustave's companion with new interest. He'd never actually roasted and devoured a human as the dragons of old had done, and honestly the thought of it turned his stomach. But one could always roast without devouring. No rule against it.

If he wanted to eat a human, he'd start with Aster, and not in the for-dinner kind of way.

His cock stirred.

Fuck, not the time.

And then it hit him. Only one thing had changed recently. Aster had been followed or tracked somehow, must have been. Almost certainly with magic, since he'd only been here a day; Lord Cezanne must have moved very quickly during the weeks it'd taken Aster to travel here, getting the king involved, organizing whatever this was, sending Sir Gustave after at once—either chartering a ship and sending him by the much shorter sea route, or hiring frequent and expensive changes of horses. And now…no need to speculate, since the man with the answers stood before him.

"Just tell me and get it over with," he said into the awkward silence his last remark had left. "I'm sure there's a private room we can—"

"No need," Sir Gustave's companion interrupted him. "We are here to ensure that the king's decree reaches you and your guest specifically, Sir Corin, but a copy will be posted for everyone to read on the notice board of the temple, also. Well. If one can call it a temple. It's more of a shack, I suppose. And assuming someone's available to read it aloud to the populace." He tittered, a hand covering his mouth.

The innkeeper, who'd been standing by their table watching the show, muttered something under his breath and turned away, his posture suggesting his guests would be getting his worst wine for the rest of the night.

Corin didn't blame him in the slightest.

"Sir Gustave," he said, "control your companion, or I'll be forced to do it for you." The young courtier started to speak, but apparently he wasn't completely stupid, either, because a glare from Corin's narrowed eyes was enough to deflate him. "Read the fucking thing, then. Let's have it."

"The fu—the royal proclamation, you mean?" Sir Gustave demanded.

"Yes. That." Corin crossed his arms and glowered, a move he'd found to be effective in the past. If he'd been wearing a sword he'd have fingered the hilt instead. Worry raced along his nerves. "Now, if you please."

Sir Gustave sniffed and held out his hand, and the other fellow reached into a satchel on the floor and pulled out an envelope.

Corin counted to ten, very slowly, during all the throat-clearing and seal-breaking and so on and so forth, but finally Sir Gustave began to read aloud.

The first part had the same nonsense as any royal decree: to all subjects and guests in the kingdom, a list of all the king's titles and honors, and on and on. Even the locals seated in the taproom, who probably hadn't had anything this interesting happen since Corin took up residence in the first place, started to fidget.

But at last Sir Gustave reached the meat of the proclamation:

"The guardianship of Lord Aster of Cezanne having been duly reverted to the crown in the person of His Majesty King Theobert the Fourth on the petition of Lord Cezanne of Cezanne, subsequent to his abandonment of his betrothal to His Grace the Duke Marellus, His Majesty King Theobert the Fourth hereby decrees that any unmarried man of noble arms and in the crown's good grace who causes Lord Aster to yield, and then brings him before His Majesty King Theobert the Fourth, shall receive, along with Lord Aster's hand in marriage, a sum of gold as a marriage portion equal to the value of the aforementioned perquisite as a token of His Majesty King Theobert the Fourth's favor."

Someone off to the side hooted with laughter and called out, "Is this procla-what-thing from His Majesty King Theobert the Fourth, then? Weren't clear on that!" And the room erupted in chuckles and agreement.

Sir Gustave bit his lip, face going alarmingly red. "It's the way these are written, and I wasn't even done read—don't make me arrest you all for treason!"

A fresh chorus of laughter and the thumping of ale mugs was his only reply.

If the proclamation had been on any other subject imaginable, Corin would've laughed right along with them. The kingdom's laws set a high bar for treason charges, and a bit of heckling in a tavern came nowhere near, as everyone present knew perfectly well.

But he had no inclination whatsoever to mirth. Lord Cezanne, Duke Marellus, and the king had somehow and for reasons yet to be determined conspired to give Aster away to anyone who wanted him, dependent on a trial by arms that Aster would be almost certain to lose to the very first comer. The kind of man who'd hear this proclamation, and see it as a way to become wealthy overnight…Aster himself, with his sweet smiles and bright eyes, his self-deprecating humor and his awkward, eager, irresistible inexperience in bed would be nothing to such a man. It chilled Corin's blood and raised his temper to the boiling point all at the same time.

"*If* I may continue?" Sir Gustave shouted, making no dent whatsoever in the din.

"You may not," Corin said. Everyone went silent. It took him a moment to understand why, and then he saw the faint haze in the air in front of his face: he'd puffed out a chest-full of smoke, and possibly a bit of flame, too. Fuck, his draconic nature had always been strong, but it'd been enhanced almost to a worrisome degree of late. "We've heard the important part. And now that everyone knows the gist, you and I are going to talk. Privately."

The other man rose, clearing his throat. "I will of course—"

"You will not," Corin said, his voice dipping to a quelling sort of growl, fists clenching. He didn't need a fucking sword. His claws would be far more than adequate.

The fucker sat back down again with a slight thump. Sir Gustave shook his head, opened his mouth, closed it, and then finally said, in a tone suffused with impotent irritation, "If you'll accompany me, then."

Corin nodded, glanced at the innkeeper, said, "Have some food and supplies packed up for me, will you? Twice as much as usual. I'll be leaving soon," and followed Sir Gustave out of the taproom.

# Chapter Fifteen

WHEN HE TUCKED ASTER into bed, Corin had strongly implied that he'd come up and join him soon—or at least eventually.

But Aster woke to an empty, silent bedroom, far less cold than he would've expected without Corin's dragon heat, but chilly enough that he'd curled into a ball in his sleep with only his nose poking out.

A few blinks confirmed the reason for the change in temperature: the part of the sky Aster could see was pure blue, and sunlight gilded the side of the southeast-facing window casement. He stretched luxuriously—and then immediately snapped back into his previous position, cursing himself, Corin, Corin's cock, and all of the decisions he'd made the day before.

Cautiously, he tried again to straighten out and stretch, more gently this time. Mmm. All right. When he experimentally clenched the muscles of his ass, that felt…God, he hadn't realized some of those muscles existed, and now they seemed to be eagerly awaiting having more to do.

He rolled to his back, cock half hard and a smile spreading across his face.

So Corin hadn't opted to spend the night with him. His smile faltered. But that didn't mean anything, necessarily. He'd said something about not wanting to keep Aster awake, so perhaps he'd simply been a gentleman. (Although gentlemanliness, after the way he'd so thoroughly and filthily wrecked Aster's body and mind yesterday, seemed a bit of a moot point.)

Anyway, it was a sunny day, he'd finally gotten a good night's sleep in a real bed after a lovely hot bath, not to mention being thoroughly and filthily wrecked by the handsomest, wickedest man in the kingdom, and he had nothing to do but seduce Corin again and see if he could get a demonstration of that licking thing. Even thinking about it made Aster's face flame hot and his heart skip a beat, but that only meant it'd probably be *amazing*.

Despite the lingering soreness between his legs and the sweet aches in every single muscle—God, fucking like that left a body sore in such different and better ways than riding or fencing did—he dressed swiftly, not bothering with looking particularly proper. He'd spent the night in his not-quite-lover's bed after a day of being fucked into oblivion, and if he wanted to let a rumpled shirt billow loose over his trousers, then he damn well would.

He went rather gingerly down the stairs, stopped at the garde-robe, and made his way to the hall. He'd heard someone moving around while coming down the stairs, so he knew Corin was in there, and he walked through the doorway with a cheery, "Good morning! It's a beautiful day!"

And then he stopped a foot inside the hall, snapping his mouth shut on anything else he might have said. Because Corin sat slumped by the hearth, elbow on the arm of his chair and head propped in his hand, even more ferociously unshaven than he'd been the day before and wearing a wrinkled shirt and trousers with holes in them. He had dark circles beneath his eyes, which gleamed moodily at Aster from under a deeply furrowed brow.

Corin had opened the shutters over the high windows, at least, but the brilliant morning sunlight only made the hall—and its occupant—look all the dustier and gloomier for the contrast.

"What's wrong?" Aster stammered, that cold knot in his stomach forming again as if it'd never been melted away. "You look—did I—"

"No, fuck," Corin said, shoving up off his elbow to sit straight in his chair. He scrubbed his hands over his face and then met Aster's eyes with his own bleak gaze. "No, you didn't do a fucking thing except the thing we already knew you did, that being run away from a marriage to a prominent nobleman and embarrass his family and yours in the process."

Oh, God. Aster didn't want to know. He didn't. But he had to.

He swallowed to try to get a little moisture into his suddenly arid throat. "What happened?"

"This." Corin leaned forward and picked up a piece of heavy parchment from the bench in front of him. Aster hadn't even noticed it in his focus on Corin. "Read it."

"Where did you—"

"I flew down to the village last night. And I wasn't the only one there who didn't belong." Corin shook the paper at him impatiently. "Just read it, would you?"

Crossing the room to take it from Corin's hand felt like walking to the scaffold. When he took it he saw the broken wax bearing the mark of the king's chancellery.

How the hell had the king gotten involved? He'd approved the marriage, and Marellus might have appealed to him to command Aster to return…his head went so light he nearly staggered. Even if his parents hadn't wanted to wring his neck before this, being publicly humiliated by the king's involvement in this affair would drive them to new heights of rage.

He skimmed through the opening nonsense and reached the part of it that mattered. And then he wondered if, rather than getting in hot water with the king, he might instead simply be going mad. *His Majesty King Theobert the Fourth…any unmarried man of noble arms…Lord Aster's hand in marriage…*

"What is—the hell is this?" he demanded, looking up from the decree. "What the hell is the king thinking? What the fuck does 'the value of the aforementioned perquisite' mean?"

"I'm assuming it means that they're calculating your marriage portion from what you're considered to be wor—"

"I fucking know what 'perquisite' and 'value' in gold mean, Corin! For fuck's sake," he snapped, and Corin shut up, raising his eyebrows. "I'm a little upset about having been classified as being one and having the other! It was a rhetorical fucking question!"

Corin grimaced and leaned back in his chair again, shoving his hands in his pockets and frowning. Despite his anger, Aster wanted nothing more than to crawl into his lap. His chest vibrated horribly with the force of his racing heart and his lungs labored and it was making him all shaky. Corin would soothe that away if Aster could only have his arms around him.

"If it makes you feel any better, Sir Gustave didn't give me a precise amount, because I got the impression that would be determined more on the basis of who was asking, but it did sound like you were calculated to be worth quite a lot."

"No, it does not make me feel better, Corin! Because that makes me a whore—or no, no, it doesn't, a whore gets paid, but they're paying whoever marries me to take me! I'm so bloody undesirable that they have to pay someone to marry me."

"At least that makes the other fellow the whore—"

"You aren't helping," Aster gritted out.

Silence. Thank God, because Aster needed to think this through, which he couldn't do while Corin kept making it worse with every word out of his mouth. He'd gotten hung up on being called a perquisite and hadn't quite...

"Wait just a bloody second. They know I'm here with you?" Corin nodded. "Yes, obviously, I'm sorry, I'm an idiot. They must have traced me with magic, I'd think. Dammit." Another nod. "And they've sent this proclamation all over the kingdom?" This time, he only got a sigh in answer. "Which means that any minute now, every fortune-hunting asshole with a sword and shield to his name will be showing up on the doorstep challenging me to a duel, which when I fight and lose, will mean he gets to drag me back to court and get paid by the king to marry me."

Corin looked grimmer than ever. "I'd say that sums up what's in the proclamation fairly well, yes."

Aster couldn't read much from his tone. Gravelly and deep, as always, maybe even a little more than usual. But a sleepless night spent flying all over the place and arguing with the likes of Sir Gustave, whom Aster knew to be a first-class pompous prick, would leave one a bit hoarse and grouchy.

He wished it were more than that: concern, anger on his behalf. But Corin really wasn't making it easy to tell.

"So what do we do?" he faltered. "I mean—when they start arriving." Corin stayed silent, and a dreadful thought occurred to him. He'd spoken without thinking. They might not be a "we" at all. "That is, if you're going to let me stay."

He had a sudden vision of Corin ushering him out the gate, all grim and silent the way he was now, and then slamming it behind him. Aster would ride down to the fork in the road and then face a choice: go back the way he'd come, almost certainly meeting some adventurer along the way who'd disarm and humiliate him and then take him home to—God, he shied away from that, unable to stomach the thought of being presented that way to the king, with snickering crowds of courtiers watching from behind their fans, his father's face red with rage and his mother's pale with a horrible mix of anger and grief. Having his value in gold announced to the world, a figure that would be bandied about and turned into every possible kind of prurient joke. And then he'd be forced to marry the bastard. And...everything that came with marriage.

He'd never see Corin again.

Aster's vision blurred. He tried to blink it away. That only made it worse, and now he had droplets clinging to his eyelashes, and even a human would be able to see he was crying, let alone a dragon with his keen vision.

"I also had a talk with Sir Gustave, and there's more—oh, the fuck," Corin spat in a tone of such disgust Aster stumbled back a step.

Corin surged to his feet, face like a thundercloud, strode across the hall, and—brushed right by him, stomping his way into the anteroom by the stairs.

What? What the hell had he been about to say? *More?*

Aster turned and trotted after him. At least Corin's anger didn't seem to be for him or his tears after all, but—and then he heard it too, his human ears catching up to Corin's senses: the clop of hooves. More than one set of hooves, in fact. He peeked his head around the corner of the anteroom by the stairs in time to see Corin opening a chest that stood by the wall in a shadowy corner where Aster hadn't even noticed it. He flipped up the lid and pulled out the longest and broadest sword Aster had ever seen. How had it even fit in that chest? It wouldn't have. And yet there it was, gleaming with a deep, bluish sheen totally unlike normal steel as Corin rotated his arm to inspect the blade on one side and then the other.

Aster gaped at it, his fingers itching with the desire to touch, everything else forgotten in his awe.

This had to be Corin's famous sword, the one they said no human could wield. Aster had only glimpsed the hilt of it before when Corin wore it while attending the king on more ceremonial occasions; he used other swords when training, and yet a different sword for dueling, as when he'd scarred Belinda's lover. This one he only drew, as far as Aster knew, when he meant to fight for real.

Corin nodded and grunted, apparently satisfied by the condition of his blade, and stomped past again, this time down the little corridor that led to the gate room.

Aster stared slack-jawed. God, he'd forgotten how Corin looked holding a sword. Not that he slouched at other times, or anything, but when he had a sword in his hand he changed subtly, his body held differently—somehow more loosely and with more tension at the same time.

Like this, Corin exuded danger in a way that practically made the air around him crackle and spark, even barefoot and with his shirt hanging untucked. He was so intimidating and so magnificent that he'd opened the gate a couple of feet—and watching him lift that heavy bar with one hand while he effortlessly held his massive sword in the other gave Aster a quiver in his belly—and stepped out onto the bridge before Aster realized he ought to have fetched his own sword.

Because wasn't he meant to be the one fighting? If he hadn't been a swordsman, then he'd have needed a champion, of course. But he was perfectly capable of fighting for himself, albeit poorly. He wouldn't even be in any danger; no one challenging him under the king's decree would be trying to hurt him. Quite the contrary. The victor couldn't claim his reward without Aster in good condition.

And yet Corin had gone out to meet whoever it was without even consulting him.

It stung more than Aster had expected to realize how little Corin truly thought of his prowess.

On the other hand, too late now. He'd spotted an arrow slit set up high on the wall just above and to the left of the gate, but he didn't see—there, an old ladder stuck in another dark corner. The ladder seemed sturdy enough when he bounced on the lower rung a couple of times, and he'd set it in place and scrambled up within a couple of seconds.

He peered out the loophole in time to see three riders rein up before the bridge. Corin stood in the center of it poised and waiting, his massive sword held out at a casual angle that would've had anyone else's arm visibly shaking.

Aster looked more closely at the three. Two of them were obviously squires or attendants, but he was surprised to realize he recognized the one in the middle: Lord Fredmund, a particularly obnoxious fop who nevertheless had a reputation as a respectably skilled duelist. He'd have outmatched Aster for certain, and clearly he knew it; he hadn't even bothered turning up in plate mail or with a lance, instead wearing only a chainmail jerkin, it looked like, with one of his servants carrying his shield. Instead of a helmet he had a jaunty yellow velvet hat with a plume long enough to nearly tickle his horse's ears.

But unfortunately for Fredmund and his lack of proper armor, it wasn't Aster on the bridge. And no matter how embarrassing it might be to have another man fight his battles for him...so far from throwing Aster out on his ass, Corin hadn't hesitated to assume the role of Aster's protector. This time, anyway.

Embarrassing, yes. But it proved he meant at least *something* to Corin, didn't it?

And at least he wouldn't need to marry the odious Fredmund, though who knew what would happen the next time someone came to the gate.

"You again," Corin said, in a tone that strongly suggested the surprise didn't delight him. Fredmund must've been with Sir Gustave last night in the village, then. Had that been what Corin needed to tell him, that Fredmund meant to come and challenge him? "The fuck are you doing here?"

No, because Corin seemed as surprised as Aster.

Fredmund made an exaggerated moue of horror, wrinkling his nose and staring down it at the same time. Aster stifled a laugh despite everything. There were established forms for this sort of thing. "The fuck are you doing here" was not one of them.

A short and fraught silence fell.

"Sir Corin of Saumur, I greet you," Fredmund said tensely, clearly trying to get back on script. "I am Lord Fredmund of Rivanne, and in the king's name—"

"Cut the crap," Corin said briskly, and Fredmund let out a little yelp of anger.

Aster leaned against the wall, closed his eyes, and gently thumped his forehead. God. He hadn't thought Corin could be any more wonderful, and yet...the feeling he didn't want to name welled up warm and desperate, irrepressible. He'd never wanted to suck someone's cock the way he did right then.

"I know why you're here," Corin went on. Aster looked out again, unwilling to miss even a moment of this. "You think you can keep yourself in stupid squishy hats by challenging Lord Aster and claiming the king's reward. But if you want to fight, you'll be fighting me. So either draw your sword or bugger off and stop wasting my fucking time."

"You—you—" Fredmund sputtered, and then stopped, closed his eyes for a second, and visibly pulled himself together. He smiled slyly. "Lord Aster can surely fight his own battles," he said, his voice pitched to carry farther than just to Corin's ears. Damn him, he'd figured out that Aster would be nearby and listening. Aster leaned back a little to make sure he couldn't be seen. "If he's not a coward, he'll come out and face me himself, rather than hiding behind you."

Aster's heart sank down to his toes. Fuck. Fredmund hadn't really left him a choice by phrasing it that way. Damn it, damn it... He opened his mouth, ready to call out through the loophole that he accepted the challenge, not at all ready to accept that he'd be going, that Corin would have to let him go, that he'd only had one night— but Corin spoke first.

"I'm afraid that won't be possible. He'd be more than willing to fight you, but he's my captive."

*Your what?* Aster mouthed, managing not to say it aloud. Shock and relief had him clutching the sides of the ladder for dear life as the world spun around him.

"Your what?" Fredmund asked blankly, blinking.

"He offered himself to me as tribute in exchange for my hospitality, which makes him my captive," Corin said, and shrugged. Aster sagged down a little more, blowing out a long breath. He wouldn't have to go. Not right now, anyway. He wouldn't have to go. "I'm a dragon, after all, and this is my dread lair, and so on. Whatever, he's staying until someone defeats me. So again, are we going to fight, or are you going to bugger off?"

Oh, fuck. Aster had to lean his head against the wall again to support himself and keep from falling off the ladder as he shook with silent laughter. Corin's indifferent, sardonic tone made the whole affair ridiculous, and made Lord Fredmund ridiculous too—but no one could argue with a dragon conducting his draconic affairs in his own way on his own land, no matter how offensive that dragon might be. Not only was that part of the well-established agreements between dragons and human authorities, but you had to be a fucking idiot to try.

"I never," Fredmund gasped. "You—sir, I think you mock me!"

"Not yet, but I'm willing. If you want to fight after all, I'd be happy to offer my honest opinions on your swordplay until I get bored and skewer you. That ought to take at least a minute, possibly two."

Aster managed to get himself under control and peeked out again. Corin lifted his sword, waggling the tip suggestively, and Aster had to clap a hand over his mouth to suppress another giggle.

Fredmund had turned an alarming shade of red, and the hand holding his reins had clenched into a tight fist. His horse tossed his head and snorted, clearly sensing his master's mood.

"You know," Fredmund said loudly, "Lord Aster's neither pretty nor amusing. I don't understand how the Cezannes produced him, frankly, nor how you're tolerating him. You know damn well I'd be doing them a favor by taking him on, though he obviously doesn't have any family feeling. And perhaps you're enjoying their discomfiture?" Aster winced. He hadn't really thought of it that way, but Corin might indeed be getting some pleasure out of seeing the

Cezannes humiliated. Fredmund added, "He's not worth my time and trouble, though I may return and defeat you if I change my mind, of course."

For a moment silence fell, broken only by the faint, distant cry of a raptor far up above the mountainside. Aster wished it'd swoop down and carry off Fredmund's ugly hat, the son of a bitch.

And then Corin chuckled, low and mellow. Fredmund went from red to purple. "I can reasonably expect to live another three hundred years, possibly four," Corin said. "Even so, I doubt I'll live to see that day, Lord Fredmund. Enjoy your ride down the mountain."

He lowered his sword, turned his back on the gasping, seething Fredmund in a pointed display of unconcern, and strolled back through the gate, shutting it firmly behind him.

# Chapter Sixteen

ASTER STARED AS CORIN lifted the bar and set it back into its cradle. He kept staring as Corin strode back down the corridor and around the corner, disappearing from Aster's sight. He couldn't seem to move, frozen there at the top of the ladder—with his cock rock hard.

Well. That motivated him to climb down, anyway, though it made the process a bit awkward. He put his feet on the floor right as Corin returned to the gate room, expression so tightly controlled Aster didn't have any idea what he was thinking.

He had a thousand questions he wanted to ask, many of which he also needed the answers to in order to plan his next move, and possibly to plan the rest of his life.

But only one sprang urgently to his tongue.

"Have you washed up since yesterday?" Aster demanded.

Corin stared, blinked, and said, "Washed up?"

Good God, people could be so frustrating. "Washed. Soap and water. Bathed." A horrible thought struck him. "Dragons do bathe, don't you? I mean, it doesn't douse your flames, or—"

"No, of course we bloody well bathe, what the fuck are you on about? We have to talk, and I need you to take this seriously!"

Corin's rumbling growl and the way he crossed his arms and glared had always had this effect on him, he realized. Only he'd never connected the pounding of his heart and his knees going wobbly with a desperate desire for Corin's cock.

"Did you bathe last night, though? Or this morning?" Aster asked again, doggedly insistent. It didn't matter how annoyed Corin became, or how serious he wanted to be, Aster would get his answer.

Corin rolled his eyes. "Yes, when I came back from the village. Why the hell do you—oh, fuck, that's why, fuck," he said, as Aster dropped to his knees right then and there, his hands already reaching up to push Corin's shirt out of the way and busy themselves with his buttons. "Aster, this isn't the time, and you don't have to."

That last sounded incredibly, overwhelmingly unconvincing, and it was Aster's turn to roll his eyes, even though he was practically panting with the need to have Corin fucking his throat *now*.

"I thought I was your captive," he said, struggling with the last button. "Your tribute. That I'd offered myself to you, and by the way, you made that sound absurdly suggestive, when Fredmund gets back and tells the story of what happened my reputation won't be worth the paper that decree's written on."

"That's the problem, we need to—oh fuck," Corin said, in tandem with Aster's, "Oh, yes, please," as the trouser button yielded at last and Corin wrapped a big hand around the back of Aster's head and pushed his face against Corin's shaft. "Mmm."

Corin groaned as Aster rubbed his cheek against his cock like a particularly slutty cat, started cursing as he nuzzled down and licked at the base, and then curled over Aster's head and let out a gut-punched gasp as he mouthed all the way to the top and wrapped his lips around the head.

God, that was satisfying, the way Corin's hand clenched in his hair, the growls he made as Aster flicked those two ridges with the tip of his tongue over and over again, the tension he could feel in that big body.

He squirmed, unable to get enough friction from his pants on his aching cock, knowing he'd probably come anyway whenever Corin got around to using him properly.

"Don't come," Corin said, and he had to have been lying when he claimed dragons didn't read minds. Of course, a command from Corin, any command, had Aster's bollocks tight and aching in half a second, especially when Corin chose that moment to thrust halfway into his throat. Sparks danced in his vision as he struggled for a breath, but he wanted it, he wanted that thick pressure, his lips stretched, his tongue held down. "If you wait, I'll suck you off when you're done," Corin added, voice rough.

Well, fuck, that wasn't helping…he let out a garbled, choking moan around his mouthful, and Corin thrust again, and again, and it didn't take long at all before he came down his throat in hard, thick, dragon-hot pulses.

Corin had spend almost like any other man's, salty and bitter and slick, but laced with spice and what Aster imagined magic might taste like. It acted on him like magic, anyway, sending a thrill along his arms to his tingling fingers, warming him from the inside out. No other man had ever made him feel like this. It had to be magic, didn't it?

He moaned again, licking his lips to chase that extraordinary flavor as Corin pulled out. He opened his eyes, blinking up at Corin looming over him.

Somehow he'd managed to obey, and his cock still throbbed heavy and desperate against the front of his trousers.

"Please," he gasped, gazing up at Corin's flushed face and glittering eyes. "I did what you told me?" Despite everything else they'd done, Corin hadn't even really touched Aster's cock yet with his hands, much less with his mouth, and Aster needed it, needed it like air. Not that he blamed him. Aster had come untouched as often as not, overstimulated by having him at all. And if he had to choose whether Corin would fuck him up the ass or touch his cock, he'd choose getting fucked. But… "Please?"

Corin caught him under the arms and hauled him up directly into a ferocious, breath-stealing kiss, licking into Aster's mouth like he was savoring the taste of his own spend there.

Aster's head was already whirling when Corin pulled back, bent suddenly, and hoisted Aster over his shoulder, head hanging down. "What are you—Corin!" Aster protested, arms waving, unable to see or do anything—and then he was bouncing against Corin's back, everything moving as well as upside down.

He managed to get a grip on Corin's waist and pinch him. An instant later, Corin's hand cracked against his ass, and he screamed and flailed and subsided, half laughing and half crying, as Corin got him the rest of the way up the stairs, every jounce tossing his head this way and that.

Then the world spun sickeningly again as Corin tossed him

down onto the bed.

Everything resettled after a moment. The bed was solid beneath him. Despite the rough handling—or, if he were being totally honest, probably because of it—his cock still strove mightily to tear its way through his pants. And above him Corin leaned down, propped on his fists to either side of Aster's shoulders.

The silence stretched.

Corin didn't touch him.

Was Aster supposed to ask?

"You're not actually my captive," Corin said abruptly at last. "I needed to fob him off. He couldn't be the one to—but you don't have to—Aster, you're not obligated to do anything. With me. I know it's easy to say that now after I already let you suck my brains out through my cock."

Oh, God give him patience with Corin and his scruples, especially since they were sometimes a little too late, and doubly especially because he apparently had to argue about this now instead of getting Corin's hands or mouth on his prick. His erection hadn't subsided, but it was losing hope.

"You said it before I sucked your brains out through your cock, too," Aster pointed out. "Not that you sounded particularly sincere—Corin, I'm joking, don't look like that. I know I'm not your captive or your tribute." *Not that I'd mind in the slightest.* "I was grateful to you for getting rid of him. I can't tell you how grateful. But that's not why I sucked you!" he added desperately, as Corin recoiled, a horrified look on his face. "You were so, I mean, how could I not after you told him 'this is my dread lair, and so on,' I mean, really? I had to practically gnaw my own hand off so that he didn't hear me laughing."

Corin's frown faded into something almost like a smile, his eyes lighting up. God, Aster could look at him forever.

"You liked that?"

"Of course I liked it. I lo—liked seeing that asshole Fredmund taken down a peg. More than a peg. Every possible peg. I'd take my chances with Marellus and Dericort every night before I married him." Damn it, he'd wanted more time, and an orgasm, before he had to have a serious conversation about this. But he had to say it, because Corin deserved to hear it. "Thank you. You didn't have to protect me. You certainly didn't have to tell him I'd be staying here. You know it means he won't be the last to turn up on your doorstep." Aster took a deep, shaky breath to try to brace himself. "In fact, I should probably go. Across the mountains, now that the snow's melting. Leave the kingdom entirely."

Corin's smile vanished like snow on a mountain pass under the summer sun. "I haven't had a chance to tell you everything. Fuck, Aster. You won't want to."

The faint frisson of worry that'd started before Fredmund arrived bloomed into a full-blown ache in the pit of his stomach, strong enough to almost compete with the clench of his arousal.

Oh, God, it had to be bad. And if he allowed Corin to tell him now, whatever it was, he might never get Corin's mouth on him. *You won't want to.*

Dread spiked into terror. "My family's all—they're all alive, aren't they? You aren't hiding—"

"They're all alive and well as far as I know," Corin said without the faintest hesitation.

Oh, thank God, thank God, and Aster went a little faint from the force of his relief. "Then don't tell me now. Please? Wait a few minutes. Until I've—a few minutes."

Corin gazed down at him, frowning, and then finally sighed. "All right," he said. "If that's what you want. That's definitely what I'd prefer," he muttered, and lowered himself down until his weight almost pressed him into the bed.

Well. Aster didn't need to be held down, exactly, since he'd hardly been trying to run away right that second. But he didn't mind. At all, in fact. His hips pushed up, cock managing to just brush Corin's stomach, hinting that holding him down a bit more might be welcome.

He needed to stop worrying about whatever Corin had to tell him, probably more horrifying details about the way everyone in the entire kingdom would be laughing at him and his entire family. Focusing on his sexual frustration had to be more enjoyable than that, at least.

Although if Corin didn't *do something*, he'd be sexually frustrated for a long damned time.

He rolled his hips more purposefully. "You made me a promise a few minutes ago."

"I did," Corin said, voice and eyes both darkening. He pushed up again and reached a hand between them, stroking the backs of his knuckles over the straining ridge of Aster's erection, eliciting a gasp, making his legs twitch and his fists clench. The corner of Corin's mouth curled in a way Aster was starting to learn meant mischief. "If you really want me to pin you down and suck your pretty cock until you're sobbing, that is. I wouldn't want to force anything on a helpless captive."

Aster's chest fluttered, a strange sensation he couldn't really define. Had Belinda felt this way when Corin teased and flirted with her? No. She couldn't have. If she'd felt like this she never would have let him go.

But that feeling buoyed him up and gave him a burst of confidence he'd never had before.

"Oh, no," he said in an exaggeratedly high-pitched voice. "Help! The dragon's sucking my cock!"

Corin stared wide-eyed. For a long, excruciating moment, Aster thought he was about to be more embarrassed than he'd ever been in his life. And then Corin's lips twitched, and his chest rumbled, and he burst out into a helpless guffaw of laughter, head dropping down and shoulders shaking.

"Fuck, Aster," he choked between paroxysms. "For fuck's— you should've screamed that out the window," and then he was off again, howling.

Fredmund's face, if he had...

And then Aster lost it himself, cackling until his eyes watered, wrapping his arms around Corin's back and shaking with laughter along with him.

"Maybe he'd have tried to offer himself as tribute too," he gasped, and that was the end for both of them. Corin collapsed on top of him, finally lifting his head enough to press his lips to Aster's on and off, and then they were rolling to the side with Corin's arms around him, kissing and laughing and tangled together, Aster with his eyes only half-open and the world outside of the bed, including anything happening at court, blurred and inconsequential, and his body and heart both singing with joy.

He couldn't have defined the moment when they went from half-embracing and half-laughing to moving with more and different intent. But Corin's hand had found its way under the waist of his trousers and drawers, cupping his ass, fingers teasing between the cheeks. And Corin's breath came faster now, heating Aster's neck where he'd nuzzled in, kissing and nipping below his ear. One of his muscular thighs pressed up between Aster's legs.

"I thought—mmm, oh—I thought you were going to suck me, not fuck me, fuck, Corin—"

"They're not mutually exclusive," Corin murmured against his collarbone. "Which one do you want me to force on you first?"

"How will I ever survive such brutality?" Aster squeaked as Corin pinched his ass, and added, "You monster!"

Too late, the words already flown, he remembered the way his sister had screamed that word at Corin after he'd fought her lover. His heart stuttered, a jolt of horror going down his spine.

Corin went still.

But only for an instant. His lips moved first, pressing a kiss to the little hollow at the base of Aster's throat. And then his hands moved, one squeezing his ass and the other wrapped around his knee, pushing his legs open.

"It's all right," Corin whispered, and squeezed again, harder. "I know what you meant."

Fuck, he'd been such an ass, and Corin had forgiven him just like that. How had Belinda not held on to him with every scrap of strength she had? Corin had loved her so very much. Adored her. The way he'd gazed at her, with longing and desire shining in his eyes...Aster would give anything to have Corin look at him that way. Even for an instant. He'd die happy.

And he'd had Corin laughing with him and enjoying him for more than simple release, and of course Aster had said the wrong thing. Yes, he was still kissing his way across Aster's chest and inching closer to putting a finger inside him, but that wasn't the same.

He had to fix this.

"I meant that you've imprisoned me here in your dread lair, and so on, haven't you? Which makes you so very…" Damn it, damn it, he couldn't use another close synonym. Obviously not monstrous, but not beastly, either. Or even brutish or inhuman. Although Aster didn't see what was so wrong with any of those—Corin could monstrously brutalize him as much as he wanted, honestly. "So very rude," he finally said.

Corin's head popped up and his hands stopped moving. "Are you fucking—rude? I'm being *rude*?"

There, Aster almost had him. He squirmed underneath him and grinned. "So incredibly rude to kidnap someone and put your hand down the back of his trousers, Corin. Downright improper."

"I didn't kidnap you, you little—you showed up uninvited!"

"Ha! You're stuck with me now!" Aster hadn't thought those words through in the slightest, and they hung in the air, echoing. He could feel his smile fading as it sank in how they'd sounded.

Why, *why* couldn't he go more than three seconds without ruining everything with his stupid mouth?

But Corin simply gazed down at him, looking a little sad, if anything, rather than angry.

"For now," he said, and bent his head again, kissing along Aster's jaw to that tender spot on his throat behind the hinge of it that he seemed to enjoy rubbing his face against so much.

Not that Aster didn't enjoy it too. Relieved beyond measure that Corin hadn't stopped, he tipped his head back, moaning as Corin pushed his shirt up and traced his fingertip around one nipple and then the other, back and forth in a figure eight that had Aster arching up into the touch.

Corin was stuck with him, at least for now.

He didn't trust his voice after that; no more teasing or joking around, because he'd have managed to say something even more revealing or tactless than he already had.

And so he simply encouraged Corin with little moans and

cries—not that he could've kept them inside—and yielded to whatever he wanted to do to him. His clothes came off, he almost didn't know how, lost in a haze of Corin's touches and kisses and his heavy weight moving over him.

At last he lay completely bare, panting up at the shadowy ceiling as Corin rubbed his bristled face against his stomach. It tickled, and his hands flailed as he shivered, landing in Corin's hair. Corin's loose shirt hung down and brushed over his cockhead in an unbearably light tease. He could barely even moan, he was so overstimulated and desperate.

"Almost there," Corin said, and bit him just below his navel.

Aster lifted his head and peered down at Corin's dark one bent over him, at his hands wrapped in those black waves. He tried pushing, but Corin didn't budge, only laughed against his skin and nipped at a hipbone.

"Almost there," he said again, licking his way along the crease of Aster's thigh and groin. "Patience is a virtue."

And then he paused, took a deep breath, and pressed his lips to the tip of Aster's cock.

# Chapter Seventeen

THE CONVERSATION LOOMING OVER them could wait if it meant he could have this. Fuck, he wished it'd wait forever. Having Aster moaning under him, incoherent and practically sobbing with desire while Corin slowly kissed down his sweet body, had to be one of the most wonderful experiences of his life.

Or it would've been if he'd had the slightest idea what the fuck to do once he reached his inevitable destination.

More than a few men and women had gotten on their knees for him in the twenty years or so since his first youthful fumbles with another person. And he'd pleasured a great many lovely cunts with his mouth—and even tongue-fucked a few very pretty asses.

He had never sucked a cock.

God, he wanted to. Aster's, anyway. The taste of his skin drove Corin mad, so warm and rosy and salty all at once. Imagining how his cock might feel in his mouth had him hard again even after coming down Aster's throat.

Aster, who'd twice now sucked him off so perfectly that nothing Corin could do would compare.

Corin did *not* like to be second best.

So he stalled and pretended to be making Aster wait, undressing him slowly and playing with those delicate little nipples of his, kissing and licking his throat, squeezing and kneading his ass and teasing his hole with a fingertip. By the sounds he made, throaty whines and moans and the occasional impossibly arousing whimper, he didn't mind Corin's attentions. And Corin certainly didn't mind taking his time with Aster's beautiful body. If he'd been more confident in his cocksucking skills, he'd have relished spinning it out as long as possible, teasing and tormenting Aster until he cracked.

Finally he simply had no excuse to avoid keeping the promise he'd so rashly made when he told Aster not to come.

He lifted his head from the delicious, tender bit of skin just below Aster's hipbone, sucked in a deep breath, and lowered down again, this time touching his mouth to the flushed cockhead that'd been trying to hit him in the chin.

Fuck, that felt so soft, the skin as smooth and delicate as that of a woman's labia, only more tightly stretched and glossier, somehow. He knew how a cock felt in his hand, of course—his own and others. But it was so different against his lips.

Aster groaned, a low, desperate sound, his hands clenching almost painfully in Corin's hair.

Corin started guiltily. He'd been so caught up in the novelty of it that he'd almost forgotten this wasn't meant to be for him.

He glanced up under his eyelashes and found Aster's head raised, wide-eyed gaze fixed avidly on him. He looked almost wild, flushed and panting, chest rising and falling too quickly.

It gave Corin a new surge of confidence. At this point it hardly mattered what he did; Aster would enjoy it regardless.

But giving him pleasure wasn't the same as being the best Aster had ever had. Aster deserved it.

Keeping their gazes locked, he slowly parted his lips and flicked out his tongue, darting the tip of it into the slit of Aster's cock. Aster's head fell back for a moment as if his muscles had given out, and he let out a gratifyingly high-pitched cry.

All right. Corin could do this. He repeated the motion of his tongue, and then when Aster's cock bobbed annoyingly in a way reminiscent of that children's game with the apples on a string, he wrapped his fist around the base of it to keep it in place. That got him another satisfying moan and Aster's fingers tugging so hard on his hair that his scalp stung.

Fuck, yes.

What would Aster do if Corin swallowed him all the way down, with or without any particular skill in the act?

He didn't need to wonder. He could simply find out.

Corin filled his lungs, took a firmer grip, opened his mouth, and slid down. Aster's cock didn't have nearly the same proportions as his own; it wasn't actually small, but it looked that way by comparison.

So it took him off guard how much of his mouth it filled and how thick the head felt when it bumped the back of his throat. He almost choked, closing his eyes against the way they'd started watering almost instantly, shifting his tongue, closing his lips firmly around Aster's shaft to create as much suction as he could.

Aster thrust up, pushing his cock deeper. "I'm sorry, I'm so fucking sorry—Corin, are you all ri—ohh!" he wailed, thrusting again despite his apologies as Corin swallowed around the head of his cock.

And again, and again, because Aster writhed and cried out and pulled his hair and kicked, and that was fucking glorious. Corin didn't need to breathe as much as a human. He used it to his advantage, ignoring any discomfort in favor of making Aster believe he knew exactly what he was doing.

Aster's cock stiffened even more, the head feeling like it...twitched...and bloody hell, but that was so fucking strange buried in his throat. Could Aster feel Corin's cock doing that when he came inside him? A moment later Aster spent, hot and salty, and Corin choked, coughed, and pulled off, the last spurt hitting him in the chin.

"Oh, God," came a soft, broken whisper from above. "Fuck." And then silence.

Fuck indeed. He let go of Aster's flushed, shiny, slowly softening cock to rub his wrist across his chin and neck, cleaning off the come and panting for breath—even a dragon had his limits. Aster had subsided, completely still except for faint tremors of his too-fast heartbeat that Corin could feel in his legs to either side of his own and in his round handful of Aster's ass.

When he looked up, Aster had his eyes closed. Corin sat back and allowed himself a moment to quietly preen. He'd never sucked a cock, and yet here he was, kneeling over Aster's prone body, triumphant. Aster being easy to please could very well have been at least as responsible as Corin's abilities, but still. He deserved some of the credit.

If nothing else, he'd earned the right to enjoy the fruit of his labor: gazing his fill without interruption. Aster didn't have much hair on his body except for the golden thatches around his cock and balls and under his arms, and the curves and angles of his body flowed like a sculptor's marble masterpiece from his lovely prick to his parted lips. A strange hot sensation tightened Corin's belly and chest. He wished he could attribute it to pure arousal, but he knew bloody well how *that* felt—he'd been hard again within three minutes after he finished in Aster's mouth and stayed that way ever since.

This felt more proprietary than simple lust. More possessive. A seething desire to touch every inch of Aster's skin—and he'd made a damn good start already—and mark him as his own, so that no fucking presumptuous upstarts like that asshole Fredmund would ever think to try to claim him again.

Of course, merely touching him wouldn't leave a mark a human could detect. Only another dragon, with a keener sense of smell, might be able to sense Corin's ownership.

To keep Aster safe from the humans who'd be seeking to take him away, he'd need to depend on more visible and tangible techniques, like beating the living shit out of them if they were stupid enough not to run.

He could also always keep Aster naked and on his knees, possibly chained to Corin's bed.

Probably impractical.

And of course, also impossible. Right now Aster didn't look like someone who'd need to be restrained to keep him right where he was. He still hadn't moved, his chest finally rising and falling at a more normal speed and a slight smile tilting the corners of his lips. Keeping him in Corin's bed wouldn't have been much of a challenge under other circumstances. He could've simply killed all comers before they even crossed the bridge to the gate and told Aster to stay precisely where he was.

All of Corin's triumph and pleasure melted away as reality, pushed aside for the moment, intruded once again.

Sir Gustave had told Corin more than enough for him to know that Aster would have no choice but to leave. He loved his family even though half of them or more were total assholes, and Marellus had managed to use the marriage contract and his favor with the king to maneuver Aster's parents into a position where they'd be financially ruined if Aster didn't come back and do as he was told.

Corin would be left here alone to contemplate his empty bed, his empty life, and the certain knowledge that Aster would be utterly miserable, quite possibly for the rest of his own life.

Of course, he'd thought of an impossible but haunting alternative. He'd thought of little else during the long, miserable night.

*…any unmarried man of noble arms and in the crown's good grace…*

Those words echoed through his mind yet again. Someone who'd told King Theobert to more or less go fuck himself after being asked to apologize to the lord he'd mutilated, and then left court under a cloud of scandal, couldn't be considered to be in the crown's good grace.

No. It didn't matter, because Corin would never publicly associate himself with another Cezanne even if he hadn't resigned from the king's service on less-than-ideal terms. Not an option.

Aster still hadn't moved except for the even rise and fall of his chest. A faint smile curled the corners of his lips. Midday had come, with the sun angled straight down outside the window, and the bedroom lay in glowing shadow, floating far above the troubles of the world. This bed, the two of them. An intimate bubble of peace and satisfaction, their mingled breaths and the slide of Corin's dragon-hot skin against Aster's soft warmth.

Fuck. Corin couldn't tell him now.

He could put it off a little longer, couldn't he? Only a tiny bit. A few minutes, or an hour. What difference would it make?

Corin wanted more of those moans, the frantic ones he'd drawn out when he had Aster's cock in his mouth…and while he might not be an expert cocksucker, he knew he excelled in another closely related skill. By the way Aster had reacted when Corin mentioned it, he'd never been the recipient of it.

No other man had ever given Aster that pleasure. What a pack of fucking idiots, to pass up the chance to taste that nearly-virgin sweetness. Corin's cock gave a throb. No, he couldn't let Aster leave quite yet.

Careful not to jostle Aster's legs too much or to bounce the mattress, he lowered himself down, sliding toward the foot of the bed at the same time. He adjusted his grip, regretfully letting go of Aster's ass and then slipping that hand back under his thigh, using the other to gently lift his balls and expose the pretty pink hole hiding underneath.

Corin had to tense all his muscles to keep still, the urge to rut into the bed—or to climb up and rut into Aster—nearly overwhelming him. Even after a night and morning of rest the signs of Corin's possession of him remained obvious. He wouldn't say Aster looked *used*, precisely, because that would be ungallant, even though Corin wouldn't mean it that way. But he hadn't quite gone back to his unfucked state, either. A little bit puffy, pinker than he'd been before, and slightly stretched.

*Claimed*, not used.

Corin held Aster's balls out of the way and ran his thumb over that soft flesh, a tremor running through him as he felt the slight swelling there. His handiwork. And he'd be doing it again, knotting that hole wide open.

That gentle touch earned him his first sign of life since Aster had come on his face, a little startled jolt through Aster's body. He glanced up to find a glimmer of brilliant blue beneath Aster's heavy eyelids, his mouth forming an O of surprise.

He dipped his head and traced Aster's hole with the tip of his tongue. Aster squeaked and thrashed. Corin pulled his hand out from under Aster's thigh to pin him across the hips, pushed his thighs wider with his shoulders, and that was that for Aster's little show of rebellion.

Fuck, so soft and silky. How had skin this delicate survived Corin's rough attentions? His knot, with its subtly raised scales? Above him Aster had started cursing and moaning, interspersed with pleas to stop because it was so very wrong and strange, his high, pleasure-drenched voice saying the opposite of the words. His hands had come back to Corin's head, fingers buried in his overlong hair—and more to the point, pushing him down toward Aster's hole rather than trying to pull him up and away.

He prodded his tongue at Aster's opening, twisted the tip of it inside him, and was rewarded with a raspy, wrung-out, "Corin, fuck, *please*," which he could've listened to every moment of his life and never gotten tired of it.

Deeper, the wider part of his tongue stretching Aster open. And then out again, fastening his mouth over his hole and sucking hard, lashing with his tongue, and that made Aster scream, but he could do better than that—his tongue was longer than a human's when he chose to extend it, much longer, and he craved the taste of Aster's body, his sweetness and salty musk.

A trace of his own spend lingered, too, although not enough. Not nearly enough. Aster would need to be filled again.

Aster let out another cry, this one wavering.

Corin pulled back, nuzzling into the crease of Aster's ass, gentling him, stroking his hip with the hand he had pinning him down. He pushed his tongue inside, taking it slow this time. Fuck, he wasn't a beast. He could give Aster a moment to adjust to the idea that another part of Corin's body wasn't precisely what he'd been used to. Deeper, an inch inside him now, with probably another two inches to go. Much, much smaller than his cock, but the sensation would be entirely different. And he could rub over that little nub of flesh that he knew would drive Aster wild, sliding back and forth with control he didn't have with his inflexible cock.

Aster's fingers clenched tighter. "Corin, what are you—I noticed your tongue was—oh, *God*—" If the rest of his wail contained words, Corin couldn't understand them. It didn't matter at all, and he fucked his tongue in and out in a hard rhythm, finally remembering to move his hand across from Aster's hip, get a grip on his cock, and squeeze in counterpoint.

Aster's voice rose to a crescendo. His whole body went rigid, his hole clenching around Corin's tongue, and a trickle of spend ran down over his knuckles from Aster's still-soft cock.

Corin twisted his tongue and fucked a little deeper just to feel Aster shudder around him, teasing and tormenting his sweet spot as he withdrew, probing it with the tip of his tongue.

His own arousal hovered on the edge of unbearable, his cock

aching—but it didn't matter so much, somehow, not when all his senses sang with Aster's ecstasy. Corin rested his forehead against Aster's inner thigh and closed his eyes, breathing deeply, savoring the warmth and sweetness of his place between his lover's legs.

Aster slowly loosened his grip and then ran his fingers through Corin's hair, stroking his scalp. Corin sucked in a deep breath, the deepest he'd taken in years, maybe, and then let it out in an endlessly long sigh.

"Mmm," Aster said. "That tickles," and stroked him again, this time trailing his fingers along Corin's temple.

Corin blew out another sharp breath. Aster twitched, giggled, and tweaked a strand of his hair.

Something warm and utterly unfamiliar bloomed in Corin's chest, a heavy, almost painful sensation that drove him to—he had no idea what. Hold Aster even closer, crush him in his arms until he cried out, until they were one. Fuck him so deeply his insides would be hollowed out forever into the shape of Corin's cock. Press the softest possible kiss to the smooth skin of his thigh.

Damn it to hell. Aster would be leaving.

But he couldn't resist one kiss, one brush of his lips on that silky skin. He shivered at the touch—or maybe that was Aster.

He drew a deep breath, tensing his muscles, drawing his strength back into his body and his mind. It had to be now.

"I need to tell you," he said.

Because if he waited, he never would.

# Chapter Eighteen

HE'D THOUGHT HAVING CORIN'S cock between his legs had been the best thing he'd ever experienced, but Corin's head came in a close second. Maybe even first after all. God, that tongue. Aster didn't have the strength remaining in him to feel more than a faint clench of remembered arousal in the pit of his belly, but...that tongue. He'd never even imagined. He stroked his fingers through Corin's thick hair, felt the weight of Corin's head resting on his hip and thigh, and sank into the mattress, everything spinning gently around him in the best possible way.

Outside, he could hear the faint call of the hawk that'd been circling over Fredmund's hat, or maybe one of its friends. The bit of sky visible through the nearer window shone clear blue. A faint rustling and squeaking came from the chimney; Aster had caught a flash of striped tail in the fireplace early that morning, and he was pretty sure Corin had been willingly going without a fire over the winter rather than inconvenience a family of chipmunks.

This place might be an absurdly drafty pile of rock, with few comforts and very little food, isolated from other people and beset with a dragon's rodent pets, and the dragon himself...and no, Aster never wanted to leave.

He startled as Corin said, "I need to tell you," the words brushing hotly against his inner thigh.

And all of a sudden, the world snapped into place again.

Aster stared up at the ceiling with eyes that had popped wide open, hands gone still in Corin's hair. *I'd be doing them a favor by taking him on, though he obviously doesn't have any family feeling.* Since he hadn't returned home, Fredmund must have meant, because Aster had always been close to his mother and his elder brother, anyway, and had been loyal to all of them in word and deed until he ran away. And

Corin had told him he wouldn't want to flee the kingdom once he'd heard what had been happening at home.

Corin would be telling him he'd need to leave.

He'd had Corin's hands and mouth on him now, and he'd come twice. He didn't have any more excuses for delay.

"Go ahead," he said, his throat painfully tight.

The process of Corin lifting his head and disentangling himself from Aster's body felt like a premonition of things to come, an inevitable separation that left Aster chilled to the bone despite the warmth of the bed and the sun-heated tower.

Corin levered himself up and flopped down next to Aster on his back with a bone-deep sigh. They lay side by side, both gazing up at the fluttering cobwebs hanging from the rafters. Aster carefully, subtly shifted his weight so that their upper arms touched. Without any comforting contact at all, he might curl into himself and wither away, and even through Corin's shirt, which he still hadn't removed, it helped more than he wanted to admit.

"The bottom line is that Marellus is a fucking asshole," Corin said abruptly at last. "Your valet was probably telling the truth." He had the good grace to sound slightly embarrassed as he admitted that, and Aster had to bite his lip hard to keep from saying he'd told him so. "Since the contract only had penalties on your side for failing to consummate and for infidelity, he'd have been able to enforce it more or less at will. Why didn't you tell me that was in the marriage contract? I'd have been a lot more likely to believe your story."

Aster closed his eyes, cringing inwardly. The contract. The fucking contract, which of course Corin would reasonably assume he'd read…the silence ticked on for three seconds, five, ten.

"Oh, for fuck's fucking sake," Corin said at last, voice so void of inflection that Aster flinched. The muscles in Corin's arm went tense against his, hard as granite. "You didn't bloody well read it, did you? You didn't read your own marriage contract."

Aster pressed himself down into the bed, wishing he could disappear, squeezing his eyes even more tightly closed to try to blot out the overwhelming shame. It didn't work. "I didn't—I mean—I wasn't the one to arrange it, was I?"

"It was your—damn it. You're very young, and you trusted your parents," Corin said, and it sounded like he had his jaw clenched. "But you were the one getting married. And I'm really not saying this is all your fault, but you probably ought to have known about those clauses. And more to the point, you should've known that if you and Marellus didn't end up married at all, he'd be claiming a third of your parents' estate! Which is mortgaged to the fucking hilt. The family would be left with nothing."

*Mortgaged. Nothing. Your fault.* The words hit like barbed arrows, piercing deep and burrowing deeper. His parents hadn't told him they were in debt. He'd known nothing. He'd trusted them, because whatever their faults, they'd always loved him. Maybe they'd thought they were showing their love for him by protecting him from the truth.

Aster couldn't control the shudders in his chest, but he bit his lip until he tasted blood trying to keep even more sounds inside. By the time he managed to control his breathing enough to speak, his eyes were swimming. Hopefully Corin wouldn't look at him.

"I didn't know. They never showed me—" He stopped, taking a deep breath. No. No excuses. "I never asked, though. I should have. I suppose I wouldn't have run away if I'd known."

Aster dared to turn his head, a tear sliding down his cheek as he moved. He found Corin facing him too, dark eyes flashing. Fuck, Corin would despise him for his weakness. He reached up to rub at it, but Corin caught his wrist and turned onto his side, pushing up to loom over him. His other hand came up and he brushed his thumb across Aster's burning cheek, through the tear track, swiping it away, his swordsman's calluses rough but his touch unbearably soft.

"It's not your fault," Corin said, and he sounded as if he really meant it this time.

Probably because he'd decided Aster was too pathetic to be held responsible for anything more complicated than buttoning his own trousers.

"No, I was a fool at best," Aster managed. He had to own up to his large part in this, not least to show Corin that he could. "But I can't change any of it now. But wait a moment—he can't take

Cezanne if the contract's voided, can he? It has to be for the king to offer me up to the first comer. Thank God, I hadn't even thought of that. So why do you and Fredmund seem to think I'll need to go—"

"You have to go home because the contract isn't voided until you're actually offered," Corin said grimly. "Until the king enters you into a marriage contract with someone else, you're still betrothed to Marellus. And if you're still betrothed, the penalty still applies. You can still run, of course. Nothing's stopping you."

No, nothing at all except the impending loss of his family and his home. Cezanne, with its tall whispering sycamore trees and its mirror-clear lake, the ancient library redolent of leather and ink and aged brandy. The portraits of his ancestors and all that they'd built for hundreds of years—gone because Aster couldn't go through with a wedding. The look that would be in his mother's beautiful eyes when she walked away from her beloved rose garden, where she'd taken Aster for his evening walks as a little boy, for the last time.

Aster couldn't help laughing, a rusty, miserable sound that ended in a sob.

Corin's jaw tightened. "I assumed as much," he said, somehow understanding everything Aster couldn't put into words.

He leaned in, stroking Aster's face, closer and closer until Aster could feel his heat.

Oh, God, he was going to kiss him, and Aster parted his lips in anticipation, his breath coming faster even though tears still gathered in the corners of his eyes. Nothing would distract him more than Corin's weight on top of him, the thrust of his thick dragon cock, his hot mouth…

"I brought back some hams from the village," Corin said. "I'm starving, and you must be too. Let's have something to eat. You can't make a plan on an empty stomach."

Aster froze, staring up at him.

Ham.

Aster's entire life had collapsed into ruin, and he was lying here in Corin's bed naked and panting and practically begging for a kiss—and Corin wanted ham. Were all men so incredibly dense and obnoxious and infuriating? Was Aster himself so dense and obnoxious and infuriating at times? No, he couldn't believe it.

"Really? Right now?" He tried and failed not to sound too ridiculously disappointed.

As if on cue, Aster's stomach let out a ferocious growl.

"Apparently," Corin said, the corner of his mouth quirking up—and poked him in the belly.

And how bloody *dare* he mock Aster right then? Indignation and worry and fear and reluctant amusement all combined into an odd, giddy feeling he couldn't name, and he wrapped his arms around Corin's chest and grappled him.

"You bastard," he panted, only half joking. Corin let out an *oof* of surprise as Aster rolled, trying to turn Corin to his back.

They struggled, and Aster thrashed about, got his legs around Corin's hips and—actually succeeded in flipping him, landing on top and tugging his arms out from under Corin's back. Corin had ended up sprawled crosswise on the bed with his legs hanging off the side, Aster straddling him with his ass resting in precisely the right place to feel Corin's burgeoning erection. Corin gazed up at him with eyes half-lidded like a lazy predator, teeth gleaming white and very sharp.

It took Aster's breath away. Corin had clearly stopped thinking about ham. Greatly daring, wondering if he'd be allowed to get away with it, he caught Corin's wrists and put his hands up by his head, pinning them down. The way those strong fingers felt between his, interlaced, shouldn't have been quite so overwhelmingly erotic. They were fingers. It meant nothing. But the stretch of Aster's skin between each one sent a tremor along his nerves all the way down, his ass clenching on nothing.

He knew damn well Corin had let him win. Aster couldn't have won a wrestling match between the two of them unless Corin had been drugged, tied up, and knocked over the head first, but he'd fought just enough that Aster had the heady thrill of triumph.

When Corin squeezed his hands, he nearly fainted as all the blood in his body rushed to his cock at once.

"Well, now you've turned the tables on your cruel captor, what are you going to do with me?" Corin asked, his voice a low, spine-shivering rumble.

ELIOT GRAYSON

*Keep you forever. Lock the gate, forget the world exists, screw my family and their debts and their terrible marriage contracts, and beg you to never let me go.*

"I'm not sure what I'm going to do with you," Aster said instead, playing for time. He couldn't help rocking back and forth a little bit, shamelessly pressing the crease of his ass down onto Corin's cock, a terrifyingly large ridge in his trousers, the rough fabric a painful tease against the delicate skin behind Aster's bollocks. Corin certainly felt like he might be amenable to... "Should I ride you again?"

"No," Corin said, with a definitive emphasis. Aster's heart dropped like a stone.

And then the world spun around him, and he landed hard on his back with Corin kneeling over him, eyes aflame and scales creeping up the sides of his face.

"Like this," Corin breathed, a delicate tendril of smoke rising up from his mouth. "Flat on your back and spread open. Just like this."

ASTER WOULD BE GOING, AND it only remained to plan his exit from Corin's tower and from his life. Corin would never need to see or hear from another Cezanne so long as he lived.

Beneath him, Aster moaned and spread his legs, head tipped back, flushed from his pert nipples up to his hairline.

The prospect of living a Cezanne-free life didn't thrill him as much as he would have expected only a few days ago.

Did their family have some kind of seductive curse they could lay on any man, or dragon, foolish enough to come near? No one in his right mind would look at Belinda and Aster together and think they could have such a power in common. Belinda, yes. Aster, no.

And yet.

Belinda had made Corin into a fool, her idiot worshipper, too blind to realize she'd been fucking everyone at court except for him. He'd waited for her, pined for her, subsisted on a regimen of fucking his own hand while he fantasized about her lips and her tits and her laugh and the way she said his name.

And Aster...he'd waltzed in, unwanted and uninvited and

previously completely overlooked. And within a day he'd been leading Corin around by his cock. Which throbbed against the constriction of his trousers, desperate and aching. His hand tightened on
Aster's hip.

"Are you going to stay where I put you if I don't pin you down?"
Corin asked.

The question felt larger than it purported to be. Aster would be
leaving. He wouldn't stay where Corin had put him. He'd be leaving,
and doing so with some man who'd take him and fuck him and marry
him and bloody well own him, and Corin wouldn't have any right to
tear that motherfucker's head off of his shoulders and roast him alive
and crack his skull between his massive jaws like a fucking walnut,
possibly not in that order.

Distantly, he realized that he'd only felt it necessary to give
Belinda's lover a disfiguring but entirely not-at-all-life-threatening
wound. Aster's magic must be stronger, unlikely as it seemed.

Fuck, he needed to get his clothes off before he spontaneously
combusted from the force of his raging internal fire, and while dragons had quite a few special powers, they only had two arms like anyone else. He couldn't hold Aster down at the same time.

"I'm your captive, remember?" Aster said breathlessly. "Until—
oh, God, we'll talk about that later. But I'm obliged to obey you,
aren't I?"

Obey him? When he'd have had Corin panting after him, begging pathetically for anything he had to offer, if he'd teased and refused instead. Just like his sister had.

Except that Aster, in the process of putting Corin under his
spell, had yielded so sweetly and so generously that Corin couldn't
possibly demand anything more.

*Until.* And they'd talk about it later.

Fuck.

Corin let Aster go long enough to sit up on his heels and yank
off his shirt, but his trousers—fuck it, fuck it sideways, he'd spend
an hour sewing buttons back on all of his ruined pants once Aster
fell asleep—he simply tore those down the front, buttons pinging to
the floor, and let his cock have some breathing room at last.

Aster's eyes went wide, fixed on Corin's cock, and his mouth dropped open gratifyingly. Corin burned to fuck him senseless, but he also wanted to kiss those parted lips and nuzzle into his throat and whisper in his ear how beautiful he was, and he had to be under a curse—no other explanation seemed sufficient.

Corin's vision blurred around the edges, tinged with a red haze.

Cursed or not, it hardly mattered. He'd care about it later, much later, or maybe not at all.

He glanced down at his cock. The slick tip glistened with fluid, and more slipped out as he watched. Perfect. His body knew he needed to claim that incredibly tight human hole, force it to fit his length and girth.

He wrapped his hands around Aster's inner thighs and pushed them as wide as he could, until Aster's knees went up past his hips and his ass tilted up off the bed. Carefully, carefully, because if his claws slipped out even a fraction of an inch they'd tear into that silky skin.

Aster's exposed pink hole glistened a little, still wet from Corin's thorough tongue-fucking. It'd be even wetter soon. Gushing, when Corin pulled his knot out at last after filling Aster with as much as he could hold.

Corin looked up. Aster lay still, hands fisted in the sheets beneath him, chest rising and falling rapidly and his cock bobbing with his frantic breaths. He hadn't moved at all from where Corin had put him. Good. Corin didn't need or expect obedience in general from a mate; he wouldn't want someone who needed to be told what to do all the time in the first place.

But right now he didn't want a fight.

He pushed his hips between Aster's legs and let the head of his cock kiss Aster's hole, shifting his weight so that he brushed against him, painting him with slick and nudging him open. So soft…his muscles shook with the effort of not shoving his cock deep all at once.

"It's so strange," Aster gasped. "I mean, wonderful, and convenient, the way you get me all—but strange. It feels like I'm the one getting wet for you."

Corin nearly doubled over, groaning, keeping himself in check with more force of will than he'd thought he possessed. "Would you like that?" he rasped, sounding not human at all. "To get wet for me? To be that much of a slut for me?" Yes, his, no one else's…

Aster's face flamed crimson, and his breath hitched, but he said softly, "Yes, please, I wish I could," and something in Corin's chest snapped painfully, so hard that he almost heard it.

Even at his most enslaved, somewhere in some deeply hidden corner of his mind Corin had resented Belinda's one-sided hold on him. But now…he tumbled into Aster's eyes, leaning down, down, falling, as if he'd folded his wings and surrendered to gravity, and not giving one single fuck if it killed him when he hit the ground. Some curses couldn't be broken. It didn't matter much when he could thrust gently, pushing the head of his cock into Aster's yielding body, catch a soft, not-quite-pained whimper with his mouth. He swallowed it down and teased Aster's tongue with his. Strong hands slid around his ribs and pulled him closer. Aster's mouth tasted of sugared roses, and Corin's cock pushed in deeper, every inch swallowed up by soft warmth and incredible tightness. He could feel Aster's body stretching to take him, the tension in his body as he obeyed the command of Corin's.

A mate ought to show *this* kind of obedience. He'd have his own mind and will, always, and Corin would respect that. And if he wanted to resist when Corin wanted him, to challenge him, he'd relish it. But when he'd already given in, it ought to be total and complete: a submission as final as Corin's to Aster's magic.

"Take me," Corin whispered into Aster's mouth. "All of me." He rocked deeper, less gently this time, giving Aster another couple of inches, already more than enough to satisfy a human.

Corin didn't want to satisfy him. He wanted to ravage him.

Aster shuddered beneath him, fingers flexing against Corin's back, and let out something like a sob. Corin kissed him more deeply, thrusting into his mouth and into his hole. Almost all the way in now. Aster wouldn't be able to feel anything else. His balls brushed Aster's cheeks. There. One more push, and no one had ever been so deep in Aster's sweet body.

He still had his hands wrapped around the backs of Aster's thighs, and he lifted them higher, folding Aster in half underneath him, feeling him tremble.

Corin fell into a rhythm: a hard, sharp thrust in, a long, slow withdrawal, dragging every inch of his scale-textured cock over Aster's insides. His own pleasure rose slowly, like the tide, a little higher with each wave, every one of his muscles tensing by degrees. Aster whimpered into his mouth and clutched at his back, skin sweat-slick and almost as hot as a dragon's.

When that irresistible ecstasy crested to its highest point at last, he had to break the kiss, resting his forehead against Aster's and thrusting even deeper, Corin's whole body rigid as he flooded Aster with his claim. His knot swelled, and he had to rock his hips one more time to stuff it in past Aster's taut rim.

"Corin," Aster said, his voice a ragged little rasp.

He'd never particularly cared about his name one way or the other. Just a word people used to address him—a convenience. It'd never been beautiful before.

Corin let go of Aster's legs at last, and Aster let out a soft grunt of relief. He had to be cramping. Corin petted his thighs, lifted himself up enough that he could help Aster get his feet down, and then propped himself on his elbows and kissed along the curve of a flushed cheek and down into the hollow of Aster's throat, licking, tasting him, savoring his complete possession.

At last he rested his head next to Aster's and closed his eyes.

He had no idea which one of them was the captive and which the captor. At that moment, for a few more minutes until the world had to become real again, it didn't matter in the least.

# Chapter Nineteen

"WHAT WAS WRONG WITH that one?" Aster asked. "You didn't say anything when you came back inside."

Corin started and looked up from his mug of tea, extracting himself from the dark muddle of his thoughts with difficulty. Aster had finished his own tea and set it aside, and he sat across from Corin by the hearth, hands folded primly in his lap.

That one. He had to mean... "What? Which—the fellow I fought this morning?"

Aster cleared his throat, a soft, hesitant sound, and fidgeted with the hem of his shirt. "When we talked about it the other day, you told me you wouldn't send me back with anyone who didn't have the balls to fight you instead of running away like a rabbit. This one fought you. He even thanked you for the lesson."

He had in fact offered a courteous challenge, politely accepted Corin's explanation for why he would be fighting him and not Aster, crossed swords with a respectable amount of skill, and then lost gallantly. If Corin ever returned to the king's service, he'd invite him to join his regiment. Not that he would return, of course. That would require groveling, apologies, and eating his pride until he choked on it. No dragon would humble himself like that to one of his own kind, much less a mere human monarch.

Never. No matter what the circumstances. Even if a proclamation left out anyone not in the crown's good grace. He simply couldn't consider it.

In the meantime, though, Corin couldn't allow him to marry Aster. He had the demeanor and courage of a man who'd be formidable someday if he trained consistently, and he might not be a complete asshole. But Aster deserved better, someone who could protect him. Someone older, more experienced.

"I didn't like the look of him," he said at last, unable to find a way to articulate any of his thoughts without offending Aster's sense of his ability to protect and care for himself.

They'd agreed on a plan, over the ham they'd eventually gone downstairs to eat the other night. Once an acceptable candidate came to the gate, Corin would bow out and Aster would take his challenge and gracefully lose. They'd left the criteria to be applied to the challengers rather vague, agreeing only that if Corin thought the fellow might pass muster, he'd make some excuse to step inside for a moment and confer with Aster, who'd be watching through the loophole by the gate.

That much settled, they'd eaten their supper and returned directly upstairs to bed. They hadn't discussed it any further since then.

Aster frowned and leaned back in his chair. "I thought he was handsome enough. I mean, he wasn't old or ugly at all, and he spoke well."

Corin unclenched his jaw before the sound of his grinding teeth became audible. He had been very handsome, in fact. Young, tall, and muscular, with flowing blond hair to his shoulders rather like Aster's.

"Didn't seem all that handsome to me," he growled, and silently cursed himself as Aster bit his lip and stared down at his lap.

Fuck, he wanted to pull Aster into his own lap, kiss him and slide his hands under Aster's clothing until he had him all disheveled and flustered, and then go back upstairs, where he didn't feel so much like he hated everything. Damn it, he ought to be able to last until evening, at least. But he'd had Aster spread wide around his knot twice last night and he still didn't feel sated at all. Every time he took Aster it stoked the flame rather than dousing it.

It had been three days since Fredmund had ridden up to the bridge, three days and slightly more than twice that many new challengers. And of course three nights, on each of which he'd told himself he'd keep some distance and slope off downstairs to sulk as soon as his knot went down. He'd spent them wrapped around Aster, of course.

He'd managed to lie still most of the time instead of petting him and nuzzling him and attentively tugging the blankets over his shoulder every few minutes.

Small victories.

Fuck, he was pathetic.

"I'm sorry, I didn't mean to snap at you," he said, in lieu of getting on his knees. "These assholes are starting to piss me off, that's all." He hoped Aster wouldn't ask why they pissed him off so much, because he didn't have an answer.

"It's all right," Aster said, with a tentative smile that went straight to his cock, and far worse, straight to a spot beneath his breastbone that ached whenever he looked into Aster's pretty eyes.

Completely fucking pathetic.

And it didn't matter whether Aster had truly put him under some kind of spell or was simply oblivious to his own insidious charms. The effect was the same: another Cezanne luring Corin into a hopeless entanglement. The first had ended here, with Corin hiding in a miserable stone hovel for years, with no occupation and no friends, followed up the mountain by the jeers and sneers of the court. He'd rather jump off the fucking bridge outside without his wings than get involved with the Cezanne family a second time.

Of course, every time he claimed Aster as his captive and fought to keep him, the rumors would grow. But fucking hell, rumors were just that, rumors. And they'd forget about it altogether when Aster returned to court as another man's prize.

"Corin?" He looked up again, his vision a bit hazy. Fuck, Aster would think he'd developed a strange obsession with tea. Aster wasn't smiling now. In fact, he'd moved his hands to the arms of his chair, a bit white around the knuckles, as if he meant to either brace himself or bolt. "That's a lot of smoke. Are you—upset about something?"

Smoke. He blinked. The haze remained. His throat and nostrils had that itchy burn they got when he breathed too much dragon fire in his human shape. He exhaled, and another plume rose up, thick and heavy.

For fuck's sake.

"No," he said, and he didn't sound convincing even to himself.

"Nothing's wrong." He sucked in a deep breath and let out another rush of smoke, and this time he felt a flicker of flame in his throat.

Aster leaned back in his chair, coughing and obviously trying to suppress it.

God fucking damn it. Corin rose so abruptly he shoved his chair, sending it screeching across the flagstones, and started to turn to leave the hall.

And then he stopped even more abruptly when the smoke cleared and he got a good look at Aster's white face, expression frozen and eyes wide.

He forced himself to go still, to turn inward, to focus on the draconic part of his nature and command it to settle the hell down. Corin might be a monster, but even monsters had their limits. Terrifying Aster crossed that line and then some.

"I'm sorry," he rasped, his scorched throat making his voice even lower than usual. Fuck, he didn't sound less terrifying in the slightest, and he had no idea what to say. "It's not—I'm preoccupied. I'm not in the mood for conversation, I'm sorry."

Aster blinked at last. "I shouldn't have bothered you. I won't—"

"It's sunny," Corin cut in, speaking before he even realized the words were forming in his mind or on his tongue. "We ought to go out back and train a bit. I could use the exercise."

He shut up, nonplussed by himself, of all the things. Where the fuck had that come from? He didn't bloody well need any exercise, not on top of…being on top of Aster however many times in the last few days. Vigorously on top. Anyway, Aster wouldn't want to spar with him.

But Aster's posture relaxed a tiny bit, his hands unclenching. And that light in his eyes… "I wouldn't give you much of a challenge," he said, but the wistful desire in his voice couldn't have been clearer. God. He did want to. Had he always? A horrible thought struck him: Corin truly hadn't noticed Aster paying him any particular attention before all of this, but what if that was simply his own oversight?

Aster gazed up at him hopefully, giving him no choice at all.

"We could both use the practice, even if it's not an even match," Corin said as tactfully as he could. "But not with that sword you brought. We'll use foils. I have a set."

"Oh," Aster said, blushing a little, looking down shyly with his lashes fanned out on his pink cheeks, and Corin didn't at all want to kiss them and see if they felt as warm as they looked, damn it to hell. "All right. Should I—I'll go sweep the last of the snow out of the courtyard, shall I? And see to Etallon while I'm out there."

He rose and bustled past, leaving Corin spinning about and watching him go with his mouth hanging open.

After a moment, Aster had tugged the door open and stepped outside, taking the extraordinary view of his ass in tight trousers with him. Corin shook his head, turned, and went to fetch his foils.

To the uneducated eye, the chest in the anteroom between the hall and the stairs looked like nothing more than a dusty old piece of junk. And in fact, unless Corin himself drew attention to it by interacting with it, no one else would notice it at all—it'd fade away into the wall behind it. Costly and expertly applied blood magic keyed the chest to Corin alone. He'd have preferred to have a permanent place for his hoard. Any dragon would. But a soldier's life, particularly given his semi-estrangement from his family, hadn't allowed for it. The chest had been the best solution he could come up with.

It'd certainly come in handy when he'd had to—not flee, more of a strategic withdrawal, damn it—leave the capital in a hurry. He'd simply strapped another trunk full of his clothes and necessities on top, snatched it up in his claws, and gone up above the clouds where no human could follow him.

He opened it with a touch of his hand on the spelled lock, accustomed by now to the slight prick of the tiny blade that snicked out to drink a drop of his blood. The lid rose smoothly and silently; he'd paid the witch extra for that.

The inside of the chest, for which he'd paid the witch an absolutely excessive amount, offered far more space than the outside would suggest. Specially designed racks held all of his swords and armor, and a little crank at the corner would move them around, allowing him to reach the ones that were currently down below in an expanded pocket of reality. He kept Giant Dick at the top, of course, within easy reach. He took a moment to stroke a finger along its gleaming blade.

Damn Edwin for calling it that, anyway, but as soon as he had, all their fellows had burst into drunken laughter and repeated it, banging their tankards on the table to drown out his protests.

It'd stuck, of course. When anyone else asked, he simply said it didn't have a name. Fuck, he missed Edwin. He missed his life.

The foils were down near the bottom. He turned the crank and brought them up, checking them one at a time. They were, like everything else, in perfect condition. Both the (yet more expensive) preservation spells on the chest and Corin's own obsessive care saw to that.

He was halfway to the back door with them before it struck him: he'd never, ever, let any other person touch any part of his hoard. No one used his swords but him. They were *his*. He'd sooner ignore his spouse fucking someone else—presuming he ever managed to marry someone who hadn't already fucked someone else regardless—than allow another man to hold and touch his weapons, much less fight with them.

And yet the possessive unwillingness simply didn't come.

Odd, but…all right. There weren't any rules saying he couldn't loosen up a bit for once, were there? Maybe Aster simply didn't feel like a threat.

Aster looked up from his work as Corin appeared in the doorway, smiling as he swept a pile of churned-up slush off to the edge of the courtyard. The pale high-altitude sun washed him out a bit, leaving him ethereally blond with a pinkish halo, his eyes gleaming like pieces of the rich blue above him.

"Of course you really do have foils," Aster said as Corin stood there staring at him dumbly. "If anyone would bring extra swords to a place like this instead of extra blankets, or a supply of coffee, it's you. I'm surprised you're letting me use one, though. Are you sure you hadn't rather I sparred with my own? It's not like I'd be capable of hurting you with it, or anything," he added, his smile turning wry.

Anything Corin might have said in reply lodged in his throat.

Of course he never let anyone else wield Giant Dick, but then again, no one else would've been able to in the first place, so they wouldn't bother to ask. When he trained at the palace he used the practice swords in the armory just like everyone else. The issue of sharing had never come up. And Aster—somehow Aster knew how he felt about it anyway.

"Foils are better," Corin managed at last. "And I'm sure you won't hurt me, because you have more skill than to simply flail away willy-nilly, don't you? You're not trying to injure me in a practice bout."

That won him a wide grin and a sparkle in those eyes that nearly had him on his knees then and there. "I won't hurt you because there's no way I can get so much as a touch, and we both know it. But I'll accept your explanation."

Aster leaned the broom up against the shed; he'd opened the door a bit, and Etallon stuck his head out and eyed them, flicking his ear and munching a wisp of hay. Far above them, a hawk cried shrilly. Otherwise the mountain rested in perfect peace.

Corin handed over one of the foils and took up a fencing stance.

A moment later Aster did the same, and then paused, looking down at Corin's feet. "Don't you want boots? The stone's freezing still."

Annoyance welled up, the same kind he'd used to feel when he'd been training a squire who'd be getting himself bloody killed if he tried to take on a real fight. Aster had to learn to keep his eyes on his opponent.

And so he lunged, lightning fast, and flicked the hem of Aster's shirt with the blunted tip of his sword. Blunted or not, the edge caught and tore. Aster cried out and jumped back, raising his gaze and his own sword respectably fast but not fast enough.

Corin had already fallen back into a relaxed guard by the time Aster had reacted. He responded to Aster's wounded look with an unrepentant grin. Fuck, but he'd missed this, and that morning's two-minute duel had only whetted his appetite. Three seconds in, and his blood already sang with the joy of armed combat, no matter how uneven and unprofessional it might be. Far from making him uncomfortable, the rough, frigid stone under his bare feet felt like a conduit straight down to the center of the earth, with every stratum of rock between here and there only adding to his solidity and strength. At moments like this he could well believe that his kind sprang from the roots of mountains, formed from unyielding granite and magma and magic.

And the sword—the sword flowed from his arm, its natural extension, not a clumsy object to be maneuvered.

"Come on, then," Corin said, sidestepping a little, circling, feeling out Aster's stance. It'd been a long time since they'd been in a training yard together, but he seemed to remember Aster favored his left, overcompensating for his natural righthandedness. "Show me what you can do."

Aster fell back, his footing tentative. "We hadn't started yet, had we?"

"When someone tries to kill you, he isn't going to give you a signal for when you need to defend yourself." Corin lunged again at about half his full speed and strength and Aster parried, barely, but didn't manage a riposte. "Good. Again."

They quickly settled into a rhythm—more Corin putting Aster through his paces and teaching him than any kind of real fight, but it held Corin's interest as much as a challenging bout would have done, merely in a different way. He'd always enjoyed training the squires.

Of course, his time had been most usefully spent honing the skills of the most advanced students; a private lesson from Sir Corin had been an honor only second—and perhaps not even second, for some—to the notice of the king. Corin didn't have an inflated opinion of himself, he didn't think, but he'd have had to be blind to miss the hero worship he received from the younger contingent of knights and squires and soldiers.

Anyway, he knew damn well how good he was with a sword. That wasn't arrogance, it was realism.

Round and round they went, working up a sweat—in Aster's case, anyway, since dragons didn't perspire—and a pleasant warmth in the muscles and joints, loose and easy. The rasp of Aster's boots and the whisper of Corin's feet on the stone, the scrape and clink of their swords, Etallon's snuffling, all of it made a delightful music, the sound of life and activity. Something Corin hadn't even quite realized how much he'd been longing for until Aster came and shook up his solitary, dull routine.

"Again," Corin said, "and go slower this time. Get it right first. Speed can come with practice. I'll go slowly too."

And he did, moving through an attack steadily and smoothly, allowing Aster to counter it the way Corin had demonstrated a few minutes before. He didn't have nearly the skill of those Corin had trained before, not even close. But his eagerness, the way he hung on Corin's every word and watched him so closely, tried so hard…that made up for it.

Or perhaps watching his lovely body bend and stretch made up for it. Or the way the exercise brought a healthy flush to his cheeks and lips, or the way his eyes shone. Corin had sometimes appreciated his opponents in a general sort of way, but he'd always been more focused on the swordplay than on the possibility of…well, a different kind of swordplay.

With Aster, every time their foils touched it felt like a caress, a tease. They circled closer. Aster tried to parry Corin's thrust and failed, his eyes gone wide, his teeth digging into his lower lip in concentration.

And that was quite enough of that.

Corin twisted his wrist and neatly caught Aster's blade with his, flicking it out of his hand and sending it spinning away across the courtyard where it landed with a clatter half in a pile of slush. If someone else had treated a part of his hoard that way he'd have picked it up, cleaned it off carefully, and then used it to slit the offender's throat. But Aster had let out a little cry and then gazed at him in awe, as if he'd done something spectacular. It wasn't much of a trick, really, but he'd executed it so swiftly and neatly that maybe it'd seemed like it.

Hero worship had never affected him this way. He'd been flattered, perhaps, mostly indifferent. It'd never made his cock go from half-mast to rock hard in an instant, never set his heart hammering, never left him almost shaking with the need to touch.

If he'd ever caught Aster looking at him like this at the palace, with desire and admiration shining in his blue eyes…

He flung his sword after Aster's. Fuck it. He'd clean them later.

And he seized him around the waist, forced him back over his arm, and took his mouth ruthlessly, swallowing his cry of surprise.

Aster melted into his arms, lips parting under Corin's assault, one leg coming up to wrap around him and reel him in, closer, between his legs, God, he'd take him right here—

"Ho there, in the tower!" Three loud bangs echoed all the way out to the courtyard. "Open up! Lord Aster, come out!"

Corin wrenched his mouth away from Aster's. "You have got to be—fucking *fuck*!"

The pounding repeated, louder this time.

"I suppose you have to go," Aster said, breathlessly and with gratifying regret. He hadn't let go, and he rubbed up against Corin's cock as if he couldn't help himself. "Unless you want me to—"

Corin cut that particular bit of idiocy off with a kiss. "Don't keep asking that," he said roughly, and forced himself to let Aster go and stride for the front gate. "This one's probably as terrible as all the others."

Maybe he could adjust his shirt so as to hide his erection from whatever idiot had chosen to get brutally and efficiently cut into pieces and flung off the bridge this morning.

On the other hand, once in pieces at the bottom of the canyon he'd be unable to gossip about how the mighty but very strange Sir Corin fought duels with a cockstand. He nodded to himself, pleased with his own infallible logic, and went to rid himself of his unwelcome visitor.

He'd deal with his cock when he returned. Aster wasn't going anywhere.

# Chapter Twenty

"OH, FOR—WHAT THE fuck now?" Corin groaned, and Aster lifted his head, barely conscious, muzzily blinking at the pale squares of the windows and trying to brush hair out of his eyes. Corin flung the blankets back and rolled out of bed, cursing as he tripped over something Aster couldn't see and then hopping his way to the window.

If he hadn't been so disoriented after waking suddenly from one of the most interrupted nights of sleep of his life—not that he really had anything to complain about, given the nature of the very thick, hard interruptions—he might've laughed. What had woken him, anyway? He'd startled to consciousness a moment before Corin spoke.

"Fuck this," Corin growled. "Unfuckingbelievable. It's not even dawn." A moment later, a tinny-sounding trumpet blast—the second, no doubt, and now he knew how he'd been rousted—made Aster jump. "Damn it, I can't see much in all this mist. Who brings an actual herald to something like this? I'm going to remove one of his limbs just for that. Probably one of the herald's too," Corin added, and stomped past the bed, obviously making for the stairs.

His massive cock at morning half-mast passed within two feet of Aster's face as he went by, the double ridges flushed dark green and his heavy bollocks swinging. For a moment Aster lost all power of rational thought.

And then he rolled over in time to catch Corin on his way out the door and call out, "You're not wearing any pants!"

"The fuck do I care," came back up the stairs in such a deep, feral snarl that Aster actually fell back onto the bed in shock.

Well. Whoever was downstairs would have quite an experience.

One that Aster found he really didn't want to miss. And Corin had seemed in the mood to get it over with.

Aster had never scrambled out of bed so quickly in his life, sticking his leg into the wrong side of his trousers and stepping on the hem, tumbling down onto the bed again, lurching for the stairs with the pants half up and a shirt dangling from his hand.

He managed to career around the corner into the anteroom right as Corin flung the gate open, still stark naked and with his huge sword gripped in his hand.

It made Aster think about his other sword, the one he'd sheathed in Aster for hours the night before, and he lost his train of thought again. God, it was silent outside, what was going on, he'd missed something important—he scrambled up the ladder by the loophole and peeked out.

Corin stood where he always did when confronting their challengers. This time, two men had approached the other end of the bridge, one a huge, hulking sort of fellow in studded leather armor mounted on one of the most beautiful white stallions Aster had ever seen, and the other a tall, slender youth dressed in an improbably bright set of silk garments, tunic and trousers and cloak, sitting on a mule and holding a polished brass trumpet.

As a pair, they were improbable.

Grouped on the bridge with Corin, naked and gleaming faintly green, with smoke trailing from his nostrils to form odd swirls in the chill pink-gray of the morning mist, they boggled the mind.

The youth cleared his throat and lifted his trumpet, clearly intending to blow another blast.

A low rumble vibrated the air—Corin. But before Aster could blink or Corin could act, the armored man reached over to the herald, snatched the trumpet from his hand just as he put it to his lips, and sent it sailing over the bridge parapet and down into the canyon's depths.

"Oh!" the herald gasped, staring at his companion, cheeks gone bright red. "How dare you!"

A faint, sad clank echoed up from down below. Corin lowered his sword. The man in armor sighed, shook his head, and said, "Corin, you really couldn't have put on some pants?"

What the—did this idiot have a death wish?

Aster blinked, shook his head, and took a closer look. Both Corin and the challenger had a relaxed sort of air about them, not hostile at all now that the herald's miserable trumpet had been so thoroughly dealt with.

"You're on my doorstep with a fucking trumpeter at the ass-crack of dawn. You're lucky to still be alive. Both of you," Corin added, turning toward the herald, who lifted his chin, sniffed, and sidled his mule a little closer to the other. Aster had to give him some credit for remaining calm. "I'd be happy to see you under any other circumstances, but not these, Sig. And I'm not going to fight you, you stupid son of a bitch."

Corin's voice held obvious affection, all for this man Aster had never even heard of. Someone who had a history with Corin, a friendship Aster couldn't begin to imagine. A twinge of something he didn't want to identify as jealousy soured his stomach.

"Well, no, of course not," Sig agreed. "I wasn't planning on fighting *you*. Lord Aster's in there, right? He can come out and surrender peaceably, and we'll be on our way. Maybe a drink first, though? I ought to have visited sooner, but you know how it is."

"No, sorry. You'll have to pay whatever gambling debts you have this time another way. He's my captive. I'm fighting for him." *I'm fighting for him.* Aster closed his eyes for a moment to both savor the wave of pleasure that sent through him and mourn the fact that Corin didn't mean it the way he wished he did. It wouldn't do any good in any case. "How'd you hear about this? And what are you doing with him?" Corin gestured at the herald.

Sig shrugged again. "He won't stop following me, long story. I haven't gotten around to killing him yet. And I heard about it the way everyone else is. There are king's messengers reading out a decree about Lord Aster in all the towns between here and the capital. Probably everywhere else, too. Seemed like an easy way to set myself up as a rich nobleman, and whatnot, so I set out the next morning. Didn't expect you to be taking all comers with your," he gestured and grinned, "sword out. Thought you'd be glad to get rid of the blighter. Your captive? Seriously?"

"I won't follow you for much longer if you don't ever do

anything interesting," the herald put in sulkily. "And you owe me a trumpet."

Corin made a gesture of his own down by his hips, hidden by his body so that Aster couldn't see. Not that he really needed to. The herald went even redder, and Sig burst out laughing.

"Your *captive*. I see," Sig said, and laughed all the louder. "All right, I know when I'm unwelcome. I suppose I'll need to make my fortune another way."

Oh, for—Aster hadn't been angry at Corin yet; in fact, he'd have said it'd be impossible. Who could be angry with someone so perfect? But now. Now he knew better. God damn it, couldn't Corin restrain himself a little while joking around with his idiot soldier friend? Fredmund and the other would-be challengers had probably left with the vague impression that Aster had whored himself out for protection from the king's decree. Did Corin really need to do his best to confirm the story, so that this Sig person and his stupid herald could gossip to everyone they met?

Of course, the story wouldn't even make sense. Aster had arrived here before the decree. But that wouldn't matter in the slightest to the rumormongers. This would only be more Cezanne blood in the water for the sharks.

If they all thought Aster was Corin's actual lover he might not mind so much.

In fact, despite how much he hated being the subject of talk, he had to admit that he wouldn't mind at all.

But no one would believe it. Not after the way Belinda and Corin's engagement had ended, and not given Aster's lack of any of the attractions his sister had to offer. Not only would they assume like slutty sister like whorish brother, they'd also be sure that the only reason Corin could possibly have for keeping Aster in his tower and using him would be the satisfying revenge of adding to the family's humiliation and shame.

Aster knew Corin was better than that. He'd even begun to believe that *he* might be better than that—that Corin might want him even if he weren't lonely, desperate, and bored.

But no one else would see it that way. Would the Cezannes even have a reputation and fortune left to save by the time he went home? If the family finances had reached the dire straits Sir Gustave had suggested, then only the Cezanne name and the king's favor would be holding off the creditors. And if their standing at court and in society reached a tipping point...

Aster caught at the sides of the ladder, which swayed horribly—or no, that was vertigo, not the ladder reaching its own tipping point.

He'd been unimaginably selfish, dizzyingly so, waiting here and losing himself in Corin's touch and his kisses and the sound of his voice when every moment counted. It might already be too late, and how had he been so *stupid*? So reckless and irresponsible? Without further delay, he had to go, without allowing Corin to fight his battles for him, without pretending that there would ever be another man at the gate whom he'd be willing to marry.

Another man who'd take him away from Corin and possess him and fuck him, and Aster would lie there in the dark and close his eyes as someone else pounded into him, or be expected to pound into someone else, and it wouldn't matter who. It wouldn't be Corin. The whole court would watch his humiliation. That wouldn't matter either. He wouldn't have Corin.

The man he loved.

The man he'd always loved, although he'd tried so hard to hide it: from himself, from Belinda, from Corin, from anyone who observed them at court.

He couldn't even pretend to hide it from himself anymore, and he doubted he'd been hiding it particularly well from Corin, either.

Distantly, he thought he ought to have been shocked or surprised, that it should've come upon him like some kind of revelation. But it was more like opening a birthday present when you already knew what you'd been given.

He loved Corin, adored him, never wanted to be parted from him. If Corin would only tolerate his presence, he'd spend the rest of his life on his knees.

But he couldn't even beg for that. No matter how foolish his parents had been, he couldn't leave them and his siblings to face the family's ruin, not when he could stop it from happening. Even if he'd been powerless, he'd still have wanted and needed to go home to support his mother as best he could.

He couldn't close his eyes and cover his ears and hide away here on Corin's cock and allow it all to go to hell, allow his home to be sold and his family disgraced.

Sig had said something else loud and probably coarse, and he and Corin were both laughing now. But Aster couldn't have picked out an individual word through the rushing in his ears if his life depended on it.

The gate slammed. The world came back into focus around him so abruptly that Aster jumped, the ladder rocking back for real, this time—and he flailed and barely caught himself, landing against the wall with his heart pounding enough to make his vision jerky.

Below him, Corin dropped the bar across the gate and strode away, calling back, "Come in the hall, I'll make a fire. That was Sig, we've campaigned together four times, and gotten drunk together a hundred more. Can't believe he didn't wait until a decent hour to come to the door, the fucker…" It sounded like Corin might still be muttering about Sig's atrocious manners, but he'd gone around the corner into the hall, and his voice faded.

Aster swallowed hard around the lump in his desert-dry throat.

*I love you. Please take me captive and chain me to your bed so that I can't ever leave.*

Slowly, so slowly, feeling like he'd aged twenty years in the last three minutes, Aster climbed down the ladder and followed Corin down the corridor. He found him stirring up the fire, still buck naked.

"I'm going to make some breakfast," Corin said, "since apparently I'm done fucking sleeping for today, God damn it."

Corin was apparently also an asshole when he got woken up early in the morning.

And he didn't bother with clothes most of the time.

Possibly, the second made up for the first. Or would have, if Aster had meant to stay. He could distantly imagine a life in which he'd simply admire the view and smile tolerantly as Corin stomped around snarling in the morning.

But that life didn't exist and never would.

*I love you. Don't let me go.*

"Would your friend. Sig. Would he hurt me?" The words felt like they bruised his lips as they left. He couldn't ask Corin this, of all people. But he had to, even though his stomach churned and his heart squeezed and his vision blurred. "Would he be a good husband, do you think?"

Corin went still. A moment later he dropped the poker with a clatter that made Aster jump an inch in the air.

"What?" He spun around, and Aster fell back a step despite himself. He'd seen the flicker of Corin's flames in his eyes a dozen times, but never like this. Fire had subsumed his pupils and crept out into his irises, crimson and vermilion. Scales spread over his body in whorling patterns, increasing as Aster watched, rippling down his arms and legs and streaming up his neck. "What did you fucking ask me?"

Aster sucked in as much air as he could, lungs too shallow to hold much at all. "I need to know if Sig would—"

"He's not going to fucking touch you!" Corin's teeth, bared in a snarl, had definitely lengthened. That wasn't Aster's imagination.

Jealousy? It couldn't be, could it? Protectiveness, maybe. Or—God, he wanted it to be jealousy, and he might be sick with longing and frustration and misery.

Except that it didn't matter either way. Even if Corin—he couldn't think about love, because he knew it couldn't be true—cared about him, a little bit at least, Aster still had to be married off to *someone*. Someone willing to bow and scrape to the king, someone who'd want to marry into the nobility and make his fortune. Someone who didn't loathe the Cezanne family with all the hot rage of his dragon's heart.

Corin would almost certainly rather transform permanently into one of the chipmunks who lived in his chimney than kiss the king's ass and marry a Cezanne. Even if he—cared about Aster far more than he did. His pride, and more importantly his self-respect, would never allow it.

Sig and Corin were friends, and Corin wouldn't give any really indecent or dishonorable man that title. Sig wasn't bad looking at all,

though no one compared to Corin. If Aster had to be with him—
and no, he couldn't even think about it after all. With any luck, Sig
might not even want Aster in his bed. Perhaps they could be married
and then ignore one another. If Aster waited for someone equally
likely to come along, he could be waiting for a long time, far longer
than he had to spare.

He lifted his chin and found the courage to look Corin in the
eyes. "Maybe he won't, but that'll be something we'll need to dis-
cuss," he said, voice only wavering a little bit. "Because I think I
ought to follow him down the mountain and tell him I've changed
my mind."

"The hell you will!" Corin took a prowling step forward, then
another, fists clenched. Aster knew those fists would never be used
against him, but it took everything he had in him to stand his ground,
and even more not to fling himself into Corin's arms and scream.
"Fuck," Corin muttered, closing his eyes, shaking his head, sucking
in a deep breath and letting it out as a gust of smoke. "Fuck. Aster.
Listen to me. Not Sig. Someone better will—"

"No, someone bloody well won't," Aster snapped, at the limit
of his patience. His heart was breaking, shattering into tiny shards
with every word they spoke. He had to get this over with. He
wouldn't have the strength to argue against what he wanted for long.
"It should be him. You know him. Tell me he won't hurt me, that he
won't treat me badly, and that's all I need to know. I have to go,
Corin," and his voice cracked on the name. "You know I have to
go."

Corin blinked, his inner eyelids taking a moment to slide out of
sight. When he opened his fists, his palms gleamed with—blood.
Fuck, those were drops of blood ticking against the flagstones, and
claws flashed at the tips of his fingers before they retracted and disappeared.

"That's really what you want?" Corin said, voice thick. "You
want to go with him. Marry him."

No, of course not, and if Corin could ask him that, if he could
even imagine that, then he couldn't care that much about Aster after
all. If he did, he'd know better. "I'm out of time," Aster said. "I've

been—delaying. But Sig's better than the others who've come so far. I need to go," he repeated, praying that if he held to that he'd go through with it.

"Go, then. Follow Sig to the village and fucking go. I need to— I'm not in control, Aster, I have to fly, and if you're going, then it needs to be now."

The air around Corin seemed to vibrate with his pent-up force, his voice dipping lower, his body almost entirely covered in scales. Terror and exhilaration warred inside Aster, nearly tearing him apart, a wild urge to change his mind and beg Corin to stay, to see what would happen. But Corin looked like he was in pain, barely poised between dragon and human. It would be cruel to drag this out.

"Goodbye," he choked out, nearly doubling over with the agony of it.

Corin stared at him for an endless moment, smoke trailing from his nose and mouth, fists clenching again. And then he turned and practically ran out the door to the courtyard.

Aster raced after him. This would almost certainly be the last time he ever saw Corin. One more glimpse of his face, of his eyes. God, he couldn't breathe, and his vision had gone so blurry he wouldn't be able to see anything anyway—

He caught himself against the doorframe just in time to see Corin standing in the middle of the courtyard for an instant, still mostly human. And then wings sprouted from his shoulders faster than the eye could follow, his body lengthening and broadening and gleaming dark green, and an armored tail suddenly stretching across the courtyard—God, he was a *dragon*, right *there*, big enough to almost fill the fucking courtyard that suddenly looked so small. That dragon had kissed him and fucked him and laughed with him and given him a fencing lesson, and he was Corin, and Aster loved him more than he could contain.

As Aster gaped at him, heart pounding and with a twisted knot of arousal and grief and longing in his belly, Corin-the-dragon launched himself into the air with seeming effortlessness despite his huge bulk, massive legs bunching and then all of him going straight up. The first flap of his wings nearly blew Aster off his feet. He caught himself on the wall with one hand, shading his eyes with the other so as to keep Corin in sight for as long as possible.

But he flew so very fast, like an arrow, becoming an eye-wateringly faint speck against the deep blue sky within seconds. And then he was gone. Aster walked out into the middle of the courtyard and tried for a better view, but Corin had truly disappeared.

Corin had flown down to the village twice while Aster had been here. Aster had been asleep both times, though.

Actually watching him fly away and leave him…even on the road here, cold and hungry and panicked, he hadn't had this sense of absolute loss. Loneliness wrapped around him and crushed his ribs. He gazed up at the endless blue until his eyes burned, leaving him dizzy and blinking away bright shadows, struggling to get a full breath.

Corin had gone. When he returned, Aster would be gone. Would he miss him? Would he worry about Aster's future, his safety? Or simply pour himself a glass of brandy and sit by the fire, shaking his head over the whole affair?

Aster would never know. He'd be on the road, soon to be jeered at and mocked by the whole court, dependent on Sig's goodwill.

At least he'd be able to have his mother's arms around him again, and with his head on her shoulder he could sob out his misery in private once he'd run the gauntlet of the court.

He'd never see Corin again.

He ached, in his head and his bones and his heart and soul. His feet felt like leaden lumps at the ends of his legs.

But he moved, one in front of the other, and went to pack his things, harness Etallon, and go.

# Chapter Twenty-One

CORIN LAUNCHED INTO THE air and circled high, high above, far out of range of a human's eyesight.

Leaving him.

Aster was leaving him, now, packing his things and saddling his horse, riding away forever, and the pressure built and built...he let out a ferocious spout of flame, trying to drain the heat inside him, but it hardly made a dent.

Sig couldn't marry Aster, claim him, *take* him.

And yet someone had to, and Sig would be better than most. Aster had wanted reassurance that Sig wouldn't hurt him; Corin could've given it freely if he'd been in his right mind, rather than enveloped in a pounding haze of furious red. Sig might be a hard-drinking scoundrel who'd risk his own ass on a throw of the dice, but he'd never risk anyone else's. Aster would be safe with him, and if he said no, Sig would shrug and find his amusement elsewhere.

Aster might not want to say no. If Corin pleased him, Sig might too. They were somewhat of a type: big, broad-shouldered men of the sword, dark haired and rough.

He spiraled up and up, beating his wings hard against the thinning air, gaining another thousand feet, pushing his body until even his dragon lungs labored and rasped. He twirled to his back to stare up at the sky, which had deepened from blue to navy at this altitude, with stars peeping through the nothingness. Diamonds scattered on plush velvet, cold and loveless.

It didn't help, it didn't help one fucking bit, and he spun down and plummeted, wings folded, scales heating from his speed, pulling himself out of the dive and swooping back up at last with another gout of flame and a flick of his tail.

Sig couldn't bloody well do *that*, now, could he? Of course, that might be a point in his favor. Fucking damn it.

Corin glided down just low enough to be out of human sight but to keep a clear view of the path from his tower to the village. Watching Aster ride away might make him sick, but he had to; someone else might be coming up the mountain to issue a challenge, and Corin had to make sure Aster made it safely to the village and found Sig first. Because that was what Aster wanted.

He wanted that. Not Corin.

Of course he valued his family's well-being over Corin, but…

Fuck.

Corin took another circle. No one coming up for now…but there. There, one rider making his way down. Even if Corin's vision hadn't been able to pick out the finer details, to see the red-gold glint of the sun on Aster's shining hair, Corin would've known him by that little hitch in his breath when Aster came into view.

As he watched, Aster turned his head and looked over his shoulder. Etallon faltered as if his rider had pulled the reins too tight.

And then Aster tipped his head back and looked up. Right at Corin, it felt like, although he knew he couldn't possibly be seen against the glare of the sky. What would happen if he swooped down and transformed, tugged Aster off his horse and into his arms? Kissed him senseless. Threw him over his shoulder and carried him right back up the mountain?

Or skipped a step and scooped him up in his claws and took him far over the mountains and to another kingdom after all, somewhere they could live anonymously, without a single Cezanne or knight-adventurer or king or duke to trouble them.

Aster turned his attention back to the path and nudged Etallon into a trot. He didn't look back again.

Corin flew over Aster until he reached the bottom of the path, taking one lower circle as they both approached the village. In front of the inn, he spotted a familiar figure sprawled on a bench, dark head tipped back against the wall and booted feet propped in front of him. Another circle, and Aster had ridden into the inn yard, dismounting and tossing his reins to a lad who ran out from the stable. Two men at the side of the yard set down whatever they were holding—tankards of ale, perhaps. They stepped forward, gesturing, and Corin didn't need to hear anything to know they were saying something like, *That's him, that's Lord Aster.*

All of Corin's muscles went tense, from his snout to the tip of his tail, and he flexed his claws and poised himself to shoot down to the ground like a thunderbolt.

But Sig had gotten to his feet and crossed the yard, placing himself—too fucking close, that was where. Right where Corin ought to be fucking standing, between Aster and anything bothering him.

There were more gestures, a few hands on sword hilts, a very clear pantomime from Sig of *He's mine, boys, back the fuck off or you'll regret it.*

Corin's line in the play. Except that he'd walked off stage and left the role to his fucking understudy.

Aster stood still in the midst of it. Even at this distance Corin could see the slight hunch to his shoulders.

His unhappiness.

Fucking bloody fuck, but Corin needed to…

Except that he didn't, because the two assholes sullenly backed off, and Aster and Sig spoke for a moment and then turned, together, and walked into the inn. Corin stared down until he almost saw double from the strain.

Aster didn't look up and he didn't look back. One last gleam of sunlight on his hair, and he was gone.

"WE'LL TRAVEL BY SEA," SIG said as he poured more ale. "Much faster that way, and we won't run into anyone who wants to kill me and claim the reward for himself."

He reminded Aster of Corin, a little. The same total confidence in his own judgment, the same broad shoulders and loose-limbed stride, the same easy, natural way of handling weapons and armor. A soldier, in short, and an intelligent and skilled one, even if Sig's manners could be rough.

But no one else in the world, no matter how tall and handsome and brave and strong he appeared to everyone else, could possibly live up to Corin's…everything. Sig was a pale shadow of the man

Aster loved.

Not to mention that Sig referred to Aster and his marriage portion so casually and collectively as "the reward." Aster meant nothing to him as a person, something that Sig's total lack of malice or cruelty didn't cover in the slightest.

Aster nodded, toying with his own cup, not even bothering to correct Sig's dismissive language or to look up from the scarred surface of the taproom table. He wished the herald had stayed downstairs to keep the conversation going. But when Sig had asked him for his congratulations the fellow had sniffed haughtily, glared, and muttered something about going to pack his things. Aster still didn't know his name.

Not that he cared.

Sig laughed, said something that sounded vaguely friendly and encouraging, possibly even sympathetic. Aster didn't really pay attention, but he did attempt a smile. After all, he'd be marrying this man.

But that felt so distant, so hazy. Everything did: the taste of the ale, the chaotic noise of the taproom, people coming and going, the chair beneath him, the future, as if every one of his senses had gone simultaneously numb. He'd never have imagined that his vision and hearing and intellect were things capable of being numb...and yet.

When Sig said it was time to go, he went. They rode out of the village toward the sea, the midafternoon sun roasting the tops of their heads and starting to tip down enough to glare in their eyes. Only eight hours or so earlier, Aster had been in Corin's bed. Ten hours earlier, he'd been pinned with a muscular arm across his chest, held immobile and helpless while Corin filled him for the third time since they'd retired for the night.

He hadn't been numb then. Every breath, every heartbeat, every thrust of Corin's cock had been vivid and sharp. Corin's whispered praise still echoed in his ears. It almost drowned out the clop of three sets of hoofbeats, the wind in the trees, the herald's grumbled complaints, and Sig's admonitions to shut up and stop being such a pain in the ass.

At least Aster had a good memory. He could hold on to every word Corin had ever spoken to him, the sensation of every touch.

The journey to the coast took all of that day, with a stop that night at a roadside tavern with good ale and terrible beds, and nearly a full second day. An hour or so before sunset they reined up on top of a gentle hill overlooking a prosperous little seaside town with the glittering water like sprinkled shards of crystal beyond. The brisk scent of salt and the distant cries of gulls roused his mind from its stupor, and he dearly wished they hadn't. Misery rushed in to fill the space left by his detached indifference. He blinked at the twinkling ocean and the rosy glare of the horizon, his head starting to throb.

Reflexively, Aster glanced up, twisting to each side to get a view of as much of the sky as he could. Empty, as it had been the whole journey. He'd made sure Sig and Jules, whose name he'd learned at last, weren't watching him—but he'd looked as often as he thought he could get away with it.

Once, a faint outline against the sky had set his heart pounding, instantly and painfully, as if his ribs would burst. It was only a cloud, the shape of which had resembled a spread pair of wings at first glance. Every passing shadow had made his breath catch. But none of them had been Corin swooping down and...

At that point in the fantasy, Aster's power of imagination broke down. Perhaps he simply had too much dull practicality in his nature. But he'd gone with Sig for a reason, that reason still existed, and all of Corin's reasons for staying where Aster had left him remained in force too.

Sig nudged his horse into motion, and Aster and Jules followed him down the hill.

Before long they'd passed through the town and Aster was dismounting at the docks, stiff and exhausted and wincing as he swung his leg over. The number of times he'd been knotted open before he set off on this journey...but that ache would fade all too soon, and the pain of missing it would be much greater.

Sig had asked questions as they went along the waterfront and eventually led them to one of the larger ships in the harbor, one bound for the capital that had room to bring their mounts aboard. Aster stood staring blankly at the ripples in the water as Sig negotiated for their passage. Throwing himself in might work. He'd have to wait until they were under way, of course. Aster knew how to swim perfectly well, and that reflex would kick in and bring him right back to the dock if he jumped here. And anyway, someone would dive in after him. Out in the open sea, a rescue effort wouldn't be likely to succeed even if someone tried.

He could cry out and stumble first, make it look like he'd slipped. Surely the king wouldn't force his parents to pay Marellus's absurd penalty if Aster died accidentally on his way back to make things right. Theobert had always been reasonable, his marriage-decree-related foray into idiocy notwithstanding.

A cleared throat made Aster start and whip his head around.

Jules stood a couple of feet away, shoulders hunched and cloak wrapped tightly around his thin body against the damp chill of the ocean breeze. He gazed steadily at Aster out of his pretty jade-green eyes, usually flashing with annoyance but at the moment more serious than Aster had seen them.

"That won't solve anything," he said. His lips flattened into a line. "You'd really rather that than be married to Sig? I mean, of course it's a dreadful fate, the man's an animal. He ought to come with a warning sign so that anyone with discrimination and taste can run away. But it won't be so bad, I'm sure. Not that bad."

Aster blinked, shook his head, and stared.

How the hell had Jules known…? And as for the rest of that, he'd contradicted himself several times, and seemed to be protesting maybe a little too much to be believed.

Damn it, Jules *knew*. Aster's cheeks went red-hot against the creeping evening fog.

"I'm not—I don't know what you mean, solve anything," he stammered. "I was just standing here."

Jules tugged his cloak tighter and scowled. "The hell you were," he said flatly. "You shouldn't do that. But you also shouldn't marry someone you don't care about."

"Maybe you should be telling Sig that," Aster snapped.

"Maybe I already did, and he didn't listen!" Jules clamped his mouth shut and glanced around shiftily, as if he'd only just realized how loud he'd been. "Anyway, what do you think would happen to him if he showed up without you to report that he'd lost you at sea? He has some human decency. He'd tell your parents what happened, not disappear and forget about it like some men would."

Fucking hell, Aster hadn't even thought of that. If the king did void the penalty out of sympathy, Marellus would very possibly take out his anger on Sig. Not to mention Aster's father would be looking for someone to blame.

Damn it all.

"You're right," he said, with a faint sense of relief mingled with the regret. "He'd be in so much trouble." Giving up the one idea he'd had for escaping his dull, pointless, miserable future didn't bother him as much as he might have thought. In fact, he couldn't really bring himself to care one way or the other.

On the other hand, Jules had been such a pain in the ass. "Maybe I will, maybe I won't," he added.

"Humph," Jules sniffed, and turned his head away, gazing out across the water. The very last periwinkle-gray remnants of sunset washed everyone out, but Jules looked pale and unhappy on top of that.

Aster couldn't pretend to have more than the average sensitivity to other people's feelings, but even he couldn't miss the fact that when he married Sig, Aster wouldn't be the only one made miserable.

That didn't make him feel any better.

Damn it, pain in the ass or not... "I'm sorry," he said.

Jules's cheeks flushed dark, and he turned back, eyes boring into Aster. "Don't apologize for being pretty and rich," he hissed. "It's hypocritical and incredibly annoying."

With that he spun on his heel, nose in the air, and whisked away down the dock.

Pretty and rich? He had almost no money of his own, and pretty? Only the most powerful jealousy could account for anyone thinking that. For fuck's sake. No matter what, he'd be ruining everyone's lives.

Aster stared out at the darkening horizon until his eyes burned, until everything vanished into the same gloomy blur.

No way out presented itself.

At last, Aster slowly turned and went to the ship. He couldn't avoid his future. He could only face it with his head held high. Perhaps Corin would hear about it and be proud of him.

And perhaps he'd never think about Aster again.

# Chapter Twenty-Two

CORIN CLOSED HIS EYES, giving in to being half asleep. Well, all right, more in a brandy-assisted stupor, lying on his back in the courtyard entirely naked. A warm wind had been sweeping through the canyon all evening, rattling and rustling everything about. Before that it'd been sunny. And before that, dark...but none of it mattered much. Three days. Three days, he'd been alone. Aster had gone off to get fucking married to stupid fucking Sig.

Another image of Aster on his hands and knees with Sig behind him flashed through his mind. One of many.

Damn it, he didn't care if Aster fucked everyone in the kingdom. He couldn't.

His fingertips itched and stung as his claws did their best to push through. More brandy. Another bottle might do the trick. Or two, he'd brought a whole case from the village the other day. Yesterday? Who the fuck cared.

The tower had been lonely before, and dull.

Now it felt like it pressed in on him, its weight far greater than that of its stone and metal components. Even when he stayed outside, like now. It didn't matter. He could hardly breathe. He'd had a great deal of brandy, but it couldn't possibly be enough to numb this constant ache. Aster's laughter rang through the hall, his cries of pleasure permeated the bedroom. The softness in those beautiful blue eyes as Aster's gaze rested on Corin's face...

Out of the darkness came a sound: the soft beat of a pair of wings.

Corin cracked his eyelids open in time to see a smaller piece of blackness resolve out of the night. A crow landed directly on his chest, cocked his head, opened his beak, and let out a huffing series of caws with a familiar cadence to it.

Corin blinked at him. "Are you fucking laughing at me, you little bastard?" The crow hopped back a couple of steps, digging one set of talons into Corin's lower belly. "Feathers burn, you son of a—oh, hell," he said, as the crow lifted his other foot to show the paper tied to his leg. "Hold still."

The crow obligingly didn't move while Corin tugged the string loose and got the letter free.

"Rawk!" he said, and lowered his foot to dig both sets of talons in.

Corin sighed and yielded to the inevitable. "There's leftover bread and ham in there," he said, pointing at the door to the fort.

The crow clacked his beak and flapped off, landing by the door and stalking inside as if he bloody well owned the place.

"Well, fuck you too," Corin muttered—quietly, because while he might be a dragon who feared no one, that didn't mean he wanted to clean bird shit off of everything he owned. Crows weren't known for their good manners at the best of times, unless you were considered a friend and had an endless supply of snacks. And even the most self-righteous and ornery of wild crows couldn't compare to a witch's trained messenger.

They were even more intelligent than the average crow, and they had all the confidence of beings whose best friends could curse and destroy anyone who ruffled their feathers.

And their services were wildly expensive. Whoever had sent this letter wanted to reach Corin urgently.

Fucking hell. He sat up, blinked, and summoned his flames, twisting his neck and shooting them up into the sky, roaring as much as his human throat could roar. It burned the brandy out of him, magic surging through his veins and nerves and searing him clean.

It hurt like hell, but when he curled over his knees, panting, his head had cleared as much as he'd hoped. Letters sent this way never had good news. He needed his wits about him.

He broke the seal, tipping the paper to catch the meager light of the quarter moon—enough for his dragon eyes.

A glance at the signature told him nothing:

*Jules Aranceur*

*Sir Corin:*

*You know me as the gentleman who accompanied Sir Sigmund on his visit to your abode, if one may call it such. At present, I continue to accompany him and Lord Aster of Cezanne on a journey to see the king. Within the hour we embark upon a ship whose accommodations I will not describe, because the mere thought of them wounds my sensibilities. I've paid a local witch (I will leave her name and direction below) a small consideration to see this letter delivered to you with all haste, and have promised her that you will substantially augment this sum when you arrive here at the port.*

"Oh, like hell I will," Corin muttered, but a strange and horrible tightening sensation had started to creep through his chest, something he'd never really experienced before. He thought it might be crippling anxiety. Possibly even terror.

*Without further ado, I feel it my duty to inform you that I interrupted Lord Aster a little while ago in serious contemplation of the water of the harbor. When I urged him not to consider the sea as a means of escape from his troubles, he admitted that had been his thought. He declined to promise not to consider it again.*

*We will be traveling across a deep and occasionally rough stretch of ocean, Sir Corin. And I can't watch Lord Aster every moment of the day and night.*

*With all respect, you're a fool, and an idiot, and also a selfish tosser.*

*No one wants Lord Aster to marry Sir Sigmund. I'd have said least of all you based on even our very short acquaintance, because you have all the subtlety of a foul-smelling boot kicking a fellow in the head, but I'm beginning to think it's actually Lord Aster who wants it least of all, and that he will find another way out if none is presented to him.*

*Jules Aranceur*

> *Madame Lizette*
> *Orchid Alley*
> *You owe her a lot of money, Sir Corin. Don't be cheap,*
> *or she'll give us both boils in awkward places. And you*
> *owe* _me_ *a fucking trumpet. Asshole.*

Despite this feeling being completely new, Corin found that it was unmistakable: yes, definitely terror. The bone-chilling, nauseating kind. Corin had seen human men in this state: pale as milk, drenched in sudden cold sweat, wobbly on their watery knees.

Corin physically couldn't turn white. And he couldn't sweat. But it was a damn lucky thing that he hadn't stood up before reading the letter.

Aster standing at the railing of a ship, gazing down, swaying with the motion of the wind and waves, bracing himself…and then not troubling to brace himself at all. He'd fall like a cut flower, eyes closing, red-blond hair disappearing beneath frothy green, one pale hand reaching…and then nothing but the cold and the dark and the nothingness of the depths of the sea.

Corin swallowed down bile, the letter crumpling in his fist, closing his eyes for a moment against a wave of vertigo.

He'd thought that washing himself with fire had given him clarity. More than that, he'd been operating under the assumption, natural to a man with a fair share of intellect and generally dependable judgment, that he knew what he wanted, what was important to him, what he could and couldn't tolerate.

It had been clear to him that he couldn't possibly apologize to the king for embarrassing him by cutting up the face of that idiot. He couldn't possibly announce to the world that he'd been stupid enough to fall under the spell of not only one Cezanne—who'd humiliated him so thoroughly they'd still be laughing about it next century—but her brother, too. He couldn't shake hands with Lord Cezanne, smile, and ask his permission to marry his son, this time.

Corin would rather die.

But he wasn't the one whose life hung in the balance. And that life meant more to him than his own. More than his hoard. By comparison, he'd fling his sword into the deepest basin of the sea without a thought.

He opened his eyes and stared out at the night. The courtyard parapet, each stone as sharp as if it'd been limned with diamonds. The stars, piercingly bright.

No, the world had never been clear before.

Now, it had become so blindingly simple, like the moment before a battle when the planning and strategy had been gotten out of the way and all that was left was to level his spear and charge.

Corin's heart raced more than it ever had before a battle, though. He wouldn't use the word *frantic*. Or *panic*. That would be...unbecoming of his dignity as a dragon and a knight. Neither knights nor dragons lost their nerve under pressure. They remained cool-headed and focused.

He sprang to his feet and strode for the door. Under other circumstances, not knowing how long he'd be gone, he'd have taken his hoard with him. As a second, barely acceptable option, he'd have hidden it in a cave in the eastern peaks, somewhere that no human could reach—dragons never touched each other's hoards without permission, not unless they wanted to be hunted, ostracized, and disowned.

In this case, the cellar would do. The chest had misdirection magic on it, so good enough.

Aster would be halfway to the capital by now; by sea, the journey took less than three days, and the scrawled date in the corner of the letter had been yesterday's.

If he'd made it that far, of course.

He had. He must have, because Corin would find him either way. He'd told Aster that water didn't douse a dragon's flames—but that was relative. If Corin dived from the zenith, plummeting down, down, wings folded, at a speed and from a height that would level a small city from the impact, he'd plunge hundreds of feet into the water before he even slowed. He might not suffocate or be crushed in the depths, not for a long time, anyway. But his flames would flicker and die. He'd sink slowly, drifting to the ocean floor, appearing to be nothing more than a strangely shaped rock to the fish that'd swim uncuriously by and the little barnacles that'd make their homes on his scales. Before long he'd be no more than the stone from which his kind had sprung.

He might not find Aster, precisely. But he'd be as close as he could get.

No. Aster had to be on that ship, worried and afraid and lonely, perhaps, but safe and well.

Waiting for Corin, whether he knew it or not. And Corin would come.

Carrying the chest down to the cellar took very slightly longer than it should have due to the crow flapping beside his head and squawking what sounded like suggestions for how he ought to get it around the turn of the stairs, but at last he shoved it into a corner. He didn't bother to open it. Even Giant Dick could stay here. If he needed a sword, he'd find one. Carrying anything would only slow him down.

The same went for clothes. If anyone had a problem with him naked, they could fucking complain to the king—or to Corin's face, if they dared.

He stopped only long enough to dump a bucket of water over the hearth so that the embers couldn't blow about and burn the place down, and then he stepped outside, spread his arms, and transformed as he leapt into the air. His wings caught the wind, bearing him up a thousand feet in an instant.

Corin wheeled to the west. Salt tickled his nose, borne on the air currents that swept in from the ocean at this altitude. He beat his wings against the buffeting in time with the pounding of his heart, flying faster than any bird, any arrow, any stone flung from the greatest catapult. Nothing on earth or above it could travel as fast as a dragon in a desperate hurry.

Corin would be in time to save Aster from everything that threatened his safety and his peace of mind. He had to be.


ASTER PULLED HIS HOOD down to hide his face despite the heat, praying he'd remain unobserved and unrecognized at least until they reached the palace gates. The crowded streets would help, anyway. It seemed to be market day, with wagons full of produce rumbling over the cobblestones in every direction and making a dreadful din. After the silence of the mountains and the sea voyage, it gave Aster an almost instant headache.

Jules, riding beside him, leaned down to peer under his hood. "You're more conspicuous like that rather than less," Jules said nastily. "And no one gives a fuck about you anyway. Do you really think the average fellow on the street would care one way or the other?"

Aster did his best to ignore both him and Sig, who'd hardly spoken a word all day but glowered and sulked more loudly and obtrusively than anyone Aster had ever met. He'd had enough rum the night before to have put any three mercenaries on—or maybe even under—the ground, but he seemed steady enough, so clearly he could hold both his liquor and his hangover.

Except for being a total asshole, of course.

"No one gives a fuck about you either," Sig growled, breaking his silence at last, tugging his reins irritably and making his horse shy around a wagon full of onions. "Why don't you fuck off? We're back in the city. You're home. Go away."

"And miss the show?" Jules hissed. "Not on your disgusting, pathetic life. Besides, you still owe me a trumpet when you get paid! And you owe me more than that, you—"

Aster spurred Etallon forward, desperately not wanting to hear what Sig owed Jules. The sun beat down with force, his shoulders drooping forward under the strain and his head light and floaty.

Or maybe that was fear and worry and grief and exhaustion.

Or all of the above. No reason to limit himself to one form of crippling misery.

He'd spent most of his time on the three-day voyage gazing down at the sea speeding by, letting the slap of the waves against the hull toss spray into his face. Every time he closed his eyes, he saw Corin. He could almost feel his arms around him. It didn't do anything about the cold. The thought of diving off the side of the ship into the frigid, endless water left him even colder, and although he could still see the appeal…he couldn't do it. Terror overwhelmed even his despair, his human instinct to live no matter what reasserting itself.

He'd also caught Jules watching him throughout the day and sometimes at night, too, as if the fellow genuinely cared.

That had touched him more than he expected.

Not that it made the constant rudeness and insults and complaints any more pleasant. Jules had been horrid aboard the ship, but upon coming ashore he'd become even worse, impossible though it might've seemed. He'd dragged his feet, looked around the dock, muttered imprecations under his breath—and over it—and finally mounted up only when Sig threatened to hogtie him over his mule.

And he still hadn't stopped: "…going to end up offending the king, or committing some terrible faux pas. Really, it'd be better for all of us if you let me do the talking—"

At that, Aster's severely frayed nerves snapped at last. He stopped Etallon and wheeled him around, nearly clipping someone's giant basket of turnips. He glared at Jules, and something in his face must have been more intimidating than usual, because the herald's flow of words stopped like he'd been silenced with magic. Sig raised one eyebrow and reined his horse to a halt.

"I'm the one being summoned back to court," Aster said quietly, his voice somehow carrying over the din around them. "This has nothing to do with you, Jules. It's not about Sig, either, really. He's an instrument of another man's will, either the king's or Marellus's or my father's, it doesn't matter. This is going to be awful and humiliating enough without some self-aggrandizing blowhard inserting himself into the proceedings. Do you understand?"

Jules's mouth tightened, and he looked down, cheeks reddening. "I understand," he said after a moment.

Sig said nothing, but the glance he shot at Jules said everything: a flash of pain and confusion and desire, gone almost before it could be seen. Aster's heart sank even further, something he'd thought would be impossible. Sig claimed to want nothing but money, but not even he would be happy at the end of this.

Aster turned, nudged Etallon back into a walk, and set off for the palace again.

Another quarter hour of weaving their way through throngs of market-goers brought them out of the southern side of the city, through a quieter commercial district, and into the neighborhoods near to the palace, where the gentry and nobility had their town-houses and walled gardens. Bougainvillea in every color from cream to apricot to crimson to the deepest royal purple spilled over white-washed walls, and broad, clean boulevards held far fewer passersby.

But few were still enough. A trio of gentlemen riding by paused, stared, and laughed as Aster and his companions passed. One of them spurred away, clattering off up the street. Two ladies leaned out of their carriage, one of whom Aster thought might be a friend of his brother's. She twisted about and said something to her servants at the back of the carriage.

A moment later, a footman hopped down and bustled away.

A few would be more than enough, in fact.

Because by the time they rode through the temple plaza that occupied a huge space to the east of the palace, a small crowd had gathered: priests, ladies, gentlemen, and servants all cheek-by-jowl in their eagerness to see the show. The palace gates stood open as they always did; King Theobert believed in making himself accessible to his subjects. But the gates were far more heavily guarded than usual. Half the garrison had turned out to watch, apparently.

Fucking bloody fucking hell. This was a nightmare.

For one hopeless, desperate moment, Aster squeezed his eyes shut, hands clenched on Etallon's reins, belly twisted into a knot. Corin. He needed Corin at his side, his strength and his confidence and his ability to make this entire mob slink away in terror with one look and one hand on his sword hilt.

Aster opened his eyes, ignoring the burning ache in his chest and the sting of gathering tears. His hood wouldn't hide him now, and it'd only make him look ashamed.

Fuck it. Aster was a Cezanne, a gentleman, a knight, and he'd done nothing wrong.

He sat up straight in the saddle and threw back the hood, lifting his chin and staring out over the heads of the whispering, giggling crowd as if he couldn't even see them.

Aster rode through the palace gates with his head held high, Sig and Jules following in his wake. He paid no attention to anyone but the captain of the guard at the gate, whom he favored with a lordly nod. He could do this with only Sig and Jules to back him up. He didn't need anyone else's courage to bolster his own. He could face the king, and his parents, and Marellus, and Dericort, and every sneering, jeering courtier in the kingdom, and a future as a laughingstock married to an insignificant soldier who didn't love or even want him, and the man he loved far away and forgetting all about him and not caring enough in the first place to come with him now.

His hands shook and his lungs couldn't quite fill. Everything went a little numb around the edges, blurry and dim.

But he rode on until they reached the courtyard where the king's guests could leave their horses, and he dismounted, and he thought he probably gave some answer to the senior servant who greeted him, telling him that Sig and Jules were with him. They'd already made themselves as clean and neat as possible before disembarking, so they didn't need to stop.

The palace corridors held more satin-clad lords and ladies, more servants, more whispers, the bows and greetings of grinning acquaintances, a gauntlet to be run. Sweat broke out on Aster's forehead and trickled down his spine as he bowed and murmured replies, as he forced one foot in front of the other.

"It's Lord Aster," someone said, and another replied, "Which one do you think he'll marry?" and yet a third muttered, "Depends on whether he wants to be able to walk the next day, I suppose," and then a series of titters followed Aster and his burning cheeks down the hall.

The din of voices grew louder as he approached the throne room. A large hall served as an antechamber, with a great carved door in between. They stopped a few feet away under the glittering eyes of yet another group of lords and petitioners and officials. Aster stared straight ahead. He couldn't feel his hands and feet. Two liveried officers of the court at the door leaned in and spoke to their escort, and then one of them nodded and stepped through into the throne room.

Sig moved to stand by Aster's side, and Aster glanced up to find Sig gazing down at him with more steady, serious sympathy in his rugged face than Aster would've thought him capable of. He did his best to smile, but he could barely manage a twitch of the lips.

"If it please Your Majesty!" came from the throne room, the officer's sonorous voice ringing and echoing. "Sir Sigmund, a knight of this realm, requests an audience as Lord Aster of Cezanne's escort!"

The throne room instantly burst into an ear-splitting hubbub. "Fuck," Sig said, drawing a stern look from the servant who'd brought them here. "I didn't think they'd care this much."

Aster's vision went dim, fading in and out in big spots. Oh, God, he'd faint, right here in front of everyone.

And then distant screaming cut through the noise of the court. Shouts of alarm, cries of fear and awe, and…

"Did someone say a dragon?" Sig demanded. "You have to be fucking kidding me."

# Chapter Twenty-Three

HEEDLESS OF PROTOCOL OR the people in his way, Aster shoved his way past the distracted ceremonial guards. The palace had been built around an enormous central courtyard garden, and even larger, gilded double doors opened onto it from the throne room, allowing in the air and the sunshine. No one stopped Aster as he sprinted across the throne room toward the courtyard. They were all either running away or running to the doors themselves to see what was going on.

Aster skidded to a stop on the expanse of marble just outside the door above a broad set of shallow steps leading down into the courtyard. The sun blinded him for a moment, reflecting off of those steps and the glittering white gravel paths. A dreadful din assaulted him, the shrieks of a whole garden full of panicking courtiers and servants. He shaded his eyes with his hand and stared up, chest so tight he could hardly breathe.

A shadow passed over the garden and an ear-splitting roar shook the air.

But he couldn't see…

And then he saw. Circling in from the north and silhouetted against the sun, there was the unmistakable shape of giant bat-like wings, a long tail, and a graceful neck and massive horned head.

A dragon.

Aster's heart stopped, thudded agonizingly, and then galloped into motion again.

Corin. It had to be Corin. Here for him? He couldn't believe it. If he believed it, he might hope. No, he had to have some other reason for returning, didn't he?

Corin wheeled in the air, his shadow passing over the courtyard twice more, great wings flapping and blowing Aster's hair about as he swooped down. The roses bowed their bright blooms, hats flew away, and more cries rose up as everyone who'd been taking the air in the garden scattered and ran like a kicked anthill.

Aster hadn't understood why he'd been circling, but now he did: Corin had to keep terrifying them until they got the hell out of the way and left him a clear area to land.

Sig and Jules both ran up beside him, Sig shouldering a velvet-clad gentleman aside to make room.

"Fucking shit," Sig said. "What a goddamn asshole. He could've saved me the trouble by simply coming with us in the first place. He's paying me back for our passage on that ship. And the trumpet, Jules."

Jules muttered something that sounded like, "Oh my God, it worked."

But Aster didn't care enough to ask what the hell that meant. He could only gaze up, frozen and breathless. The others might be afraid. He wasn't—or if he did have any fear, it was that he'd run to Corin and fling himself on him and weep and beg as soon as he touched the ground. Or break his nose and scream at him for letting him go, irrational as that might be.

Perhaps both.

The center of the courtyard had cleared out at last, and Corin took advantage, landing with a thump that traveled up through the stones and Aster's legs and lodged somewhere under his breastbone. Corin shook his big head, whuffed, and let out a plume of smoke from his massive muzzle. Even if Aster had seen dozens of dragons, he didn't think any of them would've compared to Corin's gleaming green scales, like polished malachite in the sun, or his mesmerizing eyes, black on black with the faintest ring of amber around the outside of the iris. Those claws had to be at least eight inches long. No wonder everyone had run away, although Aster could hear relieved-sounding murmurs of, "It's only Sir Corin!" from the crowd that had formed around the edges of the garden.

With a great shrug of his shoulders, Corin folded his wings, laying them neatly along his sides. A flick of his great spiked tail knocked a stone bench into a lily pond with a splash.

Aster blinked, and when he opened his eyes again he'd almost missed the transformation: Corin's body shrinking, the scales fading into skin, hair reappearing and claws melting into fingers. He looked small, almost, standing there in the middle of the courtyard: an illusion born of contrast.

A new chorus of gasps and cries rose from the audience.

One particularly brave fellow stepped forward. Aster recognized him as Lord Bertram, a notable swordsman who knew Corin well. He bowed, sweeping off his plumed hat.

"Sir Corin!" Bertram cried. "You've returned! Welcome to…" His voice trailed off as Corin ignored him completely, keeping his eyes fixed on the top of the stairs.

On Aster. The weight of his gaze hit him like a hammer, nearly dropping him to his knees. He was too far away to be sure, of course, but still…he knew that Corin looked only at him. He knew it, because he couldn't look away either, and everything else in the world had faded into meaningless background.

Behind him, he heard a new commotion: familiar voices, including his father's and Marellus's, and then a sharp command in the voice of the king himself. Apparently Theobert had brought everyone out to see Corin's arrival.

But he didn't turn his head. He couldn't, because the only important thing in the world was in front of him. Corin came closer, the air between them seeming to ring like a note struck in a crystal goblet, a golden vibration that sucked all the oxygen out of Aster's lungs and left him poised, quivering, helpless.

Any other man would've looked absurd coming up the palace steps naked and unarmed.

But Corin was no mere man. And a dragon, with flashing fiery eyes and the ripple of scales beneath his skin and intent in every prowling motion, looked anything but absurd. He took Aster's breath away.

By the gasps from the crowd, he had the same effect on everyone else.

Well, too fucking bad for them. Because Corin walked straight up to Aster, not even seeming to see the king or anyone else.

He stopped only a foot away, close enough for Aster to feel the heat of his body. Aster sucked in a deep, gulping breath and caught the heady scent of fire-scorched spices. God, no, he couldn't possibly get hard standing here, could he? Apparently he could. He'd worn loose trousers, maybe that would be enough. Although he found that he couldn't care all that much. Everyone might see how much of a slut he was for Sir Corin, dragon knight—well, let them. Aster would do anything for Corin without any shame at all. Drop to his knees here on the steps for example, and let everyone be jealous of how Aster was the one Corin desired.

Corin's stony expression didn't give much away, although a muscle ticked in his cheek. And the intense heat in his eyes as they rested on Aster's face left him breathless.

Corin reached out a hand, still without a word, and cupped the side of Aster's face, thumb stroking over his cheekbone.

"You're all right," Corin said at last, in a deep, vibrating growl that had far more dragon than human in the way he shaped the words, as if his vocal cords hadn't shifted back completely when he changed forms. "You're—I was afraid I wouldn't be in time."

"Afraid," Aster repeated, unable to believe he'd heard that right. And having trouble processing any information at all, given the searing perfection of Corin's hand against his skin and the way every cell in his body strained toward that point of contact, toward Corin. "You've never been afraid in your life. Besides, you let me go!"

That last came out much more plaintive and pathetic than he'd meant it to—especially since he hadn't meant to say it in the first place.

Corin's brows drew together. "Aster, I—"

"Sir Corin," a strident voice cut in extremely loudly. "The king requires your attention!"

Corin glanced up. "Not now," he said sharply, returning his eyes to Aster's face. "Aster, I couldn't—"

"The king, sir! You will attend to the king!" the voice said again, and then Aster's father's familiar voice added, "Aster, at once!"

Bloody blast and damn it. Aster wanted to hear what Corin had been about to say more than he wanted his next breath. Turning took more effort than a motion ever had; he had to move away from

Corin's hand on his cheek, which felt like amputating one of his own limbs.

But he turned. And he found a tableau behind him that made him freeze in horror.

The king, flanked by Sir Gustave—who'd taken a step forward and had obviously been the one speaking—and several of his other close advisors on the one side, and by Marellus, Dericort, and Aster's father on the other. Everyone else had wisely gotten the hell out of the way, except for Sig and Jules, who'd been hemmed in by the guards and stood eyeing the exits longingly.

King Theobert radiated royal authority, from his flowing purple velvet robes to his neatly trimmed salt and pepper beard to the golden circlet in his hair to the stern expression on his strong-featured face. In company with the eldest princess, who was about his age, Aster had once run screaming down the halls of the palace, dodging behind priceless vases and polished antiques as the king chased them pretending to be a hungry tiger. Theobert had tickled them when he caught them, and then sent for strawberries and lemonade. Aster tried to focus on that long-ago memory, because otherwise he might have simply collapsed to the ground and started to beg for mercy.

And then Corin shifted slightly, moving closer. And he wasn't afraid anymore.

Marellus glanced between the two of them, raising his eyebrows, a nasty smirk on his handsome face, Dericort sneering beside him. Aster's father glared at him, his face nearly purple. All three of the Cezanne children resembled their mother, blond and pale, while Lord Cezanne had the look of an angry bulldog at the best of times. Right now he seemed to be straining at the leash.

Fuck, maybe Aster was still afraid after all.

"My apologies, Your Majesty," Corin said, with extremely ill grace. "My concern for Aster's safety—"

"My son's safety is no concern of yours!" Aster's father interrupted him explosively, as if he could no longer contain himself. "My family is no concern of yours. How you dare to show your face—"

"Enough," the king said, his tone extremely mild and all the more threatening for it, and Aster's father sputtered into silence. "Sir Corin, explain yourself."

"I was trying to explain myself to Aster first," Corin snapped, and then added belatedly, "Sire."

"If it please Your Majesty, I don't think there will be time for that before the joyous wedding bells ring out. I believe this…individual," Marellus said, waving a languid hand at Sig, "has claimed Lord Aster, has he not?"

Sig opened his mouth, and so did Jules, and then Sig slapped a hand over Jules's mouth, and God, this would be a disaster—

"No, I have," Corin said, and wrapped his arm around Aster's waist to yank him close.

For a moment the world stopped spinning and came to a jolting halt, even as everyone else erupted into a chorus of questions and protests and complaints, with Aster's father shouting and Marellus arguing, something about the proclamation and Corin not fitting its requirements, and Sir Gustave scolding them all.

Aster gaped up at Corin. "But you—you—"

Corin turned his head and met Aster's eyes, vermilion flames dancing in the depths of his own. "You deserve better," he said, very low, for Aster's ears only. "And I wish I could give it to you. But I only have myself to offer." His arm around Aster's waist might as well have been forged from steel. "Will you take me?"

Take him. For his own. Corin, marrying him…in front of everyone. The world had gone all wobbly again. He braced himself on Corin's solid chest, and oh, God, the texture of his faintly scaled skin, and the possibility of having Corin to lean on forever when he needed him. Or to be leaned on, when Corin needed it. Together. It didn't seem real.

"Are you serious—you can't possibly, I mean, you—"

Corin bent down so their noses almost touched. "Yes or no," he growled, and his fingers flexed against Aster's hip. Fighting his claws? All the blood in Aster's body rushed south and his eyes nearly rolled back in his head. He had to get this over with, *now*, so that he could have Corin alone somewhere, or he really would fall to his hands and knees and beg right here in front of all these people.

"Yes," he gasped. "*Yes*."

Corin's mouth opened to reply, and he leaned closer, and the look in his eyes…

"Sir Corin! I must insist that you attend!"

Corin looked up as Aster flinched. Fuck, Sir Gustave had a set of lungs on him when he needed them. And Aster might actually kill him if he kept interrupting!

"What?" Corin snapped. "I'm not allowed to propose in peace, Sir Gustave?"

"Propose?" Sir Gustave's voice rose to something like a screech. "You, sir, are before the king, and you're not wearing any pants! And as Duke Marellus has pointed out so cogently, you do not meet the requirement for claiming Lord Aster's hand in marriage or any other reward offered by His Majesty's decree. Therefore, I must ask you to leave this place at once and allow the business of court to proceed unhindered!"

Aster's belly clenched into a cold little knot.

For a shining moment, he'd forgotten about that part of the decree. Corin had come for him and nothing else mattered. But Corin would never humble himself. Not for Aster, not for anyone…

"One moment, Aster," Corin said softly, and let him go.

Aster reached out after him, but Corin had already stepped away, standing in front of the king. "Your Majesty," he said, "may I lay my petition before you?"

Theobert's lips twitched slightly. "As Sir Gustave points out, it's more traditional to approach the king wearing pants, Sir Corin. Actually—" And he gestured at his advisors, a twitch of the finger that had one of them leaping to attention, whisking off his cloak and presenting it to Corin with a flourish. Corin wrapped it around his hips and tucked it.

Marellus stepped forward, cheeks red and eyes blazing. His quick, jerky bow and the fist clenched at his side betrayed his fury. Aster wanted to enjoy it, but God, Marellus might very well ruin everything. He had to force himself to remain still.

"Your Majesty," Marellus hissed, "please allow me to interject. This is a farce, and offensive to Your Majesty's dignity. Sir Corin left court after assaulting a noble gentleman, he is by no means an appropriate husband for Lord Aster, and Lord Cezanne does not approve—"

"When we require your opinion we'll ask for it," the king said briskly. "And Lord Cezanne is right there. My lord, do you have anything to say?" His tone made it excruciatingly clear that Aster's father had damn well better keep his mouth shut. Lord Cezanne shook his head, and the king smiled. "Very well, then. Duke Marellus, must we remind you that we took responsibility for Lord Aster upon yours and Lord Cezanne's particular request?"

Oh, God. The king was taking Corin's side, and Aster's.

Aster could have kissed him. Although with Corin already pantsless, perhaps any further breaches of protocol would be best avoided.

"But, Your Majesty," Marellus choked out, turning purple. "This is not—not—"

"Not at all what you had in mind when you made that request, no," the king said, and this time his voice could have frozen a block of ice. Marellus's mouth dropped open. His cheeks went from fuchsia to white in an instant. "Sir Corin is a knight of nobility and dignity, a dragon, and honored by all. I presume you had some other type of husband in mind for Lord Aster, hmm?"

Marellus sputtered, gasped, and bowed his head, too much a courtier not to know what happened to someone who argued further with a king in this kind of mood. The look Dericort shot Aster had more venom than a whole nest of snakes.

Aster couldn't help the grin that spread over his own face. And then, although he could very well help it, he didn't want to: he winked. Dericort let out something between a groan and a squeak, fists clenched.

"Enough," the king said, and returned his attention to Corin, who'd stood patiently the while, shoulders back and hands clasped behind him, in a perfect parade rest. Even with his torso bare and a velvet cloak draped around his hips he looked every inch the knight. "Sir Corin, state your request."

Aster's jaw dropped as Corin actually—knelt down. For him,

for Aster…

"Your Majesty, I apologize for my behavior," Corin said crisply. "I embarrassed and offended you, and I deeply regret it. As for Lord Fanfelle, I also regret the action I took during our duel. In retrospect, I ought to have done something else."

The king raised one eyebrow, the corner of his mouth quirking up. That, Aster knew from many years of observation, meant he was trying not to laugh.

"We will refrain from asking what action you believe you ought to have taken instead, lest it offend our royal sensibilities," he said. "You are restored to the crown's good grace, Sir Corin. Make your request."

"I ask for Lord Aster's hand in marriage," Corin said without the slightest hesitation. "I ask you for the greatest boon any man could receive," he added more loudly, clearly pitching his voice to be heard by more than just the small group gathered at the top of the stairs—and oh, fuck, Aster twisted his head around, and yes, there were easily a hundred courtiers gathered behind him, whispering and waving their fans, eyes gleaming, fuck fuck fuck.

And then he saw her. His sister. Belinda. She stood half behind another lady, but he couldn't miss her face: eyes flashing like murderous sapphires, skin white but with brilliant spots of red, one on each cheek. Her coloring owed nothing to rouge today. That was pure rage.

Corin started to speak again, and Aster turned back to him. Fuck Belinda, anyway. He loved his sister, but she'd brought this on herself.

"Lord Aster's beauty and grace and wit are more than I deserve, and any marriage portion that accompanies him ought to belong to him and him alone. I want only him for myself." Corin glanced over his shoulder, and his smile set Aster's heart aflutter. "In the case of the Cezannes' noble offspring, I believe the third time was the charm."

"Oh," Aster said helplessly, as that hit him right in the middle of the chest.

Corin had remembered. That one, offhand remark he'd made

about his family laughing at him for being the plain youngest sibling, and Corin had remembered.

A faint shriek of fury echoed up the stairs, a sound Aster remembered from many an evening at home when Belinda hadn't gotten her way. Apparently Corin's words had reached the crowd below.

Drawn like a fragment of iron to a lodestone, Aster stepped forward, knowing that he ought to stay where he was until the king gave his answer, but unable to stop himself. He also knew everything he felt had to be shining out of his eyes, but surely he didn't need to hide it now? He'd never need to hide it again. He'd never need to be ashamed again, or worried, or nervous, because Corin had chosen him over everything and everyone else, and he'd chosen Corin, and fuck everyone else, anyway.

Corin scrambled to his feet with none of his usual grace, and Aster walked right into his arms, where he belonged. For a long moment, Corin gazed down into his eyes, searching and intense. His arms around Aster's waist were trembling. Aster petted his chest, dug in his fingertips, shaking just as much. And then Corin smiled, and he dipped his head and took Aster's mouth with his, his tongue sweeping in and claiming him.

Distantly, Aster heard Theobert say, "Well, I suppose our royal consent is second to the groom's. Lord Cezanne, enough. Lady Cezanne will be happy and that's what matters, eh?" And there was some kind of roar: laughter or applause from everyone assembled, or perhaps simply the blood rushing in Aster's ears as his heart beat so hard and so fast it almost bruised his ribs. None of it mattered at all.

Corin lifted his head, leaving Aster's lips tender and swollen. It took him a moment to blink his eyes open halfway. Somehow he'd ended up bent over Corin's arm. No wonder there were cheers and jeers from the garden, fuck.

But the pure joy shining out of Corin's eyes, and his smile, made up for it. "I think they're going to want us to get married right now," he said softly. "Will you? It's not too late to change your mind."

"Kiss me," Aster said. "And then marry me."

Corin grinned, ducked down and pressed another swift kiss to his lips—well, almost a swift kiss, except that Aster chased him, and then Corin nibbled on his lower lip, and then Aster moaned, and then finally they broke apart—and at last he let him go enough to take him by the hand.

"I think we're ready to get married now, Your Majesty," Corin said.

Theobert raised his eyebrows. "Don't hurry on our account."

"I'm not," Corin said. "I'm hurrying on my own account." He turned and smiled down at Aster.

"I told you running away was a good decision," Aster whispered. "I'd do it again."

Corin threw back his head and laughed, squeezing Aster's hand. "You can make all our decisions. Clearly you're better at it."

"We'll do it together," Aster said.

And hand in hand, they went through the sunny doorway to be married.

# Two Hours Later...

"OH GOD," ASTER GASPED, as his back slammed into the wall and Corin slammed into his front. "God—mmm—" The kiss cut off his words, his ability to breathe, and his capacity for rational thought, and Corin had ravished every crevice of his mouth before Aster tore himself away long enough to suck in a lungful of air.

Corin bit at his throat, tugged at Aster's trousers, shoved a hand down the back of them, fingers teasing the crease of his ass.

If Aster got any harder he might rip through the trousers himself.

But that didn't mean he didn't want...well...something else. They'd been separated to prepare for the wedding: Aster to be reunited with his mother, who'd been sent for from the Cezanne townhouse, and Corin to be provided with pants and a few other garments to accompany them. Aster's mother had embraced him and petted him just as he'd hoped, but they'd only had a few minutes before they had to return to the throne room.

And then—he and Corin had been married. They'd sworn to be faithful and true, to honor one another in body and soul, to bear all of life's troubles and share their joys together. There had been a lot of protocol and people being shuffled about to stand in the right places, the priest had given an endless lecture, and it had all felt so bizarre and unreal that Aster hadn't quite been able to believe that it'd happened.

Finally they'd been released to come here, to this room, where Corin hadn't even said a single word before locking the door and shoving Aster against the nearest wall.

"I thought," Aster said, panting. He tipped his head back so Corin had more room to press his face into Aster's throat and growl. They'd been given one of the palace's best guest bedchambers, and the ceiling, Aster now saw at this new angle, had a fresco of several minor deities enjoying a flagon of wine. He hoped they weren't prudish. "I thought wedding nights were supposed to be—oh," because Corin had slid two fingers between his cheeks now, and Aster's hole had started to clench around nothing, desperate to be filled.

Corin stopped.

"What?" he asked, mouth still against Aster's throat. "Wedding nights—what?"

At least Corin sounded as wrecked as Aster felt. That might have to do with flying hundreds of miles in…when had he left his mountain hideaway? And he hadn't brought anything with him, it seemed like, not even his hoard? Aster's head throbbed, not painfully, but with the pressure of too many questions and too much uncertainty, and his own desperate exhaustion.

He had Corin to husband. The man he loved. And on the crest of relief and happiness, earlier, it'd seemed like that would solve everything. But now he felt so young and tired and pathetic, and he wanted to be fucked more than almost anything, but that "almost" encompassed a place to lie down and a few moments of silence, and comforting arms around him, ideally.

But Aster had no idea how to say that, or if he even could.

After several awkward seconds, Corin lifted his head and peered into Aster's face.

His own softened at whatever he saw there, and the pressure of his hands on Aster's body eased.

"Fuck," he said. "I'm sorry."

"N-no," Aster stammered, "there's nothing to be sorry for, you haven't done anything, I mean, Corin, please—"

Corin cut him off with a kiss, this time a gentle press of the lips, with no demand to it at all.

"You're worn out," Corin murmured against his mouth, and kissed the corner of it lightly. "I wasn't thinking. Sweetheart, I'm sorry."

He ought to apologize again, oughtn't he? Even though the endearment nearly melted him into incoherency. And he tried, but every time he made a sound, Corin kissed him again, now pulling him away from the wall, across the room, over to the bed.

Corin gentled him down onto perhaps the softest mattress he'd ever felt, coming to rest beside and half on top of him, arms cradling him to Corin's chest. He tucked Aster's head under his chin and held him close.

And then he didn't say or do anything at all.

It was bliss. Pure, heavenly delight. Nothing rocked, creaked, or swayed—Aster didn't like boats. The only sound was the call of a mourning dove outside the window, quiet and sweet. Aster had always loved their song. They didn't sound mournful at all to him, merely contemplative.

"I missed the doves," Corin said quietly. "None of those up on the mountain." And then he laughed. "I need to tell you about the crow that little bastard herald sent. Fucking impertinent asshole."

For the first time that day, Corin felt familiar and safe again, the same man who'd taken Aster to bed and protected him and laughed with him. Not Sir Corin, who had to speak formally—well, relatively—to the king, or make oaths in front of priests, or terrorize a whole palace full of people.

But his lover Corin, with a filthy mouth and an absurd sense of humor.

Aster relaxed at last with a mighty sigh and nuzzled into Corin's chest. "Which one's the impertinent asshole? Jules, or the crow? And he sent a crow? Wait." Aster pulled back and stared up into Corin's face. "*He* sent you a message? That's why you're here?"

Corin's jaw set and his arms tightened. "He told me you might—he said you wouldn't promise not to."

It took him a moment to understand. When he did, his blood chilled. "Jules had no right," he said, voice shaking with his anger. He pulled away, trying to extricate himself from Corin's arms, his belly curdling with misery. "He had no—that's why you're here, fuck, that's why, you wouldn't have come if you hadn't thought you couldn't have that on your conscience, damn it—"

"No! Bloody—Aster, stop—enough!" Corin landed on top of him, hands around his wrists and the rest of his body pinning him down. His eyes blazed. "I mean, yes, but not like—stop fighting me!

Not like that!"

"How, then?" Aster demanded, forcing himself not to buck and struggle, because it wouldn't get him anywhere. And even if it did…where would he go? Even if Corin had only married him out of pity, they were married.

Aster couldn't run away this time.

Corin closed his eyes for a moment, opened them again, and took a deep breath. "You think I came for you because I didn't want you to do anything desperate, and I'd have felt guilty if you did. Is that what you're saying?"

"Of course that's what I'm saying!"

"I came for you," Corin said, slowly and carefully, "because I realized nothing mattered to me but you. Jules's letter made everything clear. I came because I'd never been so terrified in my life. No, shut up, let me finish!" He gave Aster's wrists a squeeze, and Aster subsided, seething. "I didn't come because I was afraid. I came because, damn it, I'm terrible at this. I wouldn't have been so afraid if I didn't love you. Do you understand? I love you, and I was an idiot. And here I am. I'm sorry it took me so long and that stupid Jules had to be the one to make me understand, because now I really do owe him a fucking trumpet."

Aster had to count to ten before he trusted his voice. He couldn't pinch himself, because both of his hands were out of commission.

"Say that again," he rasped, eyes blurring. Tears, probably, but if Corin loved him he wouldn't hold it against him. "Say it again?"

Corin leaned down, eyes alight and the corner of his mouth twitching. "I owe Jules a trumpet? Say that again?"

"Corin!"

"I love you," Corin said, coming so close their lips brushed. "I love you more than my hoard. Do you understand what that means?"

No, because Aster wasn't a dragon, and he'd never truly fathom what a hoard meant to one.

But he did understand what it meant to love.

"I think I've loved you for years, Corin," he said, almost too shy to get the words out, but praying Corin would understand how he meant it. "I don't have a hoard. I just have you. And—I think it means I belong to you."

"Forever," Corin agreed. "Mine. If you run away from me, there won't be anywhere you can hide. Not that I'll give you a reason to," he added hastily, and Aster had to laugh.

"I know you won't," he said, and Corin finally kissed him.

The kiss went on and on, their bodies beginning to move with the rhythm of their lips and tongues. Corin rolled his cock against Aster's and shoved a knee up, pushing his thighs apart. Heat built and built, a tight, nearly unbearable warmth behind Aster's bollocks, and God, nothing would soothe him but Corin's cock, Corin's knot, his husband fucking him until he screamed so loudly the gods on the ceiling had to cover their ears.

"We're married," he gasped into the kiss, as the reality of it burst in on him anew. "You're my *husband*." When would he grow tired of saying it? Of feeling that bubble of happiness in his chest as he did? Perhaps never.

"Yes," Corin growled. "Your husband. Which makes your happiness my job and my pleasure. What did you want for your wedding night, sweetheart?"

"Oh," Aster said, and bit Corin's lip. "Mmm."

"If you won't tell me I'll have to guess." Corin moved down, breathing hot against Aster's collarbones. "You didn't like being pushed up against the wall, I know that much."

He had, only not tonight, but saying so would sound so…silly. Weak and pathetic. It wasn't like they were virgins, separately or together.

"I like walls," he said lamely, and Corin laughed, shifting over to bite at Aster's nipple through the fabric of his shirt, making him arch and cry out.

"You tell me if I'm getting it wrong, then," Corin said, and kept moving down.

And down, pushing Aster's shirt up to mouth over his stomach and his ribs and his hipbones, letting go of his wrists to busy his hands with Aster's trouser buttons. Not wrong at all. Down further, even less wrong, licking Aster's cock through the fabric.

"Now that we're married, I'll never need to let you out of bed," Corin murmured. Married. They were married, and the word in Corin's deep voice made him moan. Of course, it was too much to hope that Corin wouldn't notice and use it against him. He lifted his head for a moment, eyes gleaming with mischief. "Married," he said again, and Aster writhed and buried his hands in that thick black hair, shoving his head down again. Corin chuckled and kissed the head of his cock.

"You bastard," Aster panted.

"That's your bastard husband to you," Corin pointed out—and bit down.

The shock of pain and the unbearable sweetness of *husband* hit him all at once, arrowing down to his bollocks. He went tense in every muscle, arching up, spine tingling, and his cock spasmed as wetness spread over the front of his trousers.

When he blinked back to reality, Corin had sat up on his heels, staring down at the evidence of Aster's pleasure.

He shook his head, clearing it perhaps, and started to unbutton his own trousers. "I'm sorry," he said. "Gentle wedding night's over. Now I'm going to hold you down and knot you open like I own you." He grinned, teeth too sharp for a human mouth. "Because I do."

Aster swallowed hard. "You do," he said, voice shaking a little, throat raw. "You do own me, Corin. I love you so much."

"Good, because I might waste away and die if you didn't," Corin said, his tone matter-of-fact. Soldierly. Like a man who dealt in practicalities, not romance. "Take your shirt off."

Well, fuck it. If he'd wanted honeyed, practiced words and poetry, he'd have wed a courtier. Instead, he'd married a dragon and a knight who said the most marvelously romantic things as if they were fact, as if nothing could shake his belief that Aster was the most wonderful being in the world.

Married. To Corin.

If the pressure of his joy didn't kill him, he might live happily ever after.

"You take yours off first," Aster said, and fluttered his eyelashes.

"You little—"

Corin lunged, wrapping Aster in his arms, kissing him breathless. And they were both laughing when Corin said, "Fuck it," and tore both their shirts off at once.

## THE END

# Acknowledgments

This book would not exist at all without Amy Pittel, my dedicated beta reader and loyal friend. Her patience with the process this time around can only be described as saintly. There are no words. Amy, thank you.

My thanks also go out with great love to Alessandra Hazard, who always finds my screw-ups in the best possible way and also picks up exactly what I'm putting down, to Kate Hawthorne, whose willingness to read a partial manuscript and talk through it with creative gusto is above and beyond, and to Cora Rose, whose kindness and support and cheerleading are invaluable and delightful. Without any of these people I probably would've given up on this one and co-cooned myself in a bucket of mint chip ice cream for all eternity. (I did that anyway, but I also finished the book.)

Lastly but not leastly, thank you to Natana Holbrook, my lovely PA and author-support gremlin, to Lori Parks, my excellent proofreader, and to Jennifer at Romance Rehab, who writes amazing blurbs.

# Get in Touch

I love hearing from readers! Find me at eliotgrayson.com, where you can get more info about my books and also sign up for my newsletter or contact me directly. You can also find out about my other books on Amazon, or join my Facebook readers' group, Eliot Grayson's Escape from Reality, to get more frequent updates. Thanks for reading!

# Also by Eliot Grayson

Mismatched Mates:
*The Alpha's Warlock*
*Captive Mate*
*A Very Armitage Christmas*
*The Alpha Experiment*
*Lost and Bound*
*Lost Touch*
*The Alpha Contract*
*The Alpha's Gamble*

Blood Bonds:
*First Blood*
*Twice Bitten*

Goddess-Blessed:
*The Replacement Husband*
*The Reluctant Husband*
*Yuletide Treasure*

Portsmouth:
*Like a Gentleman*
*Once a Gentleman*

Santa Rafaela:
*The One Decent Thing*
*A Totally Platonic Thing*
*Need a Hand?*

Beautiful Beasts:
*Corin and the Courtier*
*Deven and the Dragon*

*Brought to Light*

*Undercover*

*The Wrong Rake*

Made in the USA
Monee, IL
31 January 2025

10379549R00132